# SONS OF CORAX

# LEGENDS OF THE DARK MILLENNIUM

# SONS OF CORAX

GEORGE MANN

BLACK LIBRARY

**A BLACK LIBRARY PUBLICATION**

First published in Great Britain in 2015.
This edition published in 2016 by
Black Library,
Games Workshop Ltd.,
Willow Road,
Nottingham, NG7 2WS, UK.

10 9 8 7 6 5 4 3 2 1

Produced by Games Workshop in Nottingham.
Cover illustration by Alex Boyd.

A CIP record for this book is available from the British Library.

ISBN 13: 978 1 78496 280 7

See Black Library on the internet at

# blacklibrary.com

Find out more about Games Workshop
and the world of Warhammer 40,000 at

# games-workshop.com

Printed and bound by CPI Group (UK) Ltd, Croydon, CR0 4YY

It is the 41st millennium. For more than a hundred centuries the Emperor has sat immobile on the Golden Throne of Earth. He is the master of mankind by the will of the gods, and master of a million worlds by the might of his inexhaustible armies. He is a rotting carcass writhing invisibly with power from the Dark Age of Technology. He is the Carrion Lord of the Imperium for whom a thousand souls are sacrificed every day, so that he may never truly die.

Yet even in his deathless state, the Emperor continues his eternal vigilance. Mighty battlefleets cross the daemon-infested miasma of the warp, the only route between distant stars, their way lit by the Astronomican, the psychic manifestation of the Emperor's will. Vast armies give battle in His name on uncounted worlds. Greatest amongst his soldiers are the Adeptus Astartes, the Space Marines, bioengineered super-warriors. Their comrades in arms are legion: the Astra Militarum and countless planetary defence forces, the ever-vigilant Inquisition and the tech-priests of the Adeptus Mechanicus to name only a few. But for all their multitudes, they are barely enough to hold off the ever-present threat from aliens, heretics, mutants – and worse.

To be a man in such times is to be one amongst untold billions. It is to live in the cruellest and most bloody regime imaginable. These are the tales of those times. Forget the power of technology and science, for so much has been forgotten, never to be re-learned. Forget the promise of progress and understanding, for in the grim dark future there is only war. There is no peace amongst the stars, only an eternity of carnage and slaughter, and the laughter of thirsting gods.

# CONTENTS

# PREY

From a distance, the bleached white figure clinging to the rocky spur might have been a snowy cap upon the mountainside, if not for the fact that it was slowly, inexorably shifting its position, creeping around the outcropping in search of its prey.

The Chaplain had been tracking the creature for nineteen long and arduous days and now his body – despite being thewed with ropey muscles and hardened against the elements – was growing weary. The endurance necessary to survive up here, high amongst the soaring Diagothian mountains of Kiavahr, had proved too much for many of his brothers and he had seen evidence of their decomposing corpses, dashed on the rocks and half frozen by the altitude, as he had climbed. He felt no sadness for their passing. There was honour in such a death. To die in pursuit of a spiritual quest was akin to dying in battle, at least in the eyes of the Chaplaincy.

He'd vowed, however, that he would not join them in their isolated, deathly slumber. He would prevail, despite the fatigue burning in his upper arms, despite the pain. He would not return empty handed.

He searched the nearby rock face for evidence of his quarry. His black eyes were like glossy pools, the colour of midnight, utterly at odds with his stark white flesh. He was dressed only in a black-feathered loincloth – the ceremonial attire of the ritual hunt – although he wore a string of ivory-coloured totems around his neck. These fragile bird skulls – his *corvia* – jangled as he shifted again, straddling two broken spurs in order to finally bring the creature into view.

It was a magnificent beast, a thing of exquisite beauty. In appearance it resembled the tiny, black-beaked Kiavahrian ravens that had given their heads to become his totems, but that was where such comparisons ended. For this scarce creature was at least the size of a man, with sleek black feathers and a wingspan of four, or perhaps even five, metres. Its talons were daggers, designed to disembowel its prey long before its beak had ever set to work, and a fierce intelligence burned behind its beady eyes. It rested upon an adjacent outcropping of grey rock, studying the slopes below for any sign of prey.

The Chaplain felt only admiration for the creature but, nevertheless, he was there to kill it, to take its life with his bare hands and claim its sacred bones. The totems around his neck were as nothing compared to the spiritual significance of this glorious creature. He would haul its corpse back down the mountainside, and from there to Deliverance, to the Ravenspire, where he would fashion its skeleton into embellishments for his ancient, ebon armour. Its wings would adorn his jump pack, its beaked skull would become his Chaplain's mask. Such was the honour attributed to performing this ritual and slaying this beast – that he would carry its spirit with him into combat, a fearsome ally in the war against the enemies of the Imperium. Only then could he properly guide his brothers into battle, ensuring the purity of their hearts and minds, the honour of his Chapter.

The bird cocked its head and glanced in his direction. He was sure it could not see him from behind the outcropping, but he was in no doubt that it knew it was being pursued. For days it had taken steps to evade him, spiralling higher and higher up the mountainside, finding increasingly inhospitable perches upon which to land. Why, then, had it now settled upon this shattered ledge, as if granting him this brief opportunity to strike? Had it simply grown weary? Had his stamina and determination proved too much for the beast? He had waited so long for this moment, these few seconds of stillness before the sudden chaos of the battle.

He drew a long, calm breath, feeling the chill air swirl into his lungs. His twin hearts beat a discordant rhythm in his breast. He felt his blood sing through his veins, and coiled his muscles, preparing to strike. The leap across to the ledge was no more than three metres, although the ledge itself was treacherous and narrow. If he missed his footing on the loose scree and fell, it would all be over; the drop was near unfathomable. He would never even be aware that he had struck the bottom.

The bird glanced away, looking to the skies as if preparing to take flight.

He moved, knowing he could not allow himself to miss

this chance. With one hand he swung himself around the spur, and then sprang across the gulf, moving with an elegance and fluidity that belied his size. He struck the ledge, landing perfectly upon the balls of his feet. He rocked forwards into the sheer wall of the mountain, using his outstretched palms to break his momentum. Then, without missing a beat, he pushed himself away from the cliff face, spinning on one heel and reaching out to grasp a fistful of the beast's feathers with his left hand.

The roc squawked in fury and beat its wings, scrabbling with its claws as it tried to pull away, but he held firm, bunching the feathers tighter and willing them not to pull free. His feet skittered as he was dragged across the ledge by the creature's sheer strength, pulled dangerously close to the edge. A slurry of loose stones skittered over the side, tumbling away into the depths.

He couldn't allow the bird to take off. If it managed to get into the air, with him still clinging on, he'd have no means of killing it without dashing himself on the rocks below. He'd be entirely at its mercy.

The bird lurched suddenly, twisting and almost breaking free. He wrenched it back, his forearm burning with the strain.

An angry, ear-splitting shriek pierced the air from above. He glanced up, confused, to catch sight of a second bird diving out of the sky. It must have been half the size again of the one he now held, and it spread its immense wings as it neared the cliff face, rearing up with its claws. It swooped in, intent on spearing him upon the end of them.

He had nowhere to go, and only moments to act. He glanced across at the smaller beast, a wry smile of admiration on his lips. 'Clever...' he muttered, releasing his grip and allowing the roc to scramble away. It launched itself from the ledge and drifted off on the currents, wings outstretched.

Now he understood why his brothers had failed. The creature had tricked him. Despite his admiration, despite his acknowledgement of its intelligence, he had underestimated it. All the while the beast had known it was being hunted, and had toyed with him, leading him further and further up the mountainside. Its goal had been to tire him, to draw him ever on towards this trap.

He laughed, despite himself. The hunter had become the hunted. Now there was only the battle to decide his fate.

He waited until the last moment and then leapt sideways, trusting his instincts that the ledge would hold. The bird screeched in frustration as its claws raked the rock where he'd been standing only seconds before. He lashed out with his fist, striking it hard across the beak and sending it reeling away again, hissing and shaking its head as it attempted to right itself.

The roc circled the broken spur upon which he had stood only a few minutes earlier, cawing shrilly. He could see its beady eyes watching him, gleaming in the light of the setting sun.

He glanced around him for anything he could use as a weapon. A loose rock, about the size of his fist, was balanced on the edge of the precipice. Could he use it to down the beast? He had little chance of getting the creature to land, and if it came close again its talons would rake him to shreds. He could pitch the stone at it, but if he missed – and there was a high probability that he would – his only weapon would be gone. He longed for his jump pack, to be able to take the battle to the air. If only...

The bird suddenly went into a dive, and he was left with no other choice. He could see the only way to defeat the creature was to risk his own life, to do something it wasn't expecting. Otherwise he was simply a sitting target. He dove for the loose rock, knowing that in doing so he would be putting himself directly into the path of the swooping beast.

He felt the thunder of its gargantuan wings before the talons struck him in the chest. The knife-like claws pierced his secondary heart, collapsed one lung and shattered at least three of his ribs as they impacted, skewering him completely. The talons erupted from his back with an accompanying spray of dark blood. He cried out in pain as the creature reversed its momentum and pulled away from the mountainside, dragging him across the ledge. His trailing fingers closed around the rock as he was lifted bodily into the air, trapped and unable to free himself from the creature's deadly embrace.

The roc shrieked in triumph, soaring higher and higher, its wings beating powerfully to compensate for his dead weight. He allowed himself to go limp, encouraging the creature to think that it had won, trusting that it would not drop him to his doom in favour of finding somewhere relatively safe in order to peck him apart and consume his organs.

For almost twenty minutes they swooped and dove through the air, rising higher, up towards the pinnacle of the mountain. He had not stirred during this time, despite the throbbing agony of his wounds, and despite the constant risk that the creature might decide to discard him like an unwanted rag doll at any moment, casting him down into the abyss.

He felt the beating of the bird's wings slow, and risked twisting his neck to peer around. They were soaring low over a wide ravine, a gully at the bottom of which a dribbling stream wound and burbled down the side of the mountain. He judged the distance. It was still a risk, but he probably wouldn't get a better chance.

The bird cawed suddenly and twisted in the air, and he realised it must have felt him tense. Its grip loosened as it tried to pull its talons free from his chest and his wounds erupted in fiery pain, but he reached up and grabbed its leg with his left hand, clinging on desperately as it tried to shake him free.

The bird went into a blind panic as he shifted his weight and unbalanced it, causing them to dip suddenly in the air. They turned, spiralling out of control, the beast's wings beating frantically as it tried to gain height, to no avail. Its other foot clawed at him in desperation, raking a talon across his face and opening a wide gash on his cheek. Blood sprayed, blinding him momentarily, but still he clung on.

Screeching, the roc twisted again, opening its jaws in order to snap at him, and he took his chance, lashing out with the rock and catching it hard across the side of its head.

The bird reeled, dipping low, disorientated. He struck again, and then again, and the bird lolled suddenly, finally becoming insensate. Its wings folded back, fluttering frantically in the wind, and then they were falling, plummeting out of the sky like a black and white drop pod careening towards the earth. The white raven and the black roc, both tumbling to their deaths.

There was nothing he could do. He had to trust that his

instincts had been right, that he would survive the fall. Nevertheless, he braced himself for the impact as they dipped out of the sky.

*Falling...*

*Falling...* and then he was plunged into ice cold water, and his body, shocked, was attempting to draw breath as he was forced beneath the surface by the speed of the impact. Water was rushing up his nose, in his mouth, and the weight upon him was immense. He thrashed, feeling the wounds in his chest protesting, feeling the cold compress of the water inside him, clutching at his hearts.

He kicked, and surfaced, gasping for oxygen. His collapsed lung burned as he dragged desperately at the thin air. He swam to the bank, blinking the water out of his eyes. He glanced around urgently and was relieved to see the massive black bulk of the roc in the stream behind him, its broken wings buffeted back and forth by the ebb and flow of the water. Its head was lolling on the bank of the stream.

He took a moment to right himself, and then waded across to where it lay, still in the water. Its wet feathers shimmered in the dying light. He dropped to his haunches. The bird's chest still rose and fell with a rattling, dying wheeze.

He met its gaze and saw panic there. He, Cordae, this bloodied, pale figure, must have seemed like a vision of death itself to the dying beast. Its broken body spasmed suddenly as it made one final, desperate attempt to get away, and then, as if realising the futility of the gesture, it flopped back and lay still, regarding him with calm resignation.

He reached out and ran a hand across the top of its head, and felt a sense of peace wash over him.

'I honour your spirit, bird,' he said, his voice low. 'We go forward together. From this day on, we are kin.' Then, with both hands, he reached down and snapped its neck.

'Victorus Aut Mortis!' he bellowed in triumph, and the sound reflected off the walls of the ravine, startling a flock of small ravens that were watching him from a nearby bush. They took to the air, squawking as they wheeled like tiny shadows cast by the setting sun.

Cordae stood, hauling the corpse of the dead roc out of the water, grunting with the exertion. He hoisted its massive bulk up onto his shoulders, staggering slightly beneath the weight. The ragged wounds in his chest and face were already beginning to knit themselves together, staunching the tide of blood, and although he knew it was going to be a long and difficult climb back down the mountain with his burden, he relished the challenge. The hard work was already done, and besides, he knew that he now had the spirit of the bird to guide him.

# HELION RAIN

Amongst the ruination of the ancient scriptorium, a statue of white marble was stirring. Slowly, tentatively, the figure came to life, shifting its position to better observe the courtyard on the other side of the broken balustrade. It moved with a practised silence, resting the nose of its bolt pistol on a fragment of the shattered stairwell, its jaw set firm with grim determination.

High above, through the canopy of shattered beams and broken roof tiles, birds wheeled in an empty sky, punctuated only by the distant heat trails of drop pods bombarding the grassy savannahs to the east. The place was shrouded in an eerie cloak of stillness, as if the building itself was somehow holding its breath, waiting for something inevitable to happen.

Veteran Sergeant Grayvus of the Raven Guard peered around the debris with eyes of pure obsidian, his pale skin stark against the surrounding stonework. The alien was barely visible, even with his augmented senses. Only the occasional alteration in the quality of light or the ghost of movement betrayed its presence in the courtyard at all. He wasn't yet sure if the creature had noticed him, or whether it was toying with him, waiting for him to make his move.

Grayvus turned his head, slowly, searching for any sign of his Scouts.

*Nothing.*

He smiled. They were learning.

Grayvus returned his attention to the courtyard. His finger tensed on the trigger of his weapon. Just a second longer...

It moved again. He depressed the trigger, spraying a round of hot bolt-fire across the flank of the concealed beast.

What followed happened in a blur of movement so swift and so precise that Grayvus was almost caught off guard.

The tyranid creature emitted an angered howl, spinning around with surprising agility and leaping over a ruined wall towards its attacker. Grayvus could see now that his instincts had been correct – the thing was a lictor: three metres tall, with a hard, pink chitinous shell and a festering mouth filled with wriggling, writhing proboscises. Its eyes gleamed an angry red and two immense, bony blades scythed the air above it, the ferocious tips of extra limbs that jutted up and out from its shoulders. Its ribcage was covered in a series of angular barbs that Grayvus knew, from experience, were to be avoided at all costs. And it smelled like death. Like the very essence of death itself. It was a scent that Grayvus would never forget. Althion IV would be burned in his memory forever.

The creature raised its head towards the sky and howled once again before stalking forwards with menacing intent.

The scriptorium erupted into a cacophony of sound and a blur of movement: the roar of a chainsword, the bark of shotguns, the sound of boots crunching gravel. The ominous clacking of the lictor's claws against the broken flagstones. Where previously the only sounds had been the distant cawing of the birds, now the ruined building was filled with the riot of battle.

The Scouts materialised from the shadows like ghosts stepping between the fabric of worlds, grey camo cloaks billowing around their shoulders, weapons charged and ready; prepared, as always, for the battle to come. Grayvus backed away from the lictor as the others swarmed around it, encircling it, trapping it between them with an ease and discipline that made Grayvus's heart sing.

Grayvus squeezed the trigger of his bolt pistol again, loosing a hail of shots. The lictor thrashed around, unsure of which direction to focus its attack. Grayvus offered suppressing fire as Tyrus leapt forwards, his chainsword growling as he swung it around in a wide arc, lopping off one of the lictor's bony limbs with a single, easy movement. Green ichor gushed from the wound as the arm fell twitching to the ground. Tyrus fell back to avoid the slashing talon that threatened to decapitate him in retaliation.

'Concentrate your fire on its head,' bellowed Grayvus as he strode forwards, raising his weapon and firing directly into the nest of tentacles that swarmed around the monster's gaping mouth. The lictor screeched in defiance. It lashed out to the left, catching Corbis hard with a flick of its remaining clawed arm, sending him sprawling to the floor, his shotgun spitting wildly into the sky as his aim was knocked violently askew. He rolled across the flagstones and remained there on the ground, still, his face hidden from view. Grayvus wondered if the Scout's neck had been snapped by the ferocity of the blow. He had little time to worry about it now.

A second chainsword roared to life and Grayvus heard it biting into the thick chitin plates that covered the creature's back, whining as it cut through layers of bone and gristle. Another of the Scouts was assaulting the lictor from behind. Tyrus, meanwhile, had pulled his bolt pistol from his belt and was showering the lictor's head with a volley of hot slugs, taking Grayvus's lead. The creature buckled, one of its legs folding beneath it, as the Scouts continued their onslaught.

'Bring it down before it can call for more of its kind!' Grayvus called as he moved to the left, trying to close the gap left in the circle by the prone Corbis, all the while keeping his black eyes fixed on the beast, his weapon trained on its head. It wouldn't do to offer the monster an escape route. Lictors hunted alone, but their kind were never far behind; if they didn't bring it down swiftly, its pheromones would bring swarms of the things down on them

There was a cry from behind the lictor. Avyn or Shyal – Grayvus couldn't see which. But he could see the creature's barbed tail flick up over its shoulder, blood dripping from the bony protrusions that crested its tip.

Grayvus felt something *thunk* into his chest-plate and cursed that he'd allowed himself to be distracted. He looked down in horror to see one of the lictor's flesh-barbs had embedded itself in his armour. Extruded from the alien's chest, the barb was attached to a glistening tendril of thick, ropey flesh. The lictor jerked and Grayvus lurched forwards, only just managing to retain his footing.

The creature was drawing him in, pulling the tendril back inside itself and dragging him closer in the process. Its slavering proboscises – or, at least, those that still remained after the rounds of bolt-fire that Grayvus had shot into its face – quivered with anticipation. This was what he had seen on Althion IV. The horror of what those tendrils could do. He *wouldn't* let it happen to him.

Grayvus dropped his bolt pistol and kicked backwards, allowing his feet to come up off the ground and throwing all of his weight against the pull of the lictor's tendril. The barb held, and although the xenos staggered, it remained firm, continuing to drag Grayvus closer.

Grayvus took a deep breath. His next move was all about timing. Around him, the other Scouts were still pounding the lictor with bolt-fire and swipes from their chainswords, and he could see it was close to death. Syrupy ichor ran from numerous wounds in its torso and the air was filled with the stench of scorched bone and seared flesh. But the creature's eyes still burned with fury and he knew that it would not stop, not until it had burrowed its unholy, bone-tipped probes inside his head and stolen his memories, absorbed all of his thoughts. Death was one thing – a thing he would welcome when the time came and he knew that he had proved himself to the Emperor – but this alien, this *monster*, it represented something else. The loss of everything he was. He would not allow this creature inside his head.

Grayvus's feet skittered across the shattered floor of the scriptorium. The creature was close now, so close he could feel the heat of its foetid breath. He flexed his shoulders, readying himself. Then, in one swift movement, he reached up and clasped the grip of his chainsword, tearing it free from its holster and thumbing the power. He swung it round before him, at the same time allowing his body to go limp, forgoing all resistance so that he was pulled sharply forwards towards the straining lictor. He collided with it, caught for a moment in its bony embrace.

For a moment he thought he saw a flicker of triumph in the alien's eyes as it readied itself to feast on his mind, before it realised the chainsword was buried to the hilt in its chest, thrumming with power, wedged there by the force of its own trap.

The lictor screamed as Grayvus forced the chainsword up and out of its torso, ripping through organs and muscles and bones until, at last, the roaring blade burst free, slicing unceremoniously through its neck and finally silencing it forever. The alien wavered for a moment before toppling to one side, Grayvus still tangled in a heap of limbs beneath it.

'Get me out of here,' he barked at the others, who still stood in a circle around the dead beast, looking on with something approaching awe.

Sometimes, in the stillness, the quiet moments of anticipation before a battle, he thought of Deliverance. He remembered the clusters of smouldering venting towers, erupting from the moon's surface like bristling spines, puncturing the grey regolith to belch oily fumes into the midnight sky. He recalled the constant rumbling beneath his feet: the reverberations of subterranean mining engines, coring out the centre of the tiny world, harvesting minerals to feed the scores of ever-hungry forges and manufactories. He saw the dark, towering monolith of the Ravenspire, silhouetted against the planet-light of distant Kiavahr, and thought of home.

He hadn't returned to Deliverance for nearly a century, drawn instead by the constant need to protect these outer worlds on the fringes of the Imperium. Or – he smiled grimly – to protect the local human forces from their own incompetence.

Perhaps, in truth, there was more to it than that. Perhaps something else was keeping him away. He buried the thought.

Idos was a backwater, a long way from that half-remembered home. A world infested with the stink of xenos, fodder for the enemy spawning pools. Yet Idos had been granted the Emperor's protection, and the Raven Guard were there to ensure it was enforced. And besides, any opportunity to halt the advance of a tyranid hive fleet was an opportunity worth taking. He'd fought tyranids before, back on Althion IV, and he knew them for the abominations they were. A plague, a virus – a scourge that needed to be purged; they had infested the galaxy and obliterated innumerable worlds with their insatiable appetite for the raw materials from which they procreated. Yet the tyranids were an enemy that he could understand. Their motives were simple, their strategy pure. They wished only to feast on the biomass of a world, to conquer it and consume it completely, and they would take it through weight of numbers alone. Singleminded and devastating.

Captain Aremis Koryn surveyed the ruined landscape before him, the grassy plains covered in straw-like grass, the undulating hills and ridges that formed from the shattered wreckage of Proxima City in the distance.

It was too late for this place. He knew that already, an indisputable truth. His Raven Guard would halt the flow of the xenos, but the planet itself would never recover. Too much had been lost, and the world was too far out on the rim of the Imperium for it to be worthy of rebuilding. The native warriors knew that, too. It was what had driven them to such desperate measures, to using inferior weapons in an attempt to destroy the hive ship that hung in planetary orbit: a moon-sized abomination. Their targeting had been off, however, and instead they had inadvertently destroyed their own moon, Helion, splintering the worldlet into a billion fragments that now wracked Idos below with fierce meteor storms and gravitational instability. And all the while, the xenos kept coming, an insatiable maw devouring the planet.

Koryn looked down upon the serried ranks of Space Marines, their black armour gleaming in the morning sunlight. To his left, bike squadrons formed a protective flank, covering the line of trees in case anything emerged unexpectedly from the forest. To his right, assault squads readied themselves for the coming onslaught, their talons glinting. And between them stood the main bulk of the Fourth Company, bolters at the ready.

The Raven Guard were few, but they would hold firm. This, to Koryn, was another indisputable truth.

Koryn himself stood upon the crest of a hill, resplendent in his ancient armour. It was an antique, worn for millennia by the captains of the Fourth Company, created in the Martian forges before the time of the great Heresy. It was engraved with the names of all those who had worn it before him and given their lives in service to the Emperor. A litany for his dead brethren, covering every centimetre of its pitted black surface. Koryn felt the burden of their memory, but also the honour of their company, the pedigree from which he had come. Today he would make his forebears proud. He would honour their memory. And one day his name would be added to theirs, etched onto a pauldron or leg plate or arm brace. One day he would give his life in the service of his Emperor, and it would be glorious. The thought gave him much comfort.

Koryn flexed his shoulders. On the horizon he could see the alien swarm approaching, a hazy cloud of buzzing wings, slashing limbs and putrid, slavering jaws. Behind the flared respirator of his helmet, he smiled. Soon his talons would taste alien blood.

Grayvus kneeled beside Corbis, rolling the young Scout over onto his back to check for any signs of life. Behind him, the corpse of the lictor still quivered nervously in its final death throes.

Corbis was tall but stocky, with a square jaw and a long, puckered scar running across his cheek from his left eye to his ear. His flesh was already beginning to lose its pinkish hue, becoming pale and translucent, and his hair had darkened to the colour of dusk: a sign that his melanchromic organ was flawed. He had the mark of the Raven.

Grayvus's flesh had long since been bleached by time and experience. His eyes, too, had lost their colourful hue, becoming orbs of the purest black, glossy pools of impenetrable darkness. He was older than the others and had seen combat in all its multifarious facets, had fought xenos and traitors alike on myriad worlds throughout the Imperium. It was his role to train the fresh-faced Scouts, to shape them into fully-fledged battle-brothers... *if* they managed to survive their training. And Idos was no simple exercise. The enemy was lurking around every corner.

Grayvus stood, his boots crunching on the splintered flagstones. 'He's breathing,' he announced, without ceremony. He walked over to where Tyrus and Avyn were standing over the prone form of Shyal, stooping to reclaim his bolt pistol from where he'd dropped it during the fight. His exposed arms were covered in lacerations and scars, as well as ichor and bodily fluids spilled from the chest of the lictor when he had brought it down.

'He's dead, sergeant,' said Tyrus, without turning his head away from the body of his fallen brother.

Grayvus glanced at the corpse. He most certainly was. Half of his face was missing from where the lictor's whip-like tail had caught him beneath the chin, crushing his jaw and pulping his right eye socket at the same time. His other eye remained open, as if staring expectantly at Tyrus, willing him to do something more. Dark blood was seeping out over the grey stone floor, forming glossy pools in the midday sun.

'He was probably dead before he hit the ground,' Grayvus said, his voice a low growl. He dropped to his haunches beside the body. Shyal's camo cloak was wrapped around his ruined form like some sort of funerary shroud. Grayvus pulled it back to reveal the black armour beneath. The Scout's belt was adorned with the skulls of Kiavahrian ravens: tiny, yellowing heads with long, curved beaks, tied in a little cluster to a thin silver chain.

These totems, these corvia, were tokens of honour and skill. They were a representation of the raven spirit and a symbol of their home world. They were a measure of the Scout's aptitude and stealth, a part of the initiation rites through which the man Shyal had given himself over to the Emperor to become an Adeptus Astartes. Each initiate would prove his cunning by catching these birds in the great woodlands of Kiavahr, moving so silently amidst the lush flora that he could grab the avians where they perched, taking them with his bare hands and gently breaking their necks. It took months of practice and great skill for a Scout to be light enough on his feet and swift enough in his movements to grab the birds before they fluttered away.

Grayvus cupped the bundle of tiny skulls in his fist and pulled them free of the dead Space Marine's belt. He looked up at the others. 'Who will carry his corvia?'

Tyrus stepped forwards. 'I would be honoured, sergeant.'

Grayvus gave a swift, sharp nod and handed the totems over to the other Scout. 'Then remember that you carry with you his honour, also. He will rest when you return them to the soil from whence they came.'

The others waited in silence while Tyrus affixed the skulls to his belt beside his own. Grayvus turned to see Corbis climbing to his feet, rubbing his neck. 'You took your time,' he said gruffly, before gesturing down a ruined side street with the nose of his bolt pistol. 'Move out.'

The Scouts moved like shadows through the wreckage of Proxima City, silent wraiths picking their way amongst the dead. The city had yielded entirely to the invading alien horde. As Grayvus and his squad clambered over the debris of a toppled Administratum building, they realised the extent of the devastation. As far as they could see, in all directions, the city was in ruins. The jagged spires of fractured buildings were like misshapen teeth, clustered in a broken grin. Dead civilians lay in rotting heaps, ready for the ripper swarms that would soon devour them, processing their flesh and blood and bones, feeding their raw biomass back into the tyranid gestalt. Within hours their constituent parts would be remoulded, formed into new alien paradigms. It was this that made Grayvus's skin crawl, this that appalled him most about the nature of the enemy: not only would they annihilate an Imperial settlement, but they would inextricably absorb it too, twist it and corrupt it and reform it in their own image.

Grayvus ground his teeth. The city had been decimated, shattered by the onslaught of the rampaging xenos and pummelled by the near-constant meteor storms as the remnants of the moon, Helion, rained down upon the planet below. There was nothing he could do to change that now. But he could halt the tide of stinking xenos. He could keep them away from the dead. The Raven Guard would have their revenge upon the tyranid filth. He would be sure of it.

Grayvus scrambled down the fractured remains of a colossal statue, swinging his bolt pistol in a wide arc, alert for any signs of danger. He heard Corbis drop down beside him.

'Sergeant, over here.' He glanced over at where Tyrus had slid down the other side of the ruined statue. Here, the head and shoulders of the monument lay half submerged in the dirt, the eyes of an ancient, unknown warrior staring up at them in silent vigil.

He crossed to where Tyrus and Avyn were standing. 'What is it?'

Tyrus pointed at the ground near his feet. 'Spawning pools. They've already started work.'

Grayvus nodded. 'They'll be coming for the dead. Be on your guard.'

The Scouts edged around the glistening pools, pushing their way further through the wreckage.

As they neared the boundary of the fallen Administratum complex, Grayvus felt the hairs on the back of his neck prickle with warning. Something was close. He stopped, and the others followed suit, turning as one to regard him. The sergeant gestured for them to remain silent.

Creeping forwards, his bolt pistol tight in his fist, Grayvus approached the half-collapsed entranceway to the building, using what was left of the wall as cover. He peered out at the street on the other side.

Two enormous tyranid creatures were hovering amongst the wreckage, about thirty metres from the Scout's current position. They were unlike anything Grayvus had seen before: fat, bloated bodies crested by an array of chitinous plates and spines, each atop a long, curling tail that floated a metre above the ground. Their heads resembled that of the lictor, but bigger, their mouths ringed with squirming tendrils. Two small arms ended in vicious-looking talons. They were the colour of rotting flesh, pink and lurid, and towered at least three or four times the height of the Scout sergeant.

Grayvus watched as one of the creatures used its talons to skewer the corpse of a Guardsman from a nearby heap of shattered rockcrete, lifting it hungrily towards its tentacled maw. He turned away as the beast chewed noisily into its carrion meal. The sound of crunching bones made his skin crawl. His finger twitched on the trigger of his bolt pistol, but he held himself in check. He turned and made his way back to where the others were waiting in silence.

'We find another way around,' he said.

Tyrus offered him a quizzical expression. 'Is the way impassable, sergeant?'

Grayvus nodded. 'Enemy hostiles block our path.'

Tyrus reached for his chainsword. 'Then we cut our way through.'

Grayvus put a hand on the Scout's arm, preventing him from drawing his blade. 'Sometimes, Brother Tyrus, winning the battle means losing the fight. Remember your training. Our mission is to survey the situation behind enemy lines and report on our findings. We will not needlessly engage the enemy and put that mission in jeopardy.'

Tyrus relaxed his grip on his weapon, but Grayvus could see the fire burning behind his eyes. 'Yes, sergeant. Forgive me.'

Grayvus smiled. He recognised that same impulse himself, that burning desire to purge the enemy, to seek revenge for his fallen brothers. But he knew nothing of the strange creatures out there amidst the rubble, and would not put his squad and his mission at risk – not for his own, or for Tyrus's, satisfaction.

Grayvus glanced around the ruined building, looking for another route. Without warning, the vox-bead in his ear sputtered to life with a hissing burst of static.

'Sergeant Grayvus?' The voice sounded tinny and distant.

'Captain Koryn.' Grayvus moved further into the shattered building so that his voice would not draw the attention of the feasting xenos outside.

'State your position, sergeant.'

'We're on the eastern fringe of the city, captain. Approximately ten kilometres from the main engagement, just inside the Administratum complex.'

The vox went silent for a while. 'Captain?' Grayvus prompted after a minute had passed.

When he spoke again, Koryn sounded distracted.

'Grayvus. There's a power station three kilometres north of your position. I need you to destroy it.'

Grayvus frowned. 'Destroy it?'

'Yes. And don't leave anything standing. Cause the biggest explosion you can.'

'But we don't have any explosives, captain.'

'Then be creative, Brother Grayvus.' The voice was firm, unyielding.

'Yes, captain.'

'And sergeant?'

'Captain?'

'Be swift, too.' The link went dead.

Grayvus pulled his auspex from his belt and consulted the readout. Three kilometres of rubble and wreckage stood between them and the power station, not to mention the risk of lurking enemy combatants and the ripper swarms feasting upon the dead. And he had no idea how they were going to destroy a power station with only bolt pistols and chainswords. It would be a test of their mettle, and a test of his training.

Grayvus glanced up at the expectant faces of his Scouts. 'Our mission parameters have changed,' he said, unable to contain the wide grin that was now splitting his face.

The enemy swarm was more substantial than even the reports of his own Scouts had led him to believe. There were thousands of them, a great, shifting ocean of flesh and bone. Koryn watched from his place on the hillside as the oncoming tide of xenos swarmed in towards his Raven Guard and the Space Marines came to life; immoveable, holding firm in the face of untenable opposition. The noise was incredible: the chatter of bolter-fire, the pounding of taloned limbs, the rending of plasteel and metal, the screeching of the xenos as they fell in waves.

Heavy bolters punched the air somewhere behind Koryn, sending hellfire rounds whistling into the conflict below, splashing searing mutagenic acid over the howling aliens, burning their unclean flesh. The bike squads roared to life, churning the earth as they shot into the melee, bolter rounds spitting from their forward-facing emplacements, mowing down scores of tyranids as they ploughed through the chaotic ranks of the enemy army. To the right, talons flashed as the assault squads pinned the enemy's left flank, slicing through the mass of darting hormagaunts and termagants that clambered over one another to get at the Space Marines.

And in the distance, like an eye at the centre of a vast storm, the hive tyrant. It was immense: an abomination rendered in flesh and blood. Its great, crested head towered high above the rest of its kin, swaying from left to right, taking in the enemy positions. Its huge cannon belched fat gobbets of venom that scorched the earth where they fell. Its limbs terminated in long, scything blades that cleaved the air around it, hungry for the blood of its enemies. It carried itself with an air of intelligence uncommon to the other, more animalistic creatures that surrounded it.

The captain knew that this creature – this monster – was the node that held the aliens together, the conduit by which the orbiting hive ship organised its troops, ensured the mindless individuals of the swarm were not, in their multitudes, mindless at all. They were a gestalt – one organism formed out of many. But if Koryn could sever that link between them, if he could interrupt that flow of information from the central intelligence above... then they became nothing. They would lose their cohesion. They would lose their purpose. And an enemy without purpose was no enemy at all.

Koryn turned to see one of his veterans approaching, his ebon armour scarred by the marks of a thousand prior battles. 'Argis. It is time for us to join our brothers in the fray.'

Koryn could not read Argis's expression behind his faceplate, but there was hesitation in his voice when he spoke. 'Captain. We are few. The enemy are legion. We cannot withstand a full engagement with the xenos. If the battle becomes protracted...' He let his words hang for a moment. 'As keen as I am to spill their foul blood, this is not our way.'

Koryn nodded. 'I hear your concerns, brother. But we must have faith. The Raven Guard will triumph this day.' Koryn knew he was taking an enormous gamble, playing a dangerous game. But that *was* their way. They would not defeat this enemy through brute force alone. They would out-think it. They would lead it into a trap. It was up to Grayvus now.

'Watch the skies, brother-captain!' Koryn turned at Argis's cry to see two winged gargoyles sweeping out of the sky towards him, their fangs chattering insanely, their jaws dripping with venom. Their heads and backs were plated with the same pink armour as their larger, flightless kin. But their exposed bellies were soft and fleshy; the perfect target.

Koryn tested his lightning claws. They fizzed and crackled with energy. He held his ground, waiting as the creatures swooped closer. He became aware of the sputter of bolter-fire as others around him began firing indiscriminately into the gargoyle flock, which suddenly filled the sky in all directions. He heard the beating of a hundred leathery wings as the hillside was cast in deep shadow, the density of the baying flock momentarily blotting out the sun. Swathes of the creatures tumbled from the air like fleshy missiles, shredded by bolter-fire, colliding noisily with the ground by the Space Marines' feet. But the onslaught continued unabated.

Koryn kept his eyes trained on the two gargoyles approaching him from above. The beast on the left squeezed the trigger of its strange, bone-coloured weapon, spitting a fine spray of acid across the captain's chest-plate and pauldrons. He ignored it, remaining perfectly motionless as the venom chewed tiny holes in his armour. He dismissed the warning sigils that flared up angrily inside his helmet.

*Waiting... Waiting...*

The gargoyles manoeuvred themselves in for the kill, swinging around to offer their viciously barbed tails to the Space Marine, aiming their poison-spewing weapons at his faceplate.

*Still waiting...*

*Still waiting...*

Koryn pounced. He sprang into the air, twisting his body and uncoiling like a tightly wound spring. He extended his talons skywards to skewer the gargoyles through their exposed bellies, impaling one on each of his sparking fists. His manoeuvre was timed to perfection. The gargoyles had no time to react, screeching in pain and fury, twisting on the hissing metal claws that now punctured their pink, alien flesh. Pungent ichors coursed down Koryn's arms.

He landed neatly, his fists still held aloft as if brandishing the splayed gargoyles as obscene trophies. They thrashed for a few seconds more, their wings beating his arms and his face, their claws scrabbling at his power armour, before falling still, nothing but dead weights. Koryn roared in triumph and lowered his arms, casting the twin corpses to the ground. His ire was up.

He glanced around him, seeing only the spatter of xenos blood as his brothers tore through the gargoyle swarm, bolters chattering away at the sky, lightning claws and chainswords flashing in the stuttering light of the battle.

Below, his sergeants were holding the line, keeping the aliens back, refusing to buckle. But Koryn could see them straining against the sheer numbers and unrelenting ferocity of the tyranid assault. It was time. There was nothing more he could do from his vantage point on the hillside. He had committed the Raven Guard to this course of action and if he failed, then it would be a glorious death. All that was left was to hold the line. All that was left was the fight.

Koryn charged down the hillside, his boots pounding the earth as he ran. He leapt into the fray, his weapons ready. The blood sang in his veins. This was why he had been created, what he was made for. This: the glory of battle. This: the smiting of the Emperor's foes. This: the great war against the enemies of man. This was his purpose, his entire reason for being.

Koryn allowed the hunger for battle to consume him, gave himself utterly to the fight. He became one with his flashing talons. He danced and parried, transforming himself into a whirling dervish of death amidst a sea of pink flesh and chitin. Xenos fell in his wake. He carved through them like a spirit passing through walls of solid rock, his lightning claws spitting and humming as they cleaved skulls and separated limbs from torsos. His ancient, ebon armour glistened with alien blood. He dragged air into his lungs and bellowed as he fought: 'Victorus aut Mortis!' The aliens came at him in a relentless tide, but he cut them down. He would hold the line. Grayvus would prevail.

Behind Koryn, the Raven Guard pressed forwards anew.

Grayvus studied the hololithic readout of his auspex and glanced warily up at the sky. It had taken the Scouts over half an hour to pick their way through the rubble of the Administratum building and now a fresh meteor storm was threatening the horizon, and also their progress. He could see fragments of planetary debris beginning to burn up in the upper atmosphere, leaving long, fiery streaks across the sky in their wake.

The storms had plagued the Raven Guard's campaign ever since their arrival on Idos, rocks and boulders hurtling indiscriminately out of the sky at incredible velocities; a terrible, deadly rain. Helion rain.

Grayvus shook his head at the thought of it. An entire moon destroyed, a planet now ravaged by meteoric storms and tidal instability. A planet plagued by the stink of xenos. Idos had once been an idyllic world on the fringes of the Imperium. Now it was a living hell.

A high-pitched whistling pierced the air. Grayvus tracked the trajectory of a fist-sized rock as it smashed into the outcropping of a nearby building. The masonry exploded with the deafening echo of stone striking stone. This was followed by another, then another, fragments of the former moon clattering amongst the ruins with the explosive force of successive heavy bolter rounds.

'Incoming, sergeant!' bellowed Tyrus, and Grayvus turned to see a hail of debris showering out of the fire-streaked sky all around them. Tiny stones pinged off his carapace; a larger piece struck his right arm brace, nearly knocking him from his feet. Another tore a deep gash in his exposed forearm. The blood looked startlingly bright against the wintery paleness of his flesh.

'Take cover!' he called to the others, scrambling for the nearest building. The others scattered. Corbis fell in behind Grayvus, running over to share the shelter of an immense, arched doorway. Much of the building had been destroyed and Grayvus knew that what remained of it would be little help when faced with a major impact, but it would offer some protection from the accompanying hail of debris. If they were lucky, the larger strikes would occur further afield.

Grayvus heaved a frustrated sigh. They would have to wait for the storm to pass. This was one enemy that neither their bolt pistols nor their cunning could defeat.

The meteor storm swept in, bombarding the city, pummelling what remained of the buildings into heaps of rockcrete and stone. Grayvus dropped to his haunches, listening to the rhythmic drumming of the impacts, the bellowing echoes of the distant explosions that signalled the larger impacts elsewhere in the city. The sounds sparked memories of Haldor and the battle for Exyrian, all those years ago, trapped inside the city boundaries, besieged by the traitorous Iron Warriors. If he closed his eyes and concentrated he could still hear the screams of the dying, echoing in the darkness of the ruins. The siege had lasted for innumerable days, and it was only due to the unrelenting campaign of Captain Koryn – hitting the

Iron Warriors with a series of swift, surgical strikes, then melting away again before the traitors could muster – that the Imperial forces had broken the enemy and brought the siege to an end. By then it was already too late for the civilians, of course. They were all dead, killed by the constant bombardments, the lack of food and the raging fever, this latter a result of the sheer volume and proximity of the putrefying corpses trapped in the ruins.

A voice cut through Grayvus's memories, snapping his attention back to the present. 'You've fought them before, sergeant?'

Grayvus tore his eyes away from the hailstorm ravaging the city, glancing back at Corbis, who was regarding him with interest, leaning against a fragment of broken pillar, his shotgun clutched in his hands. Grayvus nodded. 'Althion IV. We were ambushed. Most of my squad were killed. We were inside the hive when they came out of the darkness and hit us, attacking with all the fury of the warp itself. Terrible, deadly things with four arms. Until then I'd assumed the tyranids were nothing but beasts, animals that lacked any real intelligence, a pestilence that infested human worlds because it didn't know any different. But those things – those genestealers – there was darkness behind their eyes, a keen intelligence that spoke of something else.'

Corbis was watching him intently. 'How did you survive when so many others fell?'

Grayvus stiffened. He heard no accusation in Corbis's gruff tone, but the questions, and the memories, stirred feelings of guilt within him. He could not explain why he had lived when so many of his brothers had died. 'I cannot say. I was blinded by rage. I killed five, six of the creatures, tearing them apart with my bolter and my fist. My brothers had wounded many of them before they had fallen, but my hatred spurred me on. I covered my armour with their blood. Then one of them caught me in the shoulder with its claws, splitting my armour like a tin can. I was on my back. The thing was on top of me, its sickening jaws dripping toxins, its hot breath fogging my helm. I prepared myself. I was ready to die alongside my brothers. I had fought well and made my peace with the Emperor. And then a sudden burst of bolter-fire, and the creature was dead, shredded by explosive rounds. Erynis had saved my life.

'He was dead when I got to him, disembowelled and lying in a pool of his own blood. One other – Argis – was injured but alive. I carried him back to our base outside the hive.'

Corbis nodded gravely. 'What happened?'

Grayvus studied the Scout's face. He was young and had not yet witnessed a campaign on the scale of Althion IV. He did not know of the necessary lengths they would go to, to protect the Imperium from its enemies. 'We destroyed the hive. It was lost. We were too late, and too few.'

'The entire hive?'

Grayvus nodded. 'And now we are here,' he said, turning his head to watch the hailstorm showering the street outside, 'and so are those stinking xenos. This time, the Raven Guard will have their revenge.'

Grayvus jerked suddenly and let off a series of short, sharp shots with his bolt pistol. There was a soft *thump* amongst the clatter of meteors as something fell dead to the ground nearby.

Grayvus rose slowly from his crouching position,

tracking his weapon back and forth across the street. 'Be ready, Corbis. Those things don't hunt alone.'

'What wa–' Corbis fell silent as a small tyranid creature – about the size of a large dog – hopped up onto a slab of fallen masonry just in front of him. Tiny meteor-rocks were pinging off its armoured plating, but the creature seemed unaffected by the constant pummelling from above. It turned and hissed at the Scout, baring its fangs and its long, curling tongue. It held a bone-coloured gun of some sort in its bony claws. It cocked its head and moved as if about to strike. Corbis squeezed the trigger of his shotgun and took the creature's head clean off. The stench of burning meat filled the air around them as the body slumped soundlessly to the ground.

Grayvus stepped out into the street and released a volley of bolt-rounds into the storm. He could see a pack of termagants swarming through the wreckage towards him, their heads bobbing as they ran, twitching as the debris from the shattered moon continued to stream down around them. He knew that they would not be alone: if there were termagants here, experience told him that there would be bigger and more ferocious tyranid warriors just behind them.

Grayvus waved for the Scouts to join him as he unleashed another round of bolts into the oncoming mass of aliens. Bodies shuddered and fell, but more swarmed over the top of their dead kin, drawing closer. Grayvus felt the sting of tiny stones puncturing his flesh, burying themselves in his exposed arms and cheeks. Bright, red blood began to course freely over his pale flesh. Behind him, Corbis was crouching with his shotgun balanced on some fallen masonry, picking off termagants, one at a time. The other Scouts emerged from their shelter too, following suit, dropping aliens with every shot.

A lucky blast of return fire from one of the termagants caught Avyl full in the chest, bowling him backwards. Grayvus heard him cry out as he fought at whatever it was that had struck him and was now attempting to burrow its way through his carapace armour. There was no time to help him. The sergeant raised his bolt pistol again, searching for another target.

And then he was being pitched forwards, the sound of a massive impact ringing loudly in his ears. The ground shook violently beneath him. Darkness swam at the edges of his vision. His last thought before the black cowl of unconsciousness swallowed him entirely was that they needed to get out of there as quickly as possible.

The battle raged with a fierce intensity. Koryn was surrounded by a sea of flashing claws, creatures scrabbling to climb over his power armour, striking him as they tried to get at the Space Marine inside. He fought them off with ease, carried along by his fury, swept up in a storm of death. His talons hummed and spat with electrical energy as he cut a swathe through the mass of pink flesh and bone.

He heard more than felt the meteor storm as the hail of tiny stones rained down on his armour, scoring the black ceramite where it fell.

Further afield, boulders hurtled out of the sky, decimating the clashing armies, tearing great furrows and ridges in the landscape. Impact craters formed huge pockmarks across the battlefield and chaotic piles of the dead lay all around them, xenos and Raven Guard alike swallowed indiscriminately in the waves of earth that rushed out from the site of each strike. Above, the sky looked as if it were on fire.

Koryn twisted sharply to the right, swinging his talons up to spear a hormagaunt through the head. He gave his wrist a quick jerk and the creature's face came away in a spray of sickly ichor. Its twitching body fell to the ground, but Koryn had no time to savour the moment: for every alien he killed another two took its place.

The vox-bead buzzed suddenly to life in his ear. 'Captain?'

Koryn grunted. The sound of another voice pulling him momentarily from the trance of the battle. 'Go ahead, Fabis.'

'We're ready, captain. The alien force is in position.'

Koryn grinned inside his helm, striking down another hormagaunt with a swipe of a lightning claw. 'Your timing couldn't be better, brother. Mount your attack. And may the Emperor ride with you.'

The vox crackled and went dead. Koryn spun, arcing around to catch another of the beasts that had managed to get behind him. He jabbed his fists through the hormagaunt's torso, pulling them apart to splay the creature open, spilling its organs in a bloody heap.

The ground shook as another massive meteor struck from above, gouging the landscape, ripping an immense furrow across the battlefield. Scores of aliens died in its wake, buried in the accompanying deluge of mud and loam. Koryn glanced up. The Raven Guard were still showering the tyranid army with bolter shells and frag grenades, but many of them were being thrown off course as they collided with the meteors that filled the sky, or worse, exploding in mid-air before reaching their targets.

He looked to the left. It was difficult to see through the tangle of grappling limbs, but the bike squads had now closed on the left flank of the tyranid army, closing off their escape route through the trees. Koryn laughed as he turned his attention back to the swarm of aliens, freeing his arm from the grip of a hormagaunt that was trying to scrabble up and over his leg. He crushed its skull in his fist.

His plan was working. With Fabis closing in on the xenos army from behind, flanking them with a Raven Guard force comparable in size to that under Koryn's direct command, they had the xenos pinned. To the right, like a great dam, were the walls of the ruined city. The tyranids were completely surrounded. Now it was a waiting game. All they had to do was hold the line. Koryn willed Grayvus to hurry.

Light bloomed before his eyes. Light, and the sound of raindrops striking the ground, a relentless pitter-patter, pitter-patter. Grayvus coughed and heaved himself up off the ground. He shook his head to clear the woolliness. The sound wasn't rain. It was tiny stones. It was Helion.

The memories flooded back into his consciousness. The meteor storm was still pounding the city. He couldn't have been out for long. He cast around, looking for his bolt pistol. He found it jutting out from beneath a pile of rubble and retrieved it, dusting it off. He stretched and felt a long gash on his left cheek tug uncomfortably. The flesh had already begun to knit itself back together, but his face was crusted with dry blood. Smaller wounds covered his arms like a spider's web, or a chaotic street map.

The scene all around Grayvus was one of utter devastation. Behind him, a large meteor had slammed into the street, toppling a basilica. The building's metal sub-structure had buckled and warped, and it now described a twisted skeleton against the sky, having shed its rock-crete skin. The ground itself had risen in a vast wave from the impact point, ruffling the earth like a rug pulled out from somewhere deep beneath the city. Steam rose from the impact crater like so many ethereal spirits, desperate to return to the warp. And all the while, the meteors continued to fall, stinging Grayvus's already battered flesh.

Grayvus realised he had been flung out over the lip of the crater during the impact. He began searching the immediate area for the other Scouts but found only dead termagants, their weak bodies crushed by the wreckage of the building or shattered by the force of the impact. One of them was still squirming, its back legs clawing patheti-cally at the exposed soil. It made a high-pitched mewling sound as he approached, and then hissed viciously as he stood over it, turning its lolling head with the edge of his boot. He put a bolt through its skull, not out of any sense of mercy, but simply to ensure it was dead.

'Sergeant?' He heard the call from over the other side of the crater and ran over to find Corbis crouched over the dead figure of Avyl. The fallen Scout's body was covered in a fine layer of grit and stone, and Corbis was brush-ing it away with his hand, searching for Avyl's corvia. He located the tiny bird skulls and Grayvus watched him tug them free, fixing them carefully to his own belt, a tribute to his dead brother.

'Was it the blast?'

Corbis shook his head. 'It was the xenos.' He indicated a hole in Avyl's chest carapace where the living ammunition that the termagant had fired from its weapon had bored a hole through to the Scout's chest, devouring his hearts.

'Where's Tyrus?'

'Down there.' Corbis nodded behind him. Grayvus started over, increasing his pace to a run when he heard bolt-fire coming from that same direction, assuming that the Scout had engaged the enemy. He crested a large mound of earth to discover Tyrus was in fact following his lead, quickly and effectively terminating any remaining aliens he found amidst the wreckage. He looked up when he noticed Grayvus watching.

'Avyl is dead. We have a mission to complete.' The statement was matter-of-fact, pointed. The authority behind it was implicit.

Tyrus nodded. Grayvus could see the Scout's knuckles were white where he clenched his bolt pistol hard. He was feeling the loss of his brothers keenly. Grayvus smiled grimly. Tyrus would have his chance to avenge the dead. And so would he. He would be sure of it.

The power station loomed out of the hailstorm like a jagged tooth, a towering edifice of pipework and fuel vats that spewed a constant stream of oily smoke into the sky for miles in every direction. This was the generatorium, until recently the power hub for an entire quadrant of the city. Amidst the destruction wrought around it, this leviathan was somehow still operational. Or at least, Grayvus considered as they approached through the wide, ruined street, *something* was keeping it running.

Grayvus and the two remaining Scouts ran through the pummelling rain towards their goal. Time was running out. It had been hours since their last communication from the captain, many of those hours lost to the meteor storm and their encounter with the termagants. Now was the time to act.

Grayvus scanned the approach to the generatorium before ushering the others forwards. He clipped his auspex to his belt and reached for his chainsword. He didn't know what to expect inside the building, but he wasn't about to be caught unawares.

Tyrus was first to approach the large, arched doorway. He stepped cautiously through the entrance, his bolt pistol braced and ready. A moment later he reappeared, indicating that the others should follow. Grayvus and Corbis kept their backs to the wall as they moved slowly around the doorway to join Tyrus inside.

The corridor beyond the door was dank and industrial, with bare metal plating covering the walls and floor, and exposed pipes worming their way through the passageways like a network of arteries and veins. It was dimly lit, with only flickering emergency beacons to guide them. The stench of oil and burning coal was almost palpable.

Grayvus motioned for the others to be silent. He listened for a moment, trying to discern any sounds of movement. There was nothing but the noise of a dripping pipe, echoing throughout the empty corridor. That and the continuous background sounds of the meteor storm, striking the building outside.

He looked up, meeting the eyes of the others. They were injured and bedraggled, but their eyes shone with a burning intensity. 'We need to find the reactor. That's the only way we can destroy this place without any explosives. We set it to overload, and we get out of here as quickly as possible.'

Corbis straightened his back and flexed the fibrous muscles in his neck. 'May the Emperor protect us.'

'We will do our duty,' was Grayvus's only reply.

They set off down the passageway, their boots ringing loudly on the metal floor plates. They passed along a series of almost identical corridors as they wound their way towards the heart of the structure. The low, red lighting cast long shadows, and the occasional clank of a pipe or the thrum of a power line kept Grayvus alert and ready.

'The place seems deserted, sergeant,' said Corbis, but as they turned a dogleg in the passageway it became instantly clear that it was not. A large, bulbous sphere hung in the air just ahead of them, a fleshy ball of pink and grey. A long tail hung from the base of it, which quivered like a twitching snake as they approached. The xenos had been here, and they had left this behind.

Tyrus hefted his bolt pistol and took aim.

'No!' Grayvus bellowed, foregoing all sense of stealth. But it was already too late. The bolt-fire lanced the spore mine, which exploded in a spray of searing acid, splashing across Grayvus's face and arms and raising instant welts in his pale flesh. His skin burned for a moment and he gritted his teeth and waited for the pain to subside. But Tyrus had taken the brunt of the explosion and he fell to his knees, clutching ineffectually at his face. His bolt pistol clattered to the floor.

Grayvus rushed to his side. 'Tyrus?'

'Forgive me, sergeant.' The voice was a stuttering lisp.

Grayvus prised the Scout's fingers away from his ruined face. The bioacid had done its work. Tyrus's right eye was nothing but a puddle of jelly in its socket, and where his cheek had been there was now only stringy remnants of flesh and muscle, exposing his hind teeth.

'You're alive, brother, and that's enough. Get up.' There was a hard edge to Grayvus's voice. 'We have a job to do.'

Corbis helped the wounded Scout to his feet. 'Can you see?'

Tyrus nodded but didn't speak. He stooped to reclaim his bolt pistol, and they moved on.

The corridors and passageways of the generatorium continued to wind into the dank depths of the earth. They were drawing closer to their target now, closer to the throbbing heart of the power station, closer to their mission objective.

They'd passed another three of the spore mines, but had crawled beneath them on their bellies, an undignified but necessary means of avoiding detection, ensuring the biological triggers did not detonate in the confined space of the corridors.

Now, they had come upon a bulkhead door that had been dropped across the corridor, blocking their way: one of the safety barriers that locked into place during a shutdown. Grayvus had considered turning back, finding an alternative route, but that meant doubling back and passing the spore mines again, and worse, it meant wasting time. He consulted his auspex. Going through the bulkhead was the quickest way to the reactor. They were only a matter of metres away. Once they were through they could set the reactor to overload and get out of there. They would have to break through with bolters and chainswords.

He was about to outline this plan to the others when he heard a distinctive *tap-tap* ringing out against the metal floor plates. He glanced at the others inquisitively but was met with only blank stares. He hesitated, a cold sensation spreading across his chest. There it was again, *tap-tap*, like the clicking of a claw. Grayvus stiffened. His finely tuned hearing had detected breathing now, a ragged, rasping breath. A hissing. Something drew a claw across a wall plate, scratching a loud warning. It was toying with them. He knew what it was. They'd been herded into a trap.

Grayvus turned to see not one but two genestealers appear at the far end of the corridor, their heads bobbing, their multiple, viciously clawed arms tapping the walls menacingly as they approached. Wriggling proboscises surrounded their mouths and their eyes were blood-red and shone with a startling intelligence. They crept forwards, taking their time with their cornered prey.

The Scouts formed a line, keeping their backs to the bulkhead.

'Don't let them get close!' Grayvus barked. 'Don't let them get anywhere near you.' He knew first-hand what this genus was capable of.

Grayvus squeezed the trigger of his bolt pistol, spraying the genestealers with shells. But the creatures were too fast. They pounced, launching themselves into the air, springing off the walls to land only centimetres away from the Grayvus and the others. Grayvus's bolt pistol went spinning away down the corridor, wrenched from his grip by a glistening talon.

Corbis squeezed off a series of shots with his shotgun, catching one of the genestealers across its left flank, slowing it for only a second. It whipped out a claw and pinned the Scout by the throat, dragging him closer, its proboscises writhing with anticipation.

'No!' Grayvus's chainsword roared to life. He would not let this happen again. And he would not fail his captain.

He charged the nearest alien, swinging his chainsword in a wide arc, aiming to take off its head. The creature swiped at him with a claw, battering his blade to one side and sending Grayvus sprawling to the ground. He wasn't staying down, however, and twisted quickly up onto one knee, forcing the chainsword up. The genestealer's claw came down, centimetres from his head, but clattered uselessly to the floor as Grayvus's blade tore through the alien's carapace, chewing out its belly. It squirmed and thrashed, but Grayvus pressed the blade home even harder, twisting it round to maximise the damage. He stood, grabbing a fistful of the quivering mouth tentacles, yanking the creature's head to one side. The alien's claws raked his chest-plate as it tried to pull itself free, but Grayvus was lost to his rage. He left the chainsword buried in its innards and reached for his combat knife. He looked deep into the creature's eyes as he buried the knife to the hilt in its exposed throat.

'That's for Erynis,' he whispered, as he saw the life flee its body. The genestealer squirmed once in his grasp and then fell still. Grayvus dropped the corpse to the floor.

Beside him, the other genestealer still had Corbis pinned by the throat but was also grappling with Tyrus, who had managed to draw his chainsword and was busy sawing his way through the creature's chitinous armour plating. He was bleeding freely from a long wound in his arm. Grayvus calmly pulled his own chainsword free of the corpse at his feet, stepped across the corridor and wordlessly lopped off the head of the occupied genestealer. It fell to the metal floor with a dull *thunk* and the body went limp. Corbis and Tyrus both disentangled themselves from the mass of limbs. Tyrus was breathing heavily. What with the acid burns and the fresh injuries caused by the genestealer, he was in a bad way.

'I told you not to let it get close to you,' Grayvus said, without a hint of irony in his voice.

Corbis laughed grimly. 'What now?'

Grayvus motioned to the bulkhead. 'Through there. The reactor is on the other side of this barricade. Corbis – see if you can breach it with your shotgun.' He stepped back to make room for the other Scout. 'And be quick. I don't want to be cornered by any more of these *things*.' He kicked at the dead remains of the nearest genestealer and moved off in search of his bolt pistol.

The shotgun soon punched a series of irregular holes in the thick metal plating causing the steel to splinter like rotten wood. Grayvus kept watch, keen to avoid another encounter with the genestealers that were likely haunting the corridors around them, drawn in by the sounds of the battle. Presently, however, the bulkhead issued a long groan and a large section of plating dropped inwards, clanging loudly where it fell.

Corbis called him over.

Grayvus approached the makeshift door, his bolt pistol clutched in his fist. He could see little through the hatch but a bank of winking diodes and controls: the reactor room. He dipped his head and pulled himself through the opening.

And that's when he saw it: the biggest tyranid biomorph he had ever seen, squatting inside the reactor room, its enormous, dripping maw bared in what he could only imagine was a wicked smile.

\* \* \*

Koryn thrust and cut, parried and spun: a riotous dance of destruction. He could barely see for the blood spray hanging in the air all around him. He was injured, but was choosing to ignore the warning sigils that flashed up inside his helm, alerting him to the deep gash in his thigh. Analgesics had already flooded the area and his body would have time to repair itself later. If he survived.

Many of his brothers were dead. He knew that instinctively. He had no need to witness the sorry ranks of the lost, the discarded bodies, ripped apart by uncompromising alien jaws. He knew it, and it filled his heart with sadness. The Raven Guard were few and they could ill afford to sacrifice themselves. But his brothers had died with purpose. They had died in the glory of battle, holding the tyranid army at bay while their brethren engineered the means of their victory. He only hoped that Grayvus was close to achieving his goal. They could not hold out for much longer. Koryn could see the hive tyrant was growing restless. The end was in sight, one way or another.

Grayvus eyed the creature warily. It was huge, towering at least three times his height, with a flared crest of blood-red chitin atop its massive head. Its lower jaw was wide and pink, splayed like a shovel and connected to two mandibles that twitched ominously from side to side as it regarded him. Its fangs were as big as his forearms and coated in dripping venom. Its body was long and snake-like and – Grayvus realised – disappeared into the ground, from where the monster had evidently burrowed its way into the generatorium, digging its way in from beneath the city. Three huge pairs of limbs terminated in scything talons, with two sets of smaller, more human arms bursting out from its chest. It filled the reactor room utterly.

The creature emitted a shrill chirp and shifted its bulk, lowering its head to show them its fangs. Its foetid breath smelled of moist earth and decay. It couldn't twist itself around enough to reach them with its talons.

Once again, Grayvus was taken aback by the intelligence displayed by the xenos. Had they known the Scouts were coming? Was that why the biomorph had burrowed its way here? Or worse, had they planned to use the same trick? Were the tyranids actually intending to use the power station for the same purpose as the captain, to detonate it at a time when it would prove most devastating to the Imperial forces? Either way, they had been out manoeuvred.

'What is it?' Corbis was standing beside him, staring up at the monstrous thing.

'It's between us and the reactor,' was Grayvus's only response.

Tyrus stepped forwards, brandishing his chainsword. 'This time, sergeant, I think we're going to have to cut our way through.' His slurred voice was barely recognisable.

The Scout was right. There was little else they could do. 'Corbis. Get to that reactor. Tyrus and I will keep it occupied.' Grayvus raised his bolt pistol. 'We don't have to kill it, Tyrus, just keep it busy. The reactor will do our job for us if we can get to it.'

Tyrus nodded, but Grayvus wasn't clear whether it was in understanding or something else entirely. The injured Scout seemed distant, distracted.

Corbis approached the creature tentatively, trying to search out the best route to the reactor. He moved left and it howled like a baying wolf, slamming its talons down into the churned earth, trying its best to reach him. The bony blades scratched the walls in frustration. Corbis fell back, raising his shotgun and loosing a handful of shots. They pierced its flesh but did little more than anger it.

Tyrus fired up his chainsword. He extended his arm and placed something in Grayvus's hand. It was a tiny bundle of bird skulls. 'Honour me, sergeant, in the fields of Kiavahr.'

'Tyrus!'

The Scout charged forwards towards the beast, his bolt pistol flaring as he fired round after round into the creature's open maw. It screeched in fury and lashed out with its scything talons, one of them catching him full in the chest, bursting out of his back and spattering Adeptus Astartes blood across the room.

Tyrus growled in agony as he was lifted fully from the ground. His chain-sword roared, biting deep into the monster's flesh, as it pulled him closer to its slavering jaws.

'Corbis. Get to that reactor, now!' Grayvus swung his bolt pistol around and fired into the alien's wide mouth, satisfied to see the bolt-rounds flashing inside its head as they exploded brightly, cracking its teeth. The creature reared its head and thrashed alarmingly, swinging Tyrus violently from side to side. Tyrus was still alive, barely, speared on an outstretched claw. With one hand he was firing his bolt pistol into its face, with the other he was driving his chainsword repeatedly into the thick hide of its torso, searching for any vital organs.

Grayvus moved back and forth in a wide semi-circle, keeping his weapon trained on the monster, firing clip after clip at its head, desperate to keep it from realising that Corbis had now passed it and was working on the reactor controls behind it. He reappeared a moment later, scrambling over the mound of earth and rushing towards Grayvus.

Too late, Grayvus saw the arcing talon as it swung down from above, catching Corbis square between the shoulders and pitching him forwards. The Scout stumbled and dropped. The talon raised again, ready to finish the prone Corbis.

Grayvus dived forwards, grabbing at his brother and flinging him across the reactor room. The talon sliced down, puncturing his shoulder and opening his chest, bursting a lung. Grayvus slumped to the floor. The world was spinning. The creature pulled Tyrus's now unconscious body towards its mouth and chewed off his head.

Behind it, the reactor was reaching critical levels, warning sirens blaring.

Grayvus saw only darkness.

Koryn heard the explosion from almost four kilometres away, even above the clamour of the raging battle, even above the screams of the dying aliens and the screeching of their claws across his power armour. He heard it, and he knew they were victorious.

The ground rumbled and groaned, knocking him from his feet. He heard the vox-bead buzz in his ear but made no sense of the words as, all of a sudden, the planet seemed to lurch violently to one side. He heard a sound like rending stone and scrambled to his knees in time to see the city walls give way, crumbling to the ground as titanic forces rent the earth apart. All around him, the tyranids were scrabbling for solid ground, their animal minds unable to comprehend what was happening.

Koryn caught sight of the hive tyrant, its head thrust back, bellowing insanely at the sky. He watched as the ground cracked open beneath it, sucking the creature down into its rocky depths, pulling it into the canyon opened by Grayvus's destruction of the power station. It was as if the planet itself was enacting its revenge against these insidious invaders, swallowing them whole, crushing them with its immense power. The Raven Guard had executed their plan to precision: the fault line had opened right beneath the heart of the tyranid army, exactly where the Space Marines had pinned it in place.

Scores of aliens spilled into the newly opened crevasse like a tide, unable to prevent themselves from falling. Their screams were a violent cacophony, a tortured howl that Koryn would never forget. That was the sound of triumph. That was the sound of the Emperor's might.

Those aliens that still swarmed around Koryn himself seemed suddenly to lose direction, their psychic link with the hive mind interrupted by the death of their tyrant. They pressed on with their attack, but they had lost their cohesion, their underlying purpose, and were now fighting on instinct alone. It would be a simple matter for the remaining Raven Guard forces to mop up what was left of the alien brood.

Koryn sliced another alien in two with his talons. He was covered in xenos blood and his leg wound was still causing warning sigils to flare incessantly inside his helm. He watched as a group of hormagaunts turned and fled from an approaching assault squad, who showed no mercy, mowing down the retreating aliens with their bolt pistols.

He turned to see Argis approaching from behind, striding across the battlefield towards him, his power armour rent open across the chest in a wide gash, his bolter hanging by his side. Clusters of corvia hung from his belt, signifying the losses his squad had sustained during the thick of the battle. The veteran stopped beside Koryn, surveying the scene across the battlefield. After a moment, he spoke. 'Faith, you said, captain.'

Koryn nodded. His voice was subdued. 'Faith.'

Argis put his hand on Koryn's pauldron. 'That is most definitely our way.'

Grayvus sucked noisily at the air and winced at the lancing pain it caused in his chest. He peeled open his eyes. He was outside, slumped against a wall. The meteor storm had abated and the sun was perforating the clouds. His mouth was full of gritty blood and he was gripping something tightly in his fist. He glanced down. It was Tyrus's corvia. He allowed his hand to drop to his lap. He would take them back to Kiavahr, bury them in the soil from whence they came.

Corbis was standing over him. When he saw Grayvus was awake, his pale face cracked into a wide grin. 'Sergeant.'

Grayvus spat blood. 'Corbis. You should have left me.'

Corbis didn't answer.

Grayvus stared over at the enormous cavity that had opened in the ground behind them. The power station had been completely subsumed. What remained of it after the explosion had slid noisily into the hungry earth, tumbling down into the depths of the fractured landmass. Its destruction had opened a canyon across the face of Idos like a long, puckered scar, a fault line stemming from the site of the explosion and stretching for kilometres in both directions. Much of the city had been swallowed in the ensuing devastation. And the biomorph, too, along with most of the tyranid brood.

Corbis dropped to his haunches beside the wounded sergeant. 'What now, sergeant?'

Grayvus put his hand on Corbis's shoulder pauldron. 'Now, brother? Now you may call yourself Adeptus Astartes.'

# WITH BAITED BREATH

The corpse was staring at him from across the floor of the ruined acropolis. Its one remaining eye was yellowed and fixed, and Trooper Sergei Asdic thought he could still see the terror etched into the dead man's expression, his mouth set in a rictus howl.

Could the dead still judge? Perhaps they could. Sergei couldn't help but feel his fallen comrade was somehow appraising him as he lay there, watching him die. Wondering how he had ended up dead, while he was still – just about – drawing breath. Perhaps that was just wishful thinking on his part, ascribing some modicum of continued existence to the deceased. He supposed he'd find out, soon enough.

He was slumped against a heap of fallen masonry, his now-useless legs splayed out before him. He was beginning to feel light-headed, now, and everything had taken on a slightly unreal aspect. He coughed, and bubbles of bright blood burst on his lips. The movement made his belly spasm in pain, and his hands went involuntarily to the site of his suppurating wound. He moaned as he attempted to shift himself, in order to better prop himself up and minimise the bleeding. Not that it would do him much good. He knew he was beyond saving now, even if there had been anyone there to help.

Around him, the acropolis was littered with the deceased. His corpse would soon be one among many – just another anonymous statistic, nameless in death. He almost wished the plague marine had finished him off swiftly, like the others. That way, at least he wouldn't have to sit there awaiting the inevitable, wracked with pain and fear.

Sergei surveyed the remains of his fallen comrades, a sea of limbs upon the broken flagstones. In their midst was the enormous, festering corpse of the plague marine, its outstretched fist still clutching the blade that had pierced his guts only a short while earlier. Its power armour was rusted and broken, its necrotic, bloated flesh pushing out through the cracks and seams like malleable, festering putty. Its helmet was half corroded where its acid breath had chewed large chunks in the vents. The head was lolling to one side, almost separated from the shoulders by a fortuitous, desperate shot from Sergei's lasrifle. Strange circular symbols had been daubed on its shoulder plates in livid green paint, and maggots still picked their way through its exposed, blackened entrails. The stench was nauseating. Sergei averted his eyes.

Behind the bloodied litter of the dead, above the jagged teeth of the shattered wall, the sky was the colour of burnished gunmetal, as if the war raging below had in some way scorched the very air itself.

The distant howl of projectiles and the scream of rending plasteel told him that the battle still raged on outside the strange, tomblike atmosphere of the acropolis. He would not see it end, but he knew that he had done his duty, and that the drop pods which had fallen from the sky only a few hours earlier had brought not only reinforcements, but hope of salvation. The Emperor's finest warriors had come amongst them, thundering out of the void itself, and they would drive the foul taint of Chaos from Andricor and the entire Sargassion Reach. He took comfort in that, at least. Andricor had not been forsaken.

Sergei sensed movement and turned his head toward it, wincing as the motion set off another burst of pain in his guts.

There was no one there. He fumbled by his side, his fingers searching out the barrel of his lasrifle. He snatched it up, placing it across his lap.

'Who's there?' he asked. 'Show yourself!'

If it was an enemy hostile, he would try to take them down with another well-placed shot before he died – unless, of course, they finished him off first. In his present condition, that was a distinct possibility.

He watched the entrance to the courtyard intently, blinking away the fog of weariness that threatened to overwhelm him. His ragged breath seemed as loud as a klaxon in his ears, despite the raging sounds of the battle from all sides.

Movement again. He raised his weapon, gritting his teeth as his wound screamed in protest. He caught a glimpse of something black – something immense and black, lurking by the shattered pillar that marked one side of the entrance to the complex. His finger hovered on the trigger. He heard the crunch of a heavy footstep and readied himself, looking for his shot.

'Hold your fire.'

The voice was commanding and clipped. Sergei hesitated.

'State your name and rank,' said Sergei. 'And show yourself.'

He was having trouble holding the barrel of the lasrifle straight, but he was determined not to falter in his duty now.

Another footstep crunched on the broken masonry, and then the figure emerged into the light, and Sergei was unable to withhold a gasp.

It was a Space Marine, sheathed entirely in resplendent black power armour. Even from a few metres away he towered over him, and he had to crane his neck in order to see the front of his helm, his face hidden behind the unusual flared respirator. Both of his fists terminated in massive, arcing claws, which spat and hissed with electrical charge. His shoulder pads were emblazoned with unfamiliar white symbols, and bundles of what looked like bleached bird skulls dangled on thin chains from his belt. The Space Marine stepped towards him, and he tried to scuttle back, but his legs were unable to respond and his back was already against the wall. He tried to make himself smaller, as if that would somehow protect him from the giant.

As he came closer he could see that his armour was finely engraved with hundreds of strange runes; names, he decided, although for what purpose he could not guess. They seemed to cover almost every inch of the worn, pitted surface; a record, a list.

He searched the immediate area for others of the Space Marine's kind, but he was alone, and he was utterly terrifying. He felt himself trembling in his presence.

The Space Marine came to a stop, looking down at him.

'I am Captain Koryn of the Raven Guard Fourth Company,' he said. 'Lower your weapon.'

Sergei found himself doing as the Space Marine commanded. He placed his lasrifle back on his lap, although he kept his finger curled around the trigger, just in case he needed to defend himself quickly.

The giant cocked his head to one side, regarding him. The faceplate of his helmet remained impassive, making it impossible for him to work out what he was thinking.

'You're dying, trooper.'

It was a statement of fact, nothing more. The Raven Guard's voice echoed loudly amongst the broken spurs of the building, deep and soft.

Sergei expelled a wheezing, gasping laugh, air hissing out between his clenched teeth. He glanced down at the puddle of blood that was spreading on the stone tiles beneath him.

'I'd noticed,' he said.

'What is your name?'

Sergei frowned. He'd never encountered a Space Marine before, other than the traitorous monsters who had descended on his world in order to tear it apart – but he had heard tales; stories of the giants who walked amongst men, who fought shoulder to shoulder with humans in order to protect the realms of the Emperor from the deadly reach of Chaos, or the ever-present threat of xenos. But never had he heard of a Space Marine who had spoken in such a manner to a member of the Guard. He wondered what he had done to invite such interest from such a terrifying thing.

'Trooper Sergei Asdic,' he said. 'Deceased.'

He smiled at his own grim joke.

The Space Marine was regarding the sea of corpses by his feet. He stooped low to examine the remains of the plague marine, as if anxious to ensure it was actually dead.

'What happened here?'

'Why?' Sergei spoke before he'd had time to consider his words.

The Space Marine stood again and he flinched, expecting a harsh rebuttal for his question, but his shoulders heaved in an approximation of what might have been a shrug.

'We live on through our legends. Our stories define us. Those who have committed great deeds should have their stories heard.'

Sergei laughed, and then winced at the sudden agony it caused. He glanced at the corpse of the plague marine.

'Great deeds? It took twenty of us to bring down one of them. You might have done the same in a moment.'

Koryn seemed to consider this.

'Yet you were victorious, and you sacrificed your lives in the name of the Emperor. You did so in the face of overwhelming odds. It is true that to one such as I, felling a single enemy might be nothing more than a moment's work, but for you and your brethren, it took courage and the lives of twenty men and women. I see the greatness in this. I see sacrifice and honour. Tell your tale, trooper. Have it heard before you die.'

Sergei nodded.

'Very well.'

He closed his eyes, summoning up the memories. They seemed like dreams to him now. It was as if years had passed, as if there had never been anything else but the battlefield, the howl of the enemy weapons, the tortured screams of the dying and the deep, throbbing pain in his belly. As if the events of just a few hours earlier had happened in another lifetime. And so he told his tale.

'It began in darkness. The enemy came out of the night on a tide of pestilence, dragging their rotten carcasses across the muddied fields of Andricor.

'Led by the fearsome giants of Empyrion's Blight – lumbering, ancient warriors who had long since invited the taint of the dark gods to infest their once glorious bodies – they seemed intent upon only one thing: utter devastation. Planets had fallen in their wake, and the conquered had swelled their ranks, infected by the foul plague that lay siege not only to their flesh, but to their very souls.

'I had known they were coming. My comrades and I had been deployed to defensive positions along the bastion walls after the transmissions from the neighbouring world, Auros, had suddenly ceased.

'The Navy had formed a tight ring around the planet, warships creating a deep blockade. The path between the two worlds – difficult to navigate because of stray asteroids and rocky debris – had been shut down by a vast flotilla, and I felt confident that I would not have cause to raise my weapon or put my training to the test. The invaders would never actually set foot upon the planet. It was utterly inconceivable that they would find a way through such a dense and impenetrable blockade.

'That night, however, I watched the flotilla burn up in the

atmosphere as the enemy barges forced their way through, making short work of the Navy warships. The Imperial vessels burst against the canvas of stars like detonating fireworks, shimmering as they fragmented and burned, the wreckage tumbling to the planet below like so many falling stars. It would have been almost beautiful if I hadn't known what it represented, how many people had died in that terrible display of firepower and brutality.

'I had a sense then of the sheer ferocity of the enemy, the momentum with which they came at us, and I cowered. They would soon be upon us, and there was very little anyone could do.

'Hours passed in dreadful anticipation, huddled in the cold as we awaited our fate.

'When they finally arrived it was in their thousands, huge landing craft disgorging legions of bilious, grotesque cultists and their towering, shambling masters. They did not pause to erect a beachhead, but simply trudged across the landscape towards the Imperial fortifications and laid siege, ignoring the spitting weapon emplacements and the hail of lasfire we rained down on them from above. Scores of them fell, but others simply took their place, scrabbling over the piles of the dead, using their fallen as stepping stones to better reach the walls of the Imperial bastion.

'The Plague Marines, no matter what we threw at them, seemed practically impervious to harm. They would judder with the impact of weapons fire, sometimes even sprawling back upon the ground with the sheer momentum of the attack, and then, damaged but unfazed, they would clamber back to their feet and continue their assault. They were relentless and unstoppable. They were death incarnate.

'The bastion walls soon gave. It was inevitable that they

would. Terrifying war engines ploughed across the battle-field, discharging explosive rounds into the foundations of the structure, chewing massive holes in the walls. We were forced to fall back, readying ourselves for the oncoming surge.

'We knew then that the bastion was lost. And with it, all hope of survival. The Chaos forces were all-consuming. We were powerless to stop them. All we could hope for was a swift death, and to take as many of them with us as possible.

'They burst through the metre-thick walls as if they were passing through rotten timber, bringing with them a cor-rosive stench that was enough to overwhelm my senses and leave me reeling with nausea. Unable to hold the line, my platoon fell back to this ancient, ruined acropolis on the hillside, where we took our positions behind the walls and tried to pick off as many of the enemy as possible.

'It was a good defensive position, and we held out for some time. Whether it was sheer luck, or that the enemy had more pressing concerns, I cannot say, but the hours ticked by, and still we survived.

'The battle raged on through the night. I lost all sense of time. Existence shrank to the fight, and little beyond. I became nothing but a pawn in a great game, a tool – a means of depressing the trigger on a weapon. There on the battlefield, that was the entirety of the universe. My sole aim was to stop the enemy getting any closer, to hold back the tide of their relentless assault. Somewhere at the back of my mind I knew it was all in vain, but my sense of duty and purpose, my will to protect my home world, compelled me to go on.'

Sergei started at a percussive bang from somewhere close to the acropolis, and broke off from his tale. He glanced, frightened, from side to side, attempting to ascertain what had happened.

'What was that?'

Koryn twisted, looking back over his shoulder. Sergei caught sight of something moving in the distance behind him, a giant, lumbering form, hazy and indistinct: an enemy war machine, stomping inexorably toward them. He could hear the insistent thud of its footsteps. It must have seen Koryn standing there, his back to the narrow entranceway, or else picked up the sound of their voices and decided to investigate.

'Ignore it,' the Space Marines said. 'Continue with your tale.'

Sergei shook his head, and then wished he hadn't. The world seemed to keep on spinning for a moment. He felt woozy, and allowed his head to fall back against the masonry, resting for a few seconds.

' No, I can't. That thing... it's coming this way.'

He struggled to raise his lasrifle.

'Leave it,' insisted Koryn. 'You have little time left. Make it count.'

Koryn turned back towards him. Sergei shrugged, suppressing a laugh. It just seemed so absurd, that he should find himself here, dying amidst the corpses of his friends, talking to an armoured giant. Perhaps he was hallucinating; perhaps all of this was a feverish dream caused by his festering injury. It was difficult to tell. He decided to continue with his story.

'Morning came suddenly, weak sunlight bleaching the horizon.

'I continued to fire indiscriminately at the enemy lines,

the backwash from my super-heated lasrifle scalding my hands and wrists. I barely noticed it any more. My flesh was blistered, my legs barely able to support me due to fatigue. Yet still I pressed on, mowing down those traitorous wretches as they came upon us.

'They were the pus-ridden runts that had once been Imperial troops like my comrades and I, but had given themselves up to the festering giants who now walked among them, submitting to the sickening rot. I could not fathom what it was that made a man turn to the dark gods. The Plague Marines – they were something different, something entirely unknowable – but I detested those traitorous men who scuttled about in their wake, betrayers of all that was dear to me. They had forsaken their humanity, and for that alone, they deserved to die.

'All around me the ground shook with the quaking thunder of artillery guns barking at the dawn. The Chaos forces had brought with them vast engines of war, and they trundled across the muddy loam, churning the ground and the ruins of the bastion as they searched out pockets of survivors.

'As the light had blossomed over the battlefield, I realised for the first time the true scale of the devastation. The hillocks and undulations I had sensed in the gloaming were, in fact, innumerable heaps of human corpses, forming grisly dunes upon a wasteland of death. I knew then that it was over. We could hold out for no more than a few hours. We were outnumbered, and alone.

'It was then that I heard shouting from the others and looked up to see white streamers crisscrossing the sky. Drop pods tearing furrows through the amber morning, thudding indiscriminately into the battlefield, the impacts causing even the ground to tremble in fear and anticipation.

'The drop pods flowered open to disgorge their cargo. At first we did not know whether they represented friend or foe, and feared the enemy was swelling their own ranks for the final push, but then something changed.

'I was unable to see the figures who struck from the shadows, but their presence was evident in the alteration of the enemy's behavior – the lumbering hulks of the Plague Marines turned their attentions away from the serried ranks of men and women, focusing instead on the living shadows that flitted amongst them, cutting them down where they stood. Suddenly the entire tone of the battle had changed. The enemy was confused, and in their confusion, they were falling. I sensed something from them that I had not sensed before: fear.

'I felt emboldened by this realisation, reinvigorated. I felt hope. Help had come to Andricor. Shadows that killed. Space Marines.

'I heard a scream from behind me and turned in time to see the lumbering bulk of a plague marine ripping the arm off a trooper no more than a few feet away. It had made its move while we'd been distracted, while our minds had turned to salvation, rather than death.

'The thing was disgusting to look upon: its putrid organs hung limply from its yawning belly on stringy threads of mucus and rotten flesh. Its corroded armour was split and broken, its helmet parted by the stump of an enormous horn that had sprouted from the centre of its forehead. It carried in its hand a dripping, noxious blade, and swung it widely, cutting down swathes of my comrades as they rushed to join combat.

'I brought my lasrifle up and loosed off a series of shots, catching the beast square in the face, but it barely seemed to notice the searing burns as it swatted at more of the troopers, snapping their necks or crushing them underfoot. I saw Dole try to get close enough to plant a grenade, but the thing simply grabbed him up in its huge fist and collapsed his ribcage, casting him away like a broken doll.

'Panic gripped me. I had no idea how to kill it. To me it seemed as if it was already dead, a nightmare made flesh.

'I knew I had no choice. I rushed forward, raising my lasrifle and squeezing off shot after shot, thinking that perhaps if I could somehow separate its head from its shoulders, I might be able to stop it.

'I screamed in rage as I ploughed through the corpses of the fallen, firing over and over, and to my amazement I saw that it was working. The plague marine staggered back, away from me, and I pressed on, relentless. Its throat – the flesh already corroded by its own acidic bile – burst in a splatter of yellow pus and its head yawned backwards, twisting on top of its damaged spine. I stood, watching in awe, as the creature wobbled unsteadily on its feet for a moment, before toppling forward in a heap.

'A stream of foul-smelling gas hissed from the stump of its neck.

'It was only then that I realised the creature's foul blade was jutting out of my belly, and I pulled it free, screaming in agony, and slumped to the ground, defeated.

'This is how I was when you found me.'

'You have honoured yourself and those of your kin who gave their lives for the Emperor,' said Koryn. 'You die knowing you have done your duty. That is the greatest of honours.'

The lumbering, wheezing sounds from behind him were growing closer now, and Sergei tightened his grip on his lasrifle. The Raven Guard, however, seemed entirely unperturbed by the approaching monstrosity, content to remain standing with his back to the battlefield. He must have represented a clear target, directly in its line of sight. He was taking a hell of a chance – and for what reason? Sergei could not be sure. The ways of the Adeptus Astartes were a mystery to him, utterly unfathomable.

He found himself straining to catch a glimpse of the thing, but didn't have the strength to haul himself up to get a better view, and Koryn almost entirely blocked his line of sight. It didn't seem as if he were planning to move any time soon.

'Have you fought them before?' asked Sergei.

His teeth had begun to chatter with the cold. He didn't know if that was the weather, or the loss of blood. He suspected the latter.

Koryn nodded.

'On many occasions I have sent their foul kind to their deaths.' Koryn's voice was level, betraying no emotion.

The tension was excruciating now and Sergei wanted to scream at the Space Marine to turn around. He was convinced that the thing would be upon them at any moment; that it would unleash some horrific barrage from its weapons and that Koryn would be incinerated where he stood. Had he not realised? Did he not know it was there?

He squeezed his eyes shut, drawing a deep breath in preparation for the coming onslaught. There was nothing he could do but add his fire to the battle, to squeeze off as many shots as possible before it was upon them. Assuming, of course, that Koryn even intended to put up a fight.

He opened his eyes to see the Space Marine had gone. He hadn't even heard him move. For a moment, panicked, he thought he'd abandoned him, left him to face the monstrosity alone, but then he realised he had simply moved, stepping to one side to afford them both a better view.

The enemy machine was near the top of the steps now, and as Sergei watched, it lumbered forward, each footstep causing the ground beneath him to shudder. It was tall – taller even than Koryn – and was, without doubt, the most terrifying thing he had ever seen. His heart raced in his chest, hammering against his ribcage, and he felt warm blood oozing out through the rent in his belly. He knew he did not have long left to live, one way or another.

The creature might once have been a Space Marine such as Koryn, encased in the thick armour plating of a Dreadnought, but now it was some sort of nightmare monster dragged from the very depths of the warp itself. The green plasteel of its casing had twisted and parted, fusing with the dead, pustulant flesh beneath, so that the thing inside had become one with the machine that once housed it. The exposed skin rippled and quivered as he watched, as if fist-sized creatures shifted nervously beneath the surface, trying desperately to break free.

The creature's face sat in a pit of this rippling flesh-armour, surrounded by a haze of putrid gas and buzzing flies. The flesh here had been almost entirely flayed from the skull, and the eye sockets were hollow and empty: staring, unforgiving, but – somehow – still seeing. The skeletal jaw worked constantly up and down; as if the thing were attempting to intone some foul litany as it walked, or else laugh insanely and silently at the thought of what it might inflict upon its prey.

One arm had morphed into an immense, double-barrelled flamer that spat yellow fire, the other had split and altered, separating into three distinct tentacles that writhed and twisted like mechanised snakes, dripping with ichor. Once the limb had terminated in a bulky power fist, and now each of the tentacles had claimed a fragment of this broken weapon, each end weighted with a misshapen lump of green plasteel. A blow from any one of them, Sergei knew, would be enough to crush a human body to pulp.

Most disturbing of all, the immense, bloated body of the creature was covered in mouths. Fanged orifices of all shapes and sizes puckered arms, legs and torso alike. Dripping tongues lolled hungrily from within, tasting the air. There must have been dozens of them, snapping in anticipation.

The Helbrute stormed forwards, flicking out its tentacles and demolishing one of the stone pillars that marked the narrow entrance to the acropolis. Broken stone clattered to the ground in a spray of dust and chippings as the creature pushed on, smashing its way through the too-small opening. The walls parted like water in its wake. It bellowed again, although the voice seemed not to emanate from the skeletal mouth but from its myriad grotesque counterparts.

Flames gushed from the end of its weapon, under-lighting its harrowing face. Sergei raised his lasrifle, trying to draw a bead on its head. He was shaking so violently now that he couldn't be sure he'd even manage to hit the thing at all. He slowly depressed the trigger, but at the last moment felt the barrel of the rifle being forced down so that the shot went wide, discharging harmlessly into the wall. He hadn't even managed to get the thing's attention, so intent it was upon closing the gap between itself and Koryn.

He glanced up to see Koryn stooping over him. The Space Marine shook his head.

'Watch.'

Sergei was about to protest, to ask him what good watching would do, when Koryn suddenly released his grip on his weapon and stepped away, moving toward the oncoming Helbrute. It was standing now in the dead centre of the ruined structure, its mechanical feet crushing the remains of his fallen comrades, and it was spoiling for a fight. It could have doused them both in flames in a matter of moments, but something – vanity, he suspected, or perhaps simple arrogance – had caused it to hesitate. It seemed to beckon Koryn forward, urging him on as if willing him to close the gap between them and make good his attack. It wanted to meet him in hand-to-hand combat, to test its mettle against a captain of the Raven Guard.

Koryn raised his lightning talons, blue electrical light crackling across their surface. He lowered himself into a crouch, coiling as if to spring...

'No!' Sergei called out, his body wracking with pain. He knew even Koryn did not stand a chance against the thing alone. He could do little to assist with his lasrifle and his wavering sight. He was about to watch him die.

But then, almost as soon as the words had passed his lips, he sensed movement out of the corner of his eye. He turned his head fractionally to see the shadows were moving. All around the acropolis, Ebon-clad figures were peeling away from the walls. He glanced from side to side. They were coming from all directions. He counted them – at least nine, maybe more, entirely encircling the creature that now stood in their midst. A circle of black death.

Sergei gasped. They must have been there all along, ever since Koryn first arrived. He hadn't noticed them as they'd fanned out around the inside of the ruins, taking up their positions, ready for the attack: an entire squad of Raven Guard, their black, beaked helms shining in the weak sunlight, bleached bird skull totems dangling from chains around their belts.

It was an ambush. Koryn had lured the Helbrute into the ruins. He had shown himself in order to draw it closer, close enough for his brothers to ensnare it in their trap. That was why he had spoken with him. That was why he had left himself exposed in such a way. He'd counted on the arrogance of the creature, anticipated its desire to face him in hand-to-hand combat.

The sound of their voices would have alerted the enemy to their presence. Sergei had been nothing but bait.

He gave a wet, spluttering laugh as he watched the circle of Space Marines close in on their prey.

The Helbrute screeched, twisting and turning, its tentacles whipping out in desperate frenzy as the black-armoured warriors danced around it, weapons barking. It was beautiful to watch – almost balletic – as the Raven Guard systematically showered the creature with bolt-rounds, whilst their captain kept it pinned in position with his flashing, sweeping talons. He saw a severed tentacle spin away, wriggling for a moment on the dusty ground nearby, before falling still. He saw the tiny mouths that encrusted the creature scream in unison as its belly was breached by rounds, spilling its foul, semi-organic innards across the flagstones. He saw Koryn step forward and wrench the thing's head free with a single flick of his wrist, sending it spinning away into the corner of the ruins where it landed with a hollow thud.

The Helbrute's flamer issued a final spurt of burning promethium, and then it twisted half around, raised one leg as if to make a step, and pitched forward onto the flagstones. Its remaining tentacles gave two, twitching spasms, its left leg clawed at the ground, and then, with a hissing sigh, it was dead.

For a moment, everything was still. There was no cry of victory from the Space Marines; they simply looked on in silence as one of them stepped forward and doused the fallen monster with his flamer. The hungry conflagration took hold almost instantly, and within seconds the downed Helbrute had been reduced to a smoking, crackling pyre.

Sergei could feel the wall of heat from almost ten metres away, and the stench of burning meat was acrid in the back of his throat. He coughed, and more blood spilled from the corner of his lips.

He glanced down at the gash in his belly, and when he looked up again, all but one of the black-armoured figures had gone. Only Koryn remained, silhouetted against the guttering flames.

'Great deeds,' Sergei whispered, his voice barely audible. He was tired. So very tired. The lasrifle had slipped from his grasp. 'Great deeds.'

He sensed the towering Space Marine standing over him and, with enormous effort, raised his head to look up at his faceplate.

'Die well, soldier,' said Koryn. For the first time, his voice seemed imbued with a sense of sorrow. 'I will remember your tale.'

And then he was gone, whisked away into the storm of the battle, and all that was left was the eerie silence of the ruined acropolis, the crackle of the fire and the distant thunder of bolt-rounds.

Sergei closed his eyes, and sighed.

# OLD SCARS

## 07.13 HRS

'Tell me of Karos, Pradeus. I understand you have walked upon its surface once before.' Daed's voice echoed around the chapel, deep and booming, like the low rumble of an oncoming storm.

Pradeus thought his own voice seemed thin and inadequate by comparison. He sucked his teeth – a nervous habit he'd developed in childhood and been unable to shake. 'A long time ago, when the twin suns still burned, bright and bloody red in the sky. It was a lush planet, covered in vast savannahs and soaring Imperial cities. Now it is a dead world, captain. Little can survive its harsh climate. What human population there is ekes out a paltry existence in vast thermal hives, a warren of tunnels and sunken conurbations deep below ground.'

'Why?' asked Daed. He placed his gleaming bronze vambrace upon the table beside its twin, flexing his shoulders. A thick, ropey scar described a snake across his back, its head upon his right shoulder, its body curling down across his spine so that the thin tip of its tail rested just above his left hip. The flesh was purple and puckered where it had healed imperfectly, the damaged halves of the wound reforming in an uneasy truce.

Pradeus was glad the captain could not see the expression of awe on his face. The weapon that had inflicted such a grave wound must have been terrible indeed; the weapon's bearer even more so. 'Why?' he echoed.

'Yes. I want to understand. Why do the humans continue to inhabit such a blighted world?'

Pradeus nodded, although the gesture was redundant; Daed continued to remove his armour, his back to the Chapter serf. 'The planet is nothing but a shadow of what it was, but once it was glorious. Rich mines seamed with precious metals and ores, spired cities stretching as far as the eye could see, all presided over by the Ecclesiarchy, high in their fortress-monastery. Now the people, I believe, cling to that former greatness, refusing to give up.'

'I admire their tenacity,' said Daed, flexing his shoulders. His thick, braided hair hung down between his shoulders. 'So the surface is utterly inhospitable?'

'Karos's suns have grown pale and thin, with only the merest hint of warmth ever shining upon the surface. The entire world is now encased in a wintry glove of ammonia ice, which shrouds the ruins of the old cities. The people have been driven below ground, making what they can of the ancient mining tunnels that riddle the rocky crust beneath the ice.' Pradeus glanced over his shoulder, looking to the door, where he had sensed movement. He saw nothing.

'And now the greenskins have arrived,' said Daed, darkly.

'Yes, captain, although for what purpose, I do not know.'

'Murder, pillaging, the sating of their foul appetites... They are not so difficult to understand,' said Daed.

'You have fought them before?' ventured Pradeus.

Daed laughed. 'I have spilled their stinking blood on a hundred worlds, Pradeus, and will do so on a hundred more.' He stooped to remove a leg brace and the scar on his back twisted and flushed.

'And they have spilled yours, captain, lest you forget.' The newcomer's voice echoed from the doorway, close to where Pradeus had sensed movement just a few moments before. He turned to see Theseon, the Chief Librarian of the Brazen Minotaurs, standing in the open archway, resplendent in his azure armour. He glanced back at Daed, waiting to see his reaction.

Daed turned towards his battle-brother. 'And I still bear the scars to prove it,' he said, levelly.

'Old scars,' said Theseon, walking into the room. 'And yet they still trouble you.'

Daed removed his second leg brace, but kept his eyes fixed firmly on the Librarian. 'Karos is an Imperial world. The Guard cannot weather the climate, and so the green-skins, impervious to the cold, run riot upon its surface. What would you have me do, Theseon?'

Theseon placed a gauntleted hand upon Daed's shoulder. 'Nothing but your duty, captain,' he said, and Pradeus could sense the statement was loaded with a meaning he could not understand.

Daed nodded. 'Then we deploy within the hour. We shall liberate Karos from the xenos scum that have infected it.'

Theseon nodded but did not speak. He lowered his hand.

'Pradeus?'

'Yes, captain?' said Pradeus, stepping around the bulk of the Librarian so that his master could see him.

'My armour is still ingrained with the blood of traitors. See that it is cleaned and prepared for battle.'

Pradeus's heart sank. *Within the hour?* 'Yes, captain,' he said, trying to keep the apprehension from his voice.

'And Pradeus?'

Pradeus nodded.

'I want it to gleam as I fell the foul brutes with my axe. I want them to know the Brazen Minotaurs have arrived.' He turned and stalked from the room, dressed only in his parchment-coloured loincloth.

Theseon turned to look at Pradeus, his face impassive behind the faceplate of his helm. 'You'd better get started,' he said, without a hint of irony.

## 08.09 HRS

The battle-barge *Pride of Tauron* disgorged its payload of Thunderhawks, Storm Eagles and Stormtalons into the upper atmosphere of Karos in muted silence, as if the orks below, so intent on subjugating the human population and seizing control of the underground hives, had not even considered looking to the skies above. If they were aware of the Space Marines' presence, they did not show it. There was no bark of surface-to-air fire, no evidence of ork vessels hurriedly scrambling to launch. This, Daed considered, spoke of either their ignorance or their sheer, animalistic arrogance. Both would prove useful in their undoing.

From the viewing port of the command ship, the barge

hung in space like a vast whale, attended by a school of tiny fish. As Daed watched, the flotilla of landing vessels banked and fanned out in unison, swimming down towards the planet, their engines burning. These, however, were the deadliest of fish: they harboured teeth and claws. The orks would be destroyed, and the planet cleansed – no matter the inhospitable nature of the climate or the ferocity of the xenos. There were, as Theseon had intimated, old scores to settle.

The Thunderhawk banked, sliding easily through the thin air. Daed reached for the stabilising bar above his head, holding firm as the vessel accelerated towards the planet.

He could hear nothing but the sharp whine of the engines, as if the sound itself filled his head, drowning out everything, muffling his very thoughts. He focused on the fact that soon he would once again be in the thick of battle, bloodying his axe on the fresh corpses of his enemy.

He glanced at Theseon, who sat immobile in webbing close by, his head bowed, his gauntleted hands folded upon his lap. Something was troubling the Librarian, and it was more than simple concern over Daed's order to deploy to the planet below. Daed decided he would speak with Theseon upon planetfall.

The Thunderhawk bucked suddenly and banked to the left, the engines stuttering as the pilot fought to maintain control. Daed maintained his grip on the stabilising bar as the vessel went into freefall, spiralling around as it dove nose-first towards the frozen planet, like water circling a drain.

He opened a vox-channel, shouting over the noise of the screeching engines. 'Report!'

'We're under fire!' came the immediate reply from Caedus, the pilot. 'We took a direct hit to the primary engine.'

'Get this vessel under control, Caedus,' replied Daed, firmly. He released his left hand from the bar, holding on with the right, and allowed himself to fall against the side of the ship, his power armour clanging loudly against the plasteel. He peered out of the viewing port, fighting the momentum as the Thunderhawk continued to spin. Bright tracer fire scratched at the sky, indiscriminately showering Daed's small flotilla as they emerged from the cover of the clouds. As he watched, one of the Stormtalons detonated in a shower of burning shards, while a second Thunder-hawk streamed out of the heavens on a wild trajectory, trailing black, oily smoke.

So, the orks had woken up. Daed couldn't suppress a grin. They were going to have a fight on their hands.

The metal footplates buckled slightly beneath his feet, the plasteel screaming with the stress, and he wondered for a moment whether the vessel would maintain its integrity as they spun towards the ground. Then Daed felt the nose coming up once again, the ship levelling off. A quick glance out of the window told him they were only a few hundred metres from the ground: a pallid landscape punctuated with eccentric hulking shapes – the remains of an ancient city, now entirely encased in ice.

'We need to set down.' Caedus's voice burred over the vox. 'We're losing altitude.'

'Then get us as close to the rendezvous point as you can,' replied Daed. Through the viewing port, he watched as his brothers broke through the clouds, dropping beneath the cover of the ruined city, picking their way through the valleys and channels formed by the ice. Around them, burning rain scattered across the white expanse, showering down in glittering fragments: the remains of the fallen, taken out by the ork batteries.

'Now we all have something to avenge,' said Theseon, quietly, from behind him.

## 10.34 HRS

The rendezvous point was, it transpired, a ramshackle structure erected by the Guard in an attempt to raise a defensible position on the ice. It was on the outskirts of the frozen city, and Daed, Theseon, Caedus, Aramus and Throle had been forced to cover the last five kilometres on foot, running through the frozen streets, their helms fogging with crystallised moisture from the air. There was little evidence of the xenos here, other than the heaped remains of dead humans, dragged from their warrens and left to the vagaries of the extreme weather. Judging by the expressions on their frigid faces, many of them had still been alive when the ice and thin air had done its work.

The Guard's stronghold had been spliced together from plasteel sheeting and chunks of masonry excavated from the ruins. As Daed drew closer he could make out the remains of at least two Baneblade tanks, too, shoring up the barricade. Steam curled from small venting pillars that had been sunk into the ice, and he could feel the vibrating whirr of machinery deep beneath his boots. There was no sign of any actual Guardsmen, leaving Daed to conclude that the bulk of the human forces were either dead, or cowering beneath the surface, drawing what heat and sustenance they still could from the planet's core.

He was relieved to find some evidence of industry, however; the small Brazen Minotaurs contingent was out on the ice, working to strengthen the perimeter, unloading the transport vessels and unlashing the tanks and ground vehicles.

Daed thumbed his vox. 'Sharus?'

'Captain? It's about time...' came the response. 'Much longer and there wouldn't have been any greenskins left for you.'

Daed laughed for the first time that day. 'Have you located the commander of the human forces?'

'Yes, captain,' said Sharus. 'In the sinkhole, over by the venting pillars. Lieutenant Ariseth is his name. He claims there are very few of them left, that the greenskins have slowly eroded their forces over recent months.'

'I do not doubt it,' said Daed. 'The conditions favour the thick-skinned xenos. The humans are too weak to withstand the ice and the thin air of this dying world.'

'And yet we are here to protect them, all the same,' said Theseon.

'We will do what they cannot, in the name of the Emperor,' said Daed, firmly. 'We will scorch these foul greenskins from the face of this world.'

'The auspex readings suggest the xenos are many in number, captain,' said Throle.

'Then it will be necessary to hit them hardest where the most damage will be done,' replied Daed. 'To strike when they least expect it. In this I must take counsel from Lieutenant Ariseth, who knows the movements and proclivities of the enemy.'

\* \* \*

## 11.42 HRS

The underground warren was comprised of nothing but the lined tunnels of an old mine, filled with coiled cables and dim electric lumen-strips, which were strung up at intervals along the low ceiling. They cast a sickly, yellow pall upon proceedings as Daed was led purposefully deeper into the structure, towards the command centre where Lieutenant Ariseth awaited him. The walls and ceilings ran with melting ice as the thermal cables fought a constant battle with the encroaching planetary winter, corrosive ammonia gas seeping out into the stale atmosphere. He'd noticed on the way down that the humans hid their faces behind gas masks in order to survive.

Daed glanced from side to side as he walked, taking it all in. If this was representative of the manner in which the human population now lived, the invasion was barely worth the orks' trouble. Small chambers, many of them formed from passages that had been widened or simply collapsed together, branched off like satellites from the main tunnels, and in these Guardsmen trained, rested or simply sat around waiting to be given orders.

Ariseth was waiting in one such chamber, hunched over a hand-drawn map as if attempting to divine a new stratagem simply by staring at the contours of the ice fields. He looked up when Daed entered the room, and immediately got to his feet. 'Most welcome, Captain Daed,' he said, unable to suppress the nervousness in his voice.

Daed stared down at him, weighing him up. The man looked grizzled and worn down by his experiences. His face was mostly hidden behind a respirator, and the flesh around it was black and peeling from too much exposure to the cold. He was wrapped in bundled animal furs and wore a fur hat pulled down low over his brow. One of his eyes had been replaced by a mechanical equivalent, and it turned and whirred as it attempted to focus on the Brazen Minotaur now.

'Lieutenant,' said Daed, his voice echoing and hollow-sounding in the small room. 'The Brazen Minotaurs are here to assist in the removal of the xenos infestation from Karos.'

Ariseth raised an eyebrow. 'You make it sound as if we haven't been trying to do that for months,' he said, a modicum of bitterness creeping into his tone.

Daed allowed him that. 'You must tell me everything you know of the greenskins' motives and strategies if we are to prove successful.'

'Gladly,' said Ariseth. 'It's as if the damn things are able to predict our every move, our every counterstrike. Whatever we do they are ready for us, and ready to hit back, hard, when we're overextended and least prepared. We are few now, captain. Many thousands of us have been lost.'

Daed nodded. 'And their goal?'

Ariseth shrugged. 'Mayhem, destruction, cold-blooded murder... They seem only to relish the slaughter. They seize our vehicles and modify them, sending them back into battle, firing upon us with our own ammunition. They storm the hives, cutting the power to the thermal generators so that the populations freeze. They seem to find such things amusing. What's more, they seem impervious to the damn cold.'

'Have they established a base, a stronghold?' said Daed. He'd seen readouts on the *Pride of Tauron* that suggested the ork army had been massing in one particular location, but Daed knew the knowledge of the men on the ground counted for ten of any such readouts.

'They have,' said Ariseth, with a reluctant sigh. 'If you'll return to the surface, it's best if I show you.'

## 12.16 HRS

In the distance he could make out a series of dark shapes, jutting out of the tundra like black spurs.

'Venting towers,' said Ariseth, trembling with the cold, despite the thick layers of fur that rendered him almost unidentifiable.

Daed peered more closely at the distant structures, and could just make out faint trails of steam billowing from the crests of the towers. 'Siphoning off the excess heat from the thermal hives?'

'Yes. They form a chain over three hundred kilometres long, puncturing the ice at regular intervals,' replied Ariseth.

'Highly defensible,' mused Daed, scanning the horizons. The towering shapes loomed away into the distance.

'I'm afraid the orks have already established that,' said Ariseth, reluctantly. 'They're using the towers as staging posts, defending them like watchtowers or bastions. That one,' he pointed with a gloved hand to one of the towers immediately opposite them, around thirty kilometres distant, 'is their command post. That's where their warlord has established his base.'

'Then that should be our target,' said Daed, bristling. His hand closed unconsciously on the haft of his axe.

'There are hundreds of the beasts between us and that tower, captain, if not more. We don't have the men or the artillery to take it.'

Daed grinned. 'We have the will of the Emperor. That will be enough.'

'I hope so, captain. For all our sakes,' said Ariseth, although it was clear from his tone that he thought it would not.

'Do you know what the greenskins call their warlord?' asked Daed.

'I believe it is known amongst its kin as Grakka,' came the response.

Daed's grip tightened on the haft of his axe.

'Grakka?' he echoed. He felt the beating of his hearts quicken, the surge of unwanted memories from Praxis, of lying face down in the mud, his spine damaged, the flesh and muscle of his back carved into ribbons by the beast's blade. And of the yellow-tusked, black-eyed face of the creature looming over him, its rancid breath foul and warm on his face.

'Yes, sir,' said Ariseth. 'Have you heard the name before?'

'I have,' growled Daed, quietly. 'I have.'

## 15.27 HRS

'The towers are enormous vents,' said Daed, 'slowly siphoning off the excess heat from the underground hives.'

'And the greenskins are using them as defensive positions?' asked Aramus.

'Indeed. One of them represents their command post. That's where Grakka is skulking,' said Daed, gritting his teeth. Even now he could visualise the moment when he might see that greenskin's face again, how he might cleave its head from its shoulders with a sweep of his axe. The five of them – his veteran squad – stood outside on the ice in the waning light, surveying the horizon.

'You wish to mount a head-on attack on this command post?' said Caedus, incredulous. 'Even for you, captain, that's an audacious move.'

'I see no other way,' said Daed resolutely. 'According to the data provided by Lieutenant Ariseth, the greenskins outnumber us fifty to one. The Guard are half frozen and will be of no use to us on the open field of battle. Even with the Dreadnoughts and the Land Raiders we are badly outnumbered, and the greenskins have had months to learn the lay of the land and mount their defences. We would not be well served by meeting them on the tundra, as hungry as my axe is to cleave their brutish skulls.'

'But surely, captain, we risk as much by mounting an assault on their stronghold?' said Throle. 'The command position will be heavily defended, and it will prove difficult to lay siege to such an edifice when there are thousands of greenskins between us and the base of the tower.'

'An aerial assault. Ariseth argues that the xenos believe the venting towers to be a series of abandoned bastions. They are not aware of the true function of the structures. A well-placed attack could collapse the vents, causing the pressure to build up very quickly,' said Daed, glancing at Theseon, who was standing to one side of the small group, staring out across the icy plain.

'And the ensuing explosion would topple the tower, killing all of the greenskins within,' concluded Caedus. 'It might work.'

Daed nodded. 'More than that, the build up of pressure could cause a chain reaction, causing the neighbouring towers to blow in concert, taking out the entire xenos force.'

'It's too dangerous,' said Aramus. 'We've little chance of

being able to strike with such accuracy, particularly if we are harried by the enemy as we close in. We know they have surface-to-air capabilities at the very least.'

'It's our only option,' replied Daed, as if that were the end of the matter.

'What of the enemy's ability to predict the movements of the Guard? Do they have a spy amongst the humans?' said Caedus.

Daed shook his head. 'Mere superstition. There is nothing to it. It is simply that Grakka understands the strategies of the Imperial Guard, as he has encountered them so many times before. These humans rely solely on their training. They cannot flex. They have forgotten how to surprise the enemy.'

'Forgive me, captain, but we are all aware of what happened on Praxis. I cannot blame you for seeking to have your revenge upon the beast that bested you there – indeed, I would gladly join you in such a quest – but can you be sure that you are not allowing the matter to colour your judgement?' Throle looked to the others for support. 'I fear Aramus is correct. Our chances of victory are slim.'

Daed fixed Throle with a firm stare. 'I will take those odds, Throle, and we will do our duty. Grakka has burned entire worlds – *Imperial* worlds – and we do the Emperor's bidding when we set out to destroy him. We do this to avenge the dead, and to prevent the spread of his foul greenskins any further. My experience of Grakka has taught me one thing: that he must be stopped. If I seek vengeance, it is for the many who have tasted his axe and not survived, as well as for myself. For our fallen brothers.'

Throle nodded. 'As you command, captain.'

'For Tauron!' bellowed Caedus.

'For Tauron!' echoed the others, save for Theseon, who remained silent, studying Daed from afar.

## 17.32 HRS

'You are distracted, Theseon. Something troubles you.'

Theseon raised his head to look up at Daed, who towered over him, resplendent in his bronze armour, power axe clutched tightly in his fist, the pelt of a black Tauronic lion draped over his shoulders.

'I am tired, captain. I sense... another mind. A confused mind. It is watchful. It saps my strength.'

'Another psyker?' asked Daed, his voice low.

Theseon nodded. 'A xenos.'

'The truth of the matter becomes clear to me, Theseon. If Grakka is aided by a psyker, then it explains how he has so far been able to predict the movements of the Guard. We must strike soon, before he has chance to gather his forces in preparation for our attack.'

'I advise caution, captain. You must not allow your judgement to become clouded by thoughts of personal vendetta,' said Theseon. 'We are not here simply to settle a score, but to liberate an Imperial world.'

'I know that, Librarian,' spat Daed, turning to glance at Throle, who had entered the small underground chamber while Theseon had been talking.

'Theseon speaks sense, captain. If the greenskins are able to anticipate our strategies, then we might look to uncover new ways to surprise them. Perhaps the assault on the venting tower has already been compromised.'

'No,' said Daed. 'The attack must go ahead as planned. It is our best chance to neutralise the threat. If we can take out their command post, we might yet ignite a chain reaction that will envelop their entire force. I see no alternative.'

'But captain–' began Throle.

'The captain is right, Throle,' interrupted Theseon. 'The assault on the tower must go ahead as planned.'

'And the psyker?' asked Throle, clearly restraining himself.

'I shall see to the psyker,' said Theseon.

'Very well,' said Daed. 'I shall instruct the others to prepare for the attack.' He turned and strode from the room, ducking his head beneath the low lintel.

Theseon turned to Throle, holding up a hand until the sound of the captain's footsteps had died away down the passage. 'Here is what we must do...' he said, quietly.

## 19.46 HRS

The tension in the repaired Thunderhawk was palpable as it roared above the ice-shrouded ruins. The five Brazen Minotaurs sat in silence, lashed to their webbing. The Thunderhawk was flanked by two Storm Eagles and a battery of Stormtalons, which would work to draw fire away from the command ship as they approached the venting tower, engaging the greenskins whilst Daed set about taking out the vents themselves.

They had left the ground vehicles and a second Thunderhawk posted to the ramshackle base of the Guardsmen. If the mission was successful, they would be needed to help mop up any remaining xenos; if the mission failed... Well, they would be needed to protect the remaining humans from the tide of alien beasts that would soon follow. Daed was aware of the risks.

'Five kilometres and counting,' said Caedus from the pilot's pit. 'And here comes the first response.'

The Thunderhawk took a sudden evasive manoeuvre, dipping low to avoid artillery fire from below. The orks, it seemed, were ready for them.

'Return fire,' ordered Daed, and Throle set the battlecannons ablaze, churning up the ice in long furrows ahead of them. Through the viewing port, Daed could see the Storm Eagles doing the same, unleashing a barrage on the massed ranks of orks far below.

Daed consulted his auspex. 'Something is wrong. The orks are pulling back. They have amassed around the command tower.'

He was interrupted by the bark of heavy surface-to-air fire and the sound of a nearby Stormtalon detonating. Caedus banked sharply, and then levelled again, attempting to avoid becoming the weapon's next target.

'Librarian!' Daed growled. 'You said you would see to the alien psyker. But now this,' he turned the display of his auspex to present the screen to Theseon, who sat opposite him, silently regarding his captain. 'The xenos are aware of our attack. They have formed a defensive perimeter around the tower. There must be thousands of them...' He trailed off, accusation in his tone.

'Two kilometres,' came the report from Caedus.

'We'll never get through such a barrier,' said Daed, angrily. 'We'll have to turn back, remount our attack.'

'Now, Caedus!' called Theseon, and in response the Thunderhawk dipped and turned sharply to the left. Daed, glancing out of the viewing port, saw that the other vessels were following suit, pulling away from the target.

'What in the name of the Emperor?'

'Trust me, captain,' said Theseon. 'This is how I will see to the psyker.'

The chatter of the ork weapons stuttered and died as the Thunderhawk shot away at speed. 'I do not know what game you are playing, Librarian, but I expect answers,' said Daed, a warning note in his voice.

'Everything will become clear in a moment, captain,' replied Theseon, distracted, as he leaned forward, straining in his webbing in order to see out of the forward viewing ports. 'There!' he said, triumphantly. 'The second tower. That is our target, Throle. Collapse those vents.'

The battlecannons burst to life once again, chewing holes in the plasteel flank of the tower as Caedus brought the Thunderhawk around in a wide arc. Daed watched as the venting shafts shattered and collapsed in upon themselves in a cloud of steam, dust and debris.

The Thunderhawk banked again, pulling up higher and away from the tower.

'It should take only a few moments...' said Theseon.

The first sign of the coming eruption came in the form of a deep rumble that grew slowly until it reached fever pitch. As Daed watched, the ice around the tower began to fracture, opening large rents in the bedrock beneath. Steam hissed from the tectonic wounds, gushing forth as the pressure attempted to find a way out and was instead forced along through the underground channels of the old thermal hive, once inhabited by humans, and now the domain of the orks.

Caedus followed the fracturing landmass as it raced across the landscape, tracking it towards the gathered mob of unsuspecting xenos. By now the Thunderhawk was too high to be able to see clearly how the greenskins were reacting, but Daed knew they would be attempting to scatter.

And then, the mounting pressure finally found its outlet – the second venting tower. The command post of the ork warlord, Grakka.

The tower detonated in a blossom of steam and light, erupting like a thunderclap. Debris billowed into the air as the very ground around the orks began to subside, the foundations of the tower collapsing, dragging the gathered xenos down into the depths of the fractured hive, cooking them alive in the gushing steam or crushing them beneath the shattered bedrock.

'It is done,' said Theseon, as the Thunderhawk swept over the ruins of the ork invasion force. 'Return us to the base, Caedus.'

Daed stared angrily out of the viewing port as the Thunderhawk came about, offering him his last view of the ruination they had caused below.

## 21.06 HRS

Almost as soon as they disembarked from the Thunderhawk, Daed turned on Theseon. 'You disobeyed a direct order,' he barked. 'Explain yourself, Librarian.'

Theseon nodded calmly, and laid a hand upon the captain's pauldron. 'Your plan was sound, captain. I knew that destroying the venting tower would work, and the chain reaction was likely. Yet the greenskin psyker… Your anger was like a beacon to him, drawing him in. Your mind was open to him. Grakka knew you were here, and that you would come for him. His forces massed in defence around his command post as a consequence, waiting for our attack.'

'It was your duty to tell me,' said Daed. His hands were bunched into fists as he attempted to contain his anger.

Theseon shook his head. 'It was imperative that I did not. Doing so would have telegraphed our intentions to the enemy. You had to continue to believe that our goal was the command tower. It was the only way for the misdirection to work. We drew them away from the second tower, safe in the knowledge that the eruption caused by our attack would be enough to destroy the command post too.'

'I do not approve of your subterfuge,' said Daed, levelly. 'Although I grant you, Theseon – your audacity matches only my own. The beast is dead, and Karos is liberated.'

'And old scars are finally healed,' said Theseon.

Daed was silent for a moment. 'You did what was necessary, in the name of the Emperor. We shall speak no more of the matter.'

Theseon nodded. 'I see the ground troops are already deployed, mopping up the last of the enemy. Will you join them?'

Daed grinned. 'My axe hungers for xenos blood,' he said.

'Then lend them your strength, captain,' said Theseon. 'When you return from the field of battle, we must speak. There is a storm gathering in the Sargassion Reach, close to this system. Traitors mass.'

'Very well,' said Daed, gravely. 'It seems there may yet be even older scores to settle.'

'Indeed,' replied Theseon, but Daed had already turned away, hefting his axe high above his head.

'For Tauron!' called Theseon.

'For Tauron!' echoed Daed, disappearing into the maelstrom of churned ice and fog.

Theseon looked to the skies: a clear, dark blanket, peppered with scattered diamonds. 'Soon, Gideous Krall. Soon I shall come for you.'

# LABYRINTH OF SORROWS

# DAED

The planet was dead.

A rotten husk, suffocated beneath a blanket of thick, pestilent fog, Kasharat had always been a place of death – a mortuary world, bristling with the stele of glorious tombs, overgrown with forests of monumental spires and statuary. Here there was nothing but tributes to the long-dead heroes of old, the forgotten soldiers of millennia past. Yet now, even the curators of this hallowed place were dead or diseased, overcome and conquered.

If there was any indigenous life left upon this blighted world, it was now only carrion, picking over the remains of what had gone before, revelling in the reek of death and despair. Kasharat had been lost, just as its sister planets in the Sargassion Reach had been lost, swept away in a tide of blood, plague and suffering. Here on Kasharat the Imperium had buckled. Here there was only death.

Yet amongst the marble tombs of this vast necropolis,

things were stirring – things that had once resembled human beings, but were now barely recognisable as such. Things so depraved, deformed and pox-ridden that they were reduced to scuttling through the shattered ruins like animals, running errands for their foul masters. These were the pitiful wretches who had given over their lives to the Sickening. These were the disciples of Nurgle.

Amongst these former men walked the grotesque giants of the warband Empyrion's Blight, Space Marines of the heretical Death Guard Legion, traitors to the Emperor's cause; monsters – Captain Daed considered – who deserved nothing as forgiving as simple death.

These foul warriors of Chaos – polluted not only by the stink of treachery but also by the stench of unnatural sickness – had prosecuted a brief and terrible campaign throughout the Sargassion Reach. Seven Imperial worlds had been obliterated, the populations poisoned and the very soil blighted beneath the boots of their oppressors. Even now, war still raged across the surface of three of these planets, although Daed knew that without reinforcements, without some way to alter the course of the war, the Imperial cause was all but lost. The Plague Marines were legion, and they, in contrast, were few.

Nevertheless, Daed would fight on until the bitter end, clinging to those benighted worlds until the very last of them had fallen. Such was the duty of a Space Marine. Such was the honour of a Brazen Minotaur.

For now though, Daed had other priorities to attend to; the means, perhaps, by which to turn the tide of the war. At the very least, the means by which he could offer his brothers a fighting chance, a reason to hope. Somewhere on Kasharat was the key to their salvation.

If only he could find it.

Daed sat rigid in his webbing as the Thunderhawk banked, its engines howling as it dipped beneath the cover of the dark, viscous clouds. The planet's atmosphere was thick with the aura of death, a haze of green mist that cloaked the mortuary world to form a near-impenetrable shroud. The Thunderhawk sighed as its airbrakes dragged at the putrid fog, churning great funnels in its wake. It slewed around, searching for a place to set down, its search lamps penetrating the eerie gloom. It drifted along a corridor of marble spires, dipping and banking to avoid the structures that loomed out of the foetid haze, and then moments later the pilot was easing it down between two massive obelisks, its landing gear sinking into the soft loam. The engines wheezed for a moment longer, and then were still.

If the arrival of the Thunderhawk had been noticed by anyone on the planet's surface, it went unremarked. There was no chatter of autocannons, no bark of plasma guns. Either the traitors were unaware of Daed's arrival, or they were unconcerned. The latter thought didn't offer Daed much comfort as he pulled himself free of the webbing, glancing from side to side to see his battle-brothers doing the same.

A few seconds later the vessel's hatch slid open and Captain Daed of the Brazen Minotaurs Third Company stood framed in the doorway, a gleaming silhouette against the stark light spilling out from within. He was tall, even for a Space Marine, encased in shimmering golden power armour. His shoulders were draped with the pelt of one of the hulking black lions that roamed the forests of Tauron, his home world, and his left pauldron bore the blue-on-white bull's-head insignia of his chapter. In his fist he carried a slender power axe, its head finely etched with Tauronic traceries and runes.

Daed's neck was thick with ropey muscles and his face was craggy and tanned, pitted with innumerable scars, as if he wore his centuries of service to the Emperor like tally marks on his flesh.

He stood for a moment, sucking at the foul air, his nose wrinkling in distaste. His eyes narrowed as he surveyed the eerie landscape around them. 'There's nothing but death here, Bardus,' he said, his voice a low growl.

In response, another figure appeared in the hatchway behind him. He wore the same shining golden armour as his captain, but his lower face was swathed in a long plaited beard and he carried a bolter in his right hand.

'The stench of the traitor,' Bardus replied, and Daed could hear the disgust in his tone. 'Their very presence is enough to choke the life out of a world.'

'True enough, brother,' said Daed, hefting his axe. 'But remember – we are not here to reclaim Kasharat from the traitors, much as the notion galls me. We are here to retrieve what they have taken from us, so that we may use it against them. We must look to the war and not to the battle. This mortuary world will be of little use to either side in the conflict ahead.'

'Aye, but it makes for a damn good hiding place,' muttered Bardus, peering out through the open hatch. He raised his bolter as he spoke, as if he expected something diabolical to come lurching out of the fog at any moment. Daed could hardly blame him for that – it wasn't as if it hadn't happened before. They had been caught unawares any number of times in the last few months during their extended campaign against the Death Guard. There were *things* in the fog, half-dead creatures that didn't even register life signs on their auspexes, cursed monsters that had once been men but were now nothing but shambling, diseased carcasses, unholy plague spawn created only to spread the festering curse of Chaos ever further, or to soak up fire on the field of battle. Even these had proved difficult to despatch in such incessant numbers. The Death Guard had infected the populations of entire worlds as they had cut a swath through the Sargassion Reach; now they were goading the fallen into battle in their multitudes.

The damned smog gave the enemy a great advantage – that and the fact they seemed able to survive wounds that would have felled a normal Space Marine, shrugging off bolter fire and blows from Daed's power axe as if they had barely been scratched.

'You stand there talking like tacticians!' bellowed Brother Targus from behind them, laughing as he hefted his heavy bolter onto his shoulder. 'I hunger for the opportunity to put some more of those plague-ridden traitors out of their misery.'

Daed grinned. He could understand that impulse, the desire to smite the wretches where they stood. He relished the idea as much as Targus himself – burned, in fact, with the need to bring the Emperor's justice to bear on their corrupt souls.

'I assure you, Targus, there will be time enough for us all to blunt our axes in the stinking corpses of our enemies. I wish for nothing more myself. But first, we have a job to do.'

Daed turned and strode down the disembarkation ramp, his footsteps strangely muffled by the thick, diseased air.

Glancing up, he could make out only the spear-like tips of mortuary structures silhouetted against the sky, and the dull orbs of the twin moons that circled Kasharat in their stately, perpetual dance. Around him, there was nothing but an impenetrable bank of putrid fog. Yet even before it was infested with the plague, Daed mused, there would have been a grim, funereal air about the place.

He stood for a moment as the others clambered out of the hatch, coming to join him, their boots sinking in the sticky loam.

'Engage your respirators,' he said, fixing his own mouthpiece into place and activating his vox link. 'Keep this foul air from settling in your lungs.' He glanced around at his assembled squad as they followed his lead, each of them fixing their helms to their gorgets with a series of hissing, pneumatic sighs, then gestured to one of them. 'Bast, check your auspex for signs of life.'

Bast unclipped the scanning device from his belt and studied the readout. 'Nothing, Captain.' He turned it so that Daed could see the display. 'It's this fog – it smothers everything. I can't get a reading. It's as if the mist itself were alive.'

'Widen the spectrum. Look for anything at all.'

'Captain...' started another of the squad, Brother Throle, but Daed silenced his objections with a wave of his hand.

The auspex chirped momentarily before going silent again. 'Bast?'

'It's intermittent, captain, but there's something there. A beacon...' Bast turned and the auspex emitted another dull electronic bleep. 'That way.' He pointed to indicate the direction from which he had registered the distress signal.

'It's most likely a trap,' muttered Targus, moving around

to stand before Daed. 'They may be traitors but they're not fools. They know we're here.'

Daed set his jaw. He fixed Targus with a resolute stare. 'Throle?' he called over his shoulder.

'Aye, captain?'

'Move out.'

Daed watched Targus as he fell into formation behind the others, the enormous bulk of the heavy bolter balanced on his right pauldron. He understood his brother's reluctance. They probably *were* walking into a trap, but there were no other options. They had a mission to complete, and they were Brazen Minotaurs. They would face whatever the enemy put before them with unflinching determination, and they would do it in the name of the Emperor. That, or they would die trying.

Daed hefted his power axe and unholstered his bolt pistol, falling into line behind the others.

# KORYN

They moved silently, as if they had surrendered their corporeal forms to become spirits or wraiths, as if the very shadows themselves were living things that shifted and breathed – shadows that wore black ceramite armour and harboured vicious adamantium claws. Shadows that were trained to kill.

Ravens.

Shadow Captain Koryn of the Raven Guard flexed his neck and shoulders to dispel the tension. He sensed more than saw his brothers – Argis, Grayvus, Syrus and Coraan – as the five of them crept through the narrow tunnels of the maze-like mortuary complex, surrounded by the remnants of the dead. Dour faces hewn from soapstone and marble loomed out at him from all sides in the gloaming, their blank eyes watching impassively from across the centuries. Ornate tombs, stone coffins and the skeletal remains of old politicians and administrators – some of them still wearing their now-faded finery – lined the walls, embedded in roughly chiselled niches like insects in a hive.

It had once been a sacred place, a place to honour the dead in the name of the Emperor. Now, though, the blight of Chaos had infected the planet, and even here, in the bowels of this ancient mortuary complex, the evidence of corruption was all around them.

Foul mist clung to the air, turning everything a pale, putrid green. The walls were slick with ochre slime that seemed to quiver and move with the perturbations caused by their passing. Worse of all was the stench, the rotten reek of death and decay that pervaded everything, threatening to overwhelm even Koryn's hardened senses.

He didn't know what had brought the Death Guard to Kasharat, a mortuary world on the outer rim of the Imperium. Their reasons were opaque. It may simply have been a symptom of their inexorable drive to spread their foul plague – that burning, zealous desire to infect world after world with their sickening rot – but their actions hinted at some greater purpose. Koryn knew that his bull-headed brothers, the Brazen Minotaurs, would be concerned only with smiting the enemy and not with understanding their motives. To them, Koryn knew, the enemy were the enemy; faceless traitors who needed only to be vanquished. Their strategies were not subtle. They did not need to understand their enemy in order to strike them with a wall of sheer force, to overwhelm them with firepower. There was a certain honesty in that sort of combat, and Koryn respected the Brazen Minotaurs for their unwavering, unquestioning approach. He had seen them storm their way to victory on more than one occasion, a fist of iron driven into the very heart of the enemy.

The sons of Corax, however, excelled at a different kind of combat. Koryn knew how to hit an enemy where it hurt, to search out their weak points, to foil their plans. The Raven Guard struck from the shadows and were gone before their foe was even aware of what had happened. That, he knew, was what was needed here on Kasharat. That would ensure the success of their mission. The mortuary complex would be easily defended and a full assault would result only in a stand-off. That stand-off, in turn, would result in a siege that would take days, if not longer, to break. And days were a luxury the Brazen Minotaurs didn't have. Not if they wanted to retrieve their target in one piece.

Koryn hoped that their brothers might have had a chance by now to pick up the signal from the beacon he had planted earlier, amongst the corpses of the corrupted humans who had guarded the entrance to the mortuary complex.

He slowed as the passageway opened into a large, cavernous space. They were now far below ground, and looking up, Koryn could see that the space had originally been a natural formation, remodelled some time in the distant past for the mortuary builders' macabre purposes. Huge stalactites dripped from the roof like fangs encircling an enormous maw. Two colossal statues towered over the Space Marines, the figures' heads bowed in quiet repose. Each of them clutched a sword and shield and wore an unfamiliar pattern of armour. Effigies, Koryn assumed, of ancient heroes, long since forgotten.

At the feet of these towering figures stood a small group of grotesque creatures, formerly human, but now mutated and corrupted by the Sickening. One bore a writhing,

wriggling proboscis where its arm had once been, erupting from just beneath the shoulder joint to curl, snake-like,
in the air. The man's face was deformed with pustulent
growths, and his belly was distended and marred with
puckered sores. Beside him, another appeared to have
lost his lower jaw, and his tongue, now oversized and
sickly yellow, lolled across his naked chest, where his skin
erupted in innumerable boils. He clutched a lasrifle in his
disgusting, weeping fingers. There were five others, each
of them bearing the diabolical mark of Nurgle.

Koryn glanced from side to side, noting how his brothers
had fanned out in the shadows, drawing a wide semi-
circle around the group of cultists. This was how the Raven
Guard worked. So attuned were they to each other, so
practised were they in the art of subtle warfare that he
need not even issue his command. Intuitively, his veterans knew what he expected, what was necessary.

Koryn readied himself. He would enjoy this, would enjoy
despatching these foul bearers of the taint.

Silently he raised his twin lightning claws, the flashing blades glinting in the half-light. He drew his breath
and then swooped forward, barely making a sound as he
erupted from the shadows like a whirlwind of slashing
blades, spinning about so that his talons traced wide cir-
cles through the miasmic air. The lightning claws parted
the flesh of the nearest cultist like warm butter, slicing him
open from shoulder to belly so that his body collapsed
silently in a bloody heap in the dirt.

Koryn's blood sang as he twisted, knocking aside the
raised barrel of a lasrifle and skewering a second cultist through the belly. The man opened his mouth as if to
howl in agony, but was silenced a second later as Koryn's

other set of talons flashed, removing the cultist's head from his shoulders and spattering hot, festering blood over the Space Marine's ebony chest-plate.

Around him, Koryn's brothers moved silently in the dance of death, ducking and weaving and swiping as their blades and talons despatched the remaining five cultists in moments. The disciples of the Death Guard barely had time to register what was happening before it was all over. None of them had the opportunity to even squeeze off a shot or so much as raise an arm in defence. Within seconds the Raven Guard had melted away into the shadows, their work done, the only trace of their passing the quivering heap of corpulent flesh and severed limbs on the ground, writhing with the swarms of maggots that the cultists had harboured within their obscene bodies.

Talons dripping with gore, Koryn moved silently to join his brothers.

'Captain?' The voice that came over the vox was barely a whisper.

'Yes, Argis?'

'I understand, captain, that we owe the Brazen Minotaurs a grave debt, but should we not honour them on the field of battle as they honoured us, and not silently, from the shadows?'

'Argis, the Brazen Minotaurs honoured us in the only way they know how, in open combat, using their brute strength to aid us in our hour of need. Their sacrifice was great. But honour is not simply a matter of trading one life for another, of standing side by side on the field of battle. We honour our brothers the way *we* know how. The situation on Kasharat demands more subtlety than our bull-headed brothers could muster. We repay our debt the Raven's way.'

'Yes, captain,' said Argis, his tone circumspect. One of the shadows up ahead inclined its head, and Koryn smiled. Yes. The Raven's way.

Koryn watched as Argis slipped away into the darkness, and then followed silently behind.

# DAED

The corpses were hideous to look upon, and if he hadn't seen their like a thousand times before, it might have been enough to turn even Daed's iron stomach. There were at least ten of them, perhaps more, heaped one upon another like some grisly diorama, an assemblage of severed limbs, decapitated heads and spilled organs. Some of the body parts still writhed, as if by their own volition, as if the diabolical pestilence that had infected them was unwilling to release its foul grip, even now, after death. They twitched and spasmed as if trying to pull themselves back together, trying to reassemble themselves into new, blasphemous forms.

Bast was standing over this strange monument to the dead, his jaw set firm in obvious disgust. 'This appears to be the origin of the signal, Captain.'

Daed sensed movement and glanced down to see a twitching arm scrabbling in the dirt near his boots, its fingernails raking pathetically at his leg brace. He sent it spinning away into the murky fog with a sharp kick.

'Explain,' he said, sharply.

'The beacon, captain. It must be buried somewhere in there amongst the corpses, transmitting its distress signal.' Bast was still studying the readout on his auspex, and he dropped to his haunches, running the device over the slurry of bodies. One of the torsos twitched suddenly, and Throle stilled it again with a short burst from his bolter, sending a fountain of blood and gore into the air. It spattered Bast where he stood, but he continued to study the readout without comment.

'Like I said, a trap,' growled Targus. 'They're trying to lure us in.'

The five Brazen Minotaurs were standing by the pillared entrance to a vast mausoleum complex, much of which, Daed had gathered, was buried far beneath their feet. The readings he had seen suggested there was a warren of tunnels and chambers stretching for miles below ground, although given the interference caused by the green mist, he knew the veracity of any such readouts was in doubt. If they entered the labyrinthine structure, they would be going in blind.

The entrance yawned open before him, a marble staircase descending into the gloom. The traitor's icons and wards were splashed in sickly green across the pillars like a warning. Or, Daed considered, like a challenge.

'A trap?' said Throle in gruff rebuttal. 'Why would the enemy leave a distress beacon buried in a heap of their own dead?'

'The enemy are not easily fathomed,' said Bardus, his back to them as he kept watch, surveying their surroundings for anything that might come swooping out of the fog. 'There is no understanding the depths of their perversity.'

'Nor should we wish to understand it, Bardus,' replied Daed. 'For to understand it is to give yourself over to its foul corruption.' He glanced from side to side, hefting his axe as if anxious to bury it in something. 'But Targus is right. It may yet prove to be a trap.'

'Or worse,' replied Bast, his voice low and steady. 'There may be others who wish to claim our targets as their own.'

Daed nodded as he mulled this over. Were there other hostile forces here on Kasharat? Their surveillance had suggested only the presence of the Death Guard traitors and their cretinous followers. But perhaps Bast was right? Perhaps another faction had seen the opportunity to alter the course of the conflict in their favour. Perhaps even now they were winding their way through the tunnels below in search of Daed's quarry.

Targus was shaking his head impatiently, and Daed prickled with annoyance. 'Captain, we should leave this place. No good will come of it. The enemy waits for us inside. I am convinced these stinking corpses are nothing but a tribute to their vile god, intended only to lure us into their trap. We should return to where the real battle is, where we can honour the Emperor with blood on our axes, instead of skulking around here amongst the filth and the dead!'

Daed shook his head. 'No, Targus. I, too, long for the opportunity to cleave their traitorous heads from their shoulders, to spill their foul blood upon my boots. But our mission here is critical. The fate of worlds rests on what we might find inside that foul warren. If Bast is right... if it were to fall into the hands of others...We cannot risk it. So we will go on, in the name of the Emperor, and we will do what is needed of us. We are Brazen Minotaurs!'

Daed turned at the sound of a boot scraping on stone, expecting to find another of the serpentine body parts stealing away from its kin. Instead, he caught sight of a human being, squatting on a nearby rock, cocking its head as it listened in to their conversation. One of its eyes had swollen to unnatural proportions and its forearms and fingers had become bloated and fat, oozing pus and ichor. When it saw him looking it made to scramble away behind the rock, dragging its enormous, distended belly behind it.

Daed leapt forward, moving faster than his immense size belied. He shot out his gauntleted fist and grabbed the pitiful thing's head between his fingers. The creature whimpered and stared up at him, its scabrous lips parting as if about to beg for its life, but Daed did not award it the opportunity to speak. He closed his fist, bursting its fragile skull between his fingers. Its twitching corpse dropped to the ground, stinking pus and blood spurting from the stump of its neck.

Daed glanced around at his brothers.

'We press on,' he said, decidedly. 'We find what we came here for, trap or otherwise.' He didn't wait for their agreement before stalking forward and disappearing into the enveloping darkness of the mausoleum complex.

# KORYN

The incessant buzzing was growing louder.

Koryn pressed himself into an alcove, and waited. The five Raven Guard had wound their way deeper into the mortuary complex, drawing closer to what their auspexes and their intuition told them was the nexus of the labyrinth, the heart of the structure, where they reasoned the target would be found. And, Koryn considered, most likely a concentration of Traitor Marines and their pox-ridden kin, too.

They had despatched another seven cultists as they had passed through the warren of tunnels and deeper into the bowels of the structure. Here, the ornamentation of the tombs was less ostentatious, more functional, older even than those above.

In sharp contrast, evidence of inhabitation by the traitors grew all the more explicit. Rotting, fleshy membranes covered much of the walls, dripping with toxic slime, and the ground was thick with an oozing, corrosive sludge that lapped around their boots and made it harder for them to pass in silence. Bright runes flickered inside Koryn's helm, warning of airborne poisons and miasmic spores that, once lodged in the lungs, would multiply at an alarming rate, overloading even the resilient metabolism of a Space Marine. Toxic shock would follow, or worse, infection by the vile pestilence that had claimed the traitors. Koryn knew what he would do before he ever succumbed to that. He thanked the Emperor for the resilience of his respirator.

The buzzing was closer now, the screaming whine of engines churning the foetid air. Koryn watched the mouth of the tunnel, readying himself for battle, waiting to see what would round the bend.

Moments later he got his answer. Two man-sized machines came buzzing along the passageway, twin rotary engines burring. They hovered three of four feet above the ground, red lights winking in the darkness like murderous eyes. They were composed of nothing but huge sacks of decaying, quivering flesh, melded with corroded machine parts and weapons in what Koryn took to be a sick parody of life. He had seen their like before on the field of battle. Blight drones.

The drones buzzed down the tunnel towards the Raven Guard, trailing stringy mucus behind them where they brushed against the dripping walls. Koryn gave a minute shake of his head, and he hoped his brothers had seen him in the gloom. They would let the foul things pass, engaging them only if they, themselves, were engaged. The drones were guards, nothing more, and destroying them would not only be a waste of ammunition, it would also risk bringing about unnecessary attention.

The mission was everything. The instruments of the enemy could wait. Koryn watched with gritted teeth as they brushed past, filling the passageway with their disgusting bulk, their putrid flanks only inches from his helm.

Moments later, the buzz of their rotary engines had receded into the distance. Koryn eased himself out of the alcove where he'd been concealing himself. He watched as his four brothers did the same, seemingly solidifying from the shadows, their ebon armour coalescing out of the darkness. Silently, they moved on.

The tunnels continued to descend into the earth, winding and doubling back on themselves, sometimes opening into wider, uninhabited caverns, other times drawing in until they were so narrow that Koryn had to walk sideways to squeeze his bulk through them. Brother Grayvus took the lead at the head of the small squad, and it was soon after they had put an end to another clutch of cultists that Koryn saw him stop suddenly at the mouth of a T-junction and hold up his hand in warning.

'What is it, Grayvus?' breathed Koryn over the vox.

'Death Guard, Captain. Three of them, up ahead.'

Stealthily, Koryn slipped past Syrus and the others, coming to stand beside Grayvus. He peered around the corner. There, in the sickly glow of a candle sconce, stood three of the Traitor Marines. Their now deformed armour was ancient - more ancient, even, than Koryn's own venerable suit of Corvus pattern armour. Unlike Koryn's, however, that of the traitors was now so degraded and corroded that it barely appeared to offer them any protection at all. It had clearly been altered to accommodate the mutated bulk of its inhabitants, and Koryn guessed they must have worn it for aeons, ever since the warp had first swallowed them and spat them out again in new twisted, decrepit forms.

Their flesh had grown through the cracks in the ceramite plating, enveloping it, causing the suits to become intrinsically part of them, inseparable from what remained of their once-glorious bodies. Their heads bulged beneath their broken helms and Koryn could see the face of one of them through the broken visor, his eyes shrivelled and weeping toxic ichor. Poison gases spewed from vents between their armour plates. They carried bolt pistols and power swords, the blades stained rusty brown with spilled blood.

To Koryn, the sight of the Plague Marines was disgusting beyond comprehension. Their vileness extended beyond the physical, of course, but it was as if their traitorous nature had manifested in their flesh, had been made physical and real as a result of their unholy pacts. He despised everything they stood for.

One of them stood fingering his own entrails, which spilled out from a jagged crack in his power armour to hang loose around his knees. Insects and other, more unnatural, creatures picked around in the ruins of his belly. Flies circled the heads of each of the traitors, and the reek of decay was all-permeating, even through the relative protection of Koryn's respirator.

'For Corax, brothers,' said Koryn, his voice hard as iron.

'For Corax,' his squad echoed in unison.

Without even the slightest sound, Koryn slipped around the corner, keeping his back to the wall as he began to manoeuvre himself into position for the ambush. The flickering candle in the wall sconce cast the Plague Marines in a warm, yellow orb of light, and Koryn knew that to get close to them, he would have to betray his position. No matter – he and his brothers would silence the traitors before they had the opportunity to raise the alarm.

He glanced back to see the others following behind, Syrus, Grayvus and Argis across the tunnel from him, keeping to the shadows as they crept steadily towards their prey. The traitors seemed content with their own concerns, evidently still unaware of the Raven Guards' proximity.

Koryn paused, now just a few feet behind the nearest Death Guard. He could see the ancient iconography on the pauldron, the old symbol of the legion now barely visible beneath layers of grime and necrotic, rippling flesh.

He glanced at Argis, issued a hand gesture to indicate that the others should follow his lead, and then, in one swift motion, launched himself from the wall, unsheathed his combat blade from his belt, and slit the throat of the closest Plague Marine from behind.

The traitor choked and stumbled backwards, causing Koryn to do the same. Thick, yellow pus oozed from the open wound in the Death Guard's throat, seeping out from the rotten tissue between its helm and the remnants of its gorget.

Growling in anger, the Plague Marine turned, swinging its fist up and round, catching Koryn hard in the chest and sending him spinning to the ground. He could barely believe the traitor was still standing. The wound in his throat yawned open like a wet, smiling mouth, but the Plague Marine seemed utterly unperturbed by this wound.

Koryn's brothers had engaged the other two traitors and were now locked in vicious hand to hand combat, ducking and weaving to avoid the poisoned blades that threatened to open up their armour and allow the pestilence inside.

Koryn rolled, springing to his feet, his lightning claws sparking as he thrashed out, tangling them in the traitor's intestines and wrenching them free. The Plague Marine's guts spattered in a heap by Koryn's boots, but still the enemy came on wordlessly, swinging its power sword in a wide arc so that Koryn had to raise his other talons quickly to defend himself, batting aside the deadly weapon. The Death Guard staggered with the momentum, and, seeing his chance, Koryn kicked out, trying to keep the foul thing at bay. It laughed, a deep, wet splutter from somewhere within its chest, and then charged forward, ignoring a swipe from Koryn's claw that drew four long gashes across its partially exposed chest. It struck him hard on his right shoulder and he shuddered under the force of the blow, feeling his pauldron crack with the impact. Warning sigils flared up inside his helm.

Once again Koryn lashed out, his talons raking open great furrows in the Plague Marine's belly, tearing away ceramite and stringy flesh. Still it came on. The thing was near impossible to kill, so close to death was it already.

Koryn twisted at the sound of Syrus crying out beside him, and saw with horror that one of the other traitors now held his brother's beaked helm between its fists. He was appalled to see that a broken fragment of spine trailed from the base of the helm, where the Plague Marine had physically ripped Syrus's head from his shoulders. Crimson blood spurted from the stump of Syrus's neck, and as Koryn watched, his corpse toppled backwards against the passage wall, sliding to the ground in a black heap.

Koryn embraced the rage that he felt welling up inside of him, but did not allow it to overwhelm him. He ducked to avoid another swipe from the Plague Marine's fist and struck low with his lightning claw, burying his talons in the traitor's right knee and shearing away its lower leg in a flurry of sparks. The traitor twisted and buckled, dropping heavily to the floor, its power sword skittering away across the ground. Wasting no time, Koryn leapt forward, pinning one of the traitor's arms beneath his boot and forcing his talons into the throat wound he had opened earlier. He finished the job with a grunt of satisfaction, wrenching the Plague Marine's head from its body. It rolled away down the passageway amidst a shower of dark blood.

Koryn turned to see Argis had finally felled another of the Death Guard, carving out its twin hearts with his talons and his combat blade. Grayvus had the third pinned against the wall, writhing and belching foul gases as it fought to get free. It was a matter of a moment's work for Koryn to loose that one's head from its shoulders too, and Grayvus allowed the corpse to drop to the ground, still twitching.

Argis dropped to his knees before the remains of his fallen brother. He looked up at Koryn, still panting for breath. 'I will honour him, Captain, by returning his corvia to the soil of distant Kiavahr.'

'Quickly then, Argis. Do what is necessary to honour our fallen kin,' replied Koryn gravely.

Argis cupped the bundle of fragile bird skulls suspended from fine chains on Syrus's belt and gave them a sharp tug, pulling them free. He stood, hastily tying the talismans to the small cluster that hung from his own belt.

'Another brother lost in battle. He will not be forgotten.'

Koryn stepped forward, putting a hand on Argis's shoulder. 'Yes, brother. He will not be forgotten. But remember why we are here. The Brazen Minotaurs sacrificed an entire company on Empalion II in order to enable the successful completion of our mission. We owe them a debt of honour, and we owe them our lives. Syrus understood that.'

They were silent for a moment.

'Retrieve his progenoid glands, Argis,' said Koryn. 'And hurry. We don't have much time.'

'Yes, captain,' replied Argis, drawing a scalpel from his belt and setting to work. Koryn watched the mouth of tunnel while Argis carried out the necessary procedure, the means by which their chapter's future would be secured.

'Now help me to move his body out of sight,' said Koryn a moment later, when Argis had hidden Syrus's geneseed carefully in a pouch at his belt. He stooped and took up Syrus's legs while Argis hefted the corpse beneath the arms, and silently they deposited it into one of the nearby alcoves in the wall, hidden from view.

'A dusty tomb for a hero,' said Coraan.

Koryn surveyed the carnage around them, feeling his shoulder twinge with pain. The traitor had obviously done more damage than Koryn had initially realised. Not enough, however, to render the limb useless.

He turned to face the remaining three members of his squad.

'We draw closer,' he said, his voice low. 'Closer to our goal, and closer to the heart of the enemy.' He only hoped that somewhere behind them, Captain Daed of the Brazen Minotaurs could say the same.

'Move out.'

# DAED

'It's as if someone is leaving us a trail,' said Daed, staring down at the ruins of a former Traitor Marine. 'A trail marked in blood.'

The traitor's wounds were still weeping dark, corrosive fluid that scarred the stone floor where it pooled, forming hissing spirals of vapour. This was the fourth scene of its like that they had encountered as they had passed through the winding tunnels, each of them alike, all lined with tributes to the long-forgotten dead.

'Either that,' said Bast, 'or it is evidence that another faction are indeed here on Kasharat, searching for our prize.'

Daed nodded. He had yet to decide which he thought it might be. Either way, neither option offered him much comfort. Worse still, he could sense the warp-infested traitors all around him, elsewhere in the tunnels, seething like the poisonous vapour itself, like rodents scuttling about in the darkness. The notion filled him with a sharp sense of disquiet.

Something, or someone, had passed this way, tearing through the defences of the Death Guard to leave a path through the mausoleum complex. Whoever or whatever it was, they had enabled the Brazen Minotaurs to pass unmolested into the lair of the enemy. The only question that still concerned Daed was why. It felt somehow wrong that he hadn't yet had cause to bloody his axe.

'Captain?'

Daed turned to see Bardus watching the passageway behind them, eager for his attention. 'What is it, Bardus?'

'Listen.'

Daed concentrated, straining to hear anything in the echoing depths of the mortuary. There it was – a droning, buzzing sound, like that of a hovering insect.

'I hear it,' he replied.

'Whatever it is, captain, it's coming this way,' said Bardus, hefting his bolter.

Daed smiled. Perhaps, finally, they had stirred the enemy in their nest. 'Brace yourselves. Ready your weapons, I want to be prepared for them when they arrive.'

'Aye, Captain,' said Bardus, dropping to one knee and bracing himself against the tunnel wall.

The air here was thick and syrupy, denser than it had been even on the surface, and it obscured Daed's vision, making it difficult to see what was coming, what diabolical thing was responsible for the noise. He longed for the clean air of Tauron, for the lush green forests, filled with prides of the black lions that prowled through the wilds in their thousands. He longed for the hunt, for the feel of one of the great beasts struggling in his arms as he wrestled it to the ground, burying his hunting knife in its heart. He thought then of what the Sickening would do to Tauron, and he raised his bolt pistol and power axe in defiance. That was what he fought for – to hold the forces of Chaos at bay, to protect the Imperium from its terrible taint. Kasharat was already lost, but the weapon he hoped to recover here might prevent other worlds from falling. Whatever it was that had lured them there, down into that vast mortuary complex, Daed knew then that he would defeat it.

Something stirred in the swirling mist, but Daed was unable to get any real sense of bearing, of how far away the thing might be. He trained his bolt pistol on what he took to be the epicentre of the disturbance, but refrained from opening fire without knowing exactly what it was he would be shooting at. He felt the fine hairs on the back of his neck prickle in anticipation. The mist began to churn.

Daed waved his hand to signal the others to remain silent. He could hear the buzz of rotary engines now, drawing closer by the second. Bast had heard them too, and he raised his bolter in readiness. 'Incoming!' he called.

Targus strafed left and dropped to one knee, swinging the heavy bolter up onto his shoulder.

Seconds later, Daed saw the hellish machines that were responsible for the sound. They burst out of the bank of green vapour – strange, hovering contraptions about the size of a man, with twin rotary engines and bulbous fleshy torsos that hung from the metal casings like the bodies of fat maggots. The drones were half machine, half rancid flesh, and they bristled with winking lights and strange mechanical weapons.

There were two of them, and they shot down the

passageway, propelled at speed by their whirring engines. Daed hefted his axe, preparing to make a swing for one if it came close enough.

Beside him, Targus squeezed the trigger on his heavy bolter and it boomed with explosive force in the confined space, belching an explosive shell at the lead drone. Targus's aim was true, and the bolter shell pierced the soft, fleshy tissue of the machine's torso. It exploded in a shower of glistening pus and mechanical components, its rotors clattering to the floor.

The reverberating sound of the explosion was enough to stir the other Brazen Minotaurs into action. Bast sent a spray of bolter fire arcing into the air, clattering off the walls as the other drone slid noisily out of the way, churning the green miasma as it shot forward and into their midst.

'Keep away from its poisoned blades,' Daed barked. He raised his bolt pistol and fired a number of shots into the flank of the bizarre thing, opening puckered wounds that wept like silent, screaming mouths.

Targus was furiously loading another round into his heavy bolter, while the others continued to pepper the drone with shot after shot, holding the thing at bay.

'Hurry, Targus!' Daed bellowed, glancing over his shoulder to see Targus raising the weapon onto his shoulder once again.

A spray of the machine's pustulant innards spattered over Daed's arm brace then, and too late he realised their error. The gloopy stuff began to corrode his power armour almost as soon as it came into contact with the ceramite, chewing a series of deep pockmarks where it had landed.

'Hold your fire!' he screamed, but it was too late. Targus had already pulled the trigger of the heavy bolter.

The blight drone exploded in a fountain of acidic pus, showering Bardus in a concentrated burst, covering his golden armour in a spray of the nauseating yellow fluid. He staggered back a few steps as he tried to clear the stuff from his helm, and then realised what was happening as it began to chew its way into the crevices between the armour plating. He held his hand up and cried out in pain as his flesh began to disintegrate inside his armour.

The drone itself was a trap, Daed realised, like a deadly, hovering land mine. The corrosive filth inside it was a weapon, and it was eating away at the joints in Bardus's armour, seeping beneath the ceramite to burn his flesh. There was nothing they could do, no way for them to save him without succumbing to the poison themselves. All they could do was watch as Bardus was slowly, inexorably overcome, until the poison had consumed his body. He staggered back against the wall, issued a long, pained exhalation and collapsed into a crumpled heap upon the ground.

What was more, the noise of the heavy bolter fire meant they had given themselves away. Now the traitors would know they were there, and so would whoever was responsible for the trail of corpses that had led them this far into the complex.

Targus lowered his weapon and pushed past the others to stand over the corpse of his fallen brother. He turned, wordlessly, to look at Daed.

'Bardus is lost, brothers,' said Daed, 'But we will honour him.' He reached up and unclasped the black lion's pelt that hung around his own shoulders.

Foul vapour was now issuing from inside Bardus's armour as the poison burned through his corpse. A section of his helm had been eaten away, and beneath it Daed could see the damaged, half-disintegrated remains of his brother's face.

Daed stepped forward, dropped to his haunches and draped the lion's pelt almost reverently over the corpse, as if it were a death shroud.

'He was Lionguard,' said Daed. 'His name will be recorded in the annals of Tauron.' He stood, resting his hand upon Targus's pauldron. 'There is nothing you could have done. You were not to know.'

Targus nodded, but Daed could see he was grieving for the loss of his brother. 'I will avenge him, captain.'

'On the field of battle, yes,' said Daed, his voice low and commanding. 'But here, now, we must focus only on the mission. Put all other thoughts from your mind.'

'Captain?' The voice that interrupted them was insistent over the vox. Daed turned to see Bast approaching. 'We must move swiftly, captain, before the enemy mobilises. The noise of the battle will draw them to us. This foul air gives them the advantage. They know the tunnels.'

Daed nodded. 'Lead on, Bast. Follow the trail of the dead. One way or another, we will reach our goal.'

He started forward, but stopped short when his boot encountered something hard on the ground, which skittered away across the stone floor, clanging off the tunnel wall. Crossing to where it came to rest, Daed was surprised to see the beaked, ebony helm of a Space Marine. He frowned when he noticed the sheared fragment of spinal column still jutting rudely from the base of the helm, and realised with surprise that the decapitated head of its former owner was still contained within. The wound looked recent. The stump of the neck was bloody and wet.

'What is it, captain?' said Throle, coming to stand beside him.

'I'm not sure,' replied Daed, turning to glance after Bast, who was already barely visible in the soupy miasma. 'But I believe this confirms we have company on Kasharat.'

# KORYN

The echo of heavy weapons fire reverberated through the tunnels like the crack of thunder. Koryn and his Raven Guard froze in response, each of them attempting to ascertain from which direction the sound had come. It was somewhere up above, a few tunnels away, back towards the surface.

After a moment, Grayvus spoke. 'What are they doing? They'll have the whole place down upon us!'

'The blight drones,' said Argis, and the dismay was evident in his voice.

'That is their way,' said Koryn. 'They meet their enemies head on. They look them in the eye before they take their lives. There is honour in that.'

'They'll be meeting even more of them now,' said Grayvus, wryly. 'The pox-ridden scum will be swarming through these tunnels in a moment.'

Koryn nodded. 'Yes, we must press on. We must keep

the way clear. We're near to the heart of the complex now. There our brothers will find what they are looking for.'

'I hope it shall prove worth it,' muttered Coraan. Koryn let the comment pass. He knew his brothers were still smarting from the loss of Syrus. To the Raven Guard, who were so few, every fallen brother was painfully mourned, every loss keenly felt by all. But on Empalion II, the Brazen Minotaurs had helped the Raven Guard to snatch victory from the jaws of defeat. They had laid siege to a city under the sway of the Iron Warriors, sacrificing an entire company as a decoy in order to allow the Raven Guard to slip over the walls of the city and destroy the enemy from within. It was that which had brought Koryn to Kasharat, that debt of honour. The Brazen Minotaurs, bull-headed and brutal, could never have reached their target alone, and without it they risked losing the entire conflict to the enemy warband. Seven Imperial worlds had already fallen, and it was Koryn's duty to come to their aid. He would not allow another world to succumb to the Sickening.

Footsteps pounded in an adjacent passageway. Koryn felt his pulse quicken. They would have to fight their way through from here on in, carving a bloody path through the corpses of the corrupted. It was not, perhaps, how he might have chosen to proceed with their mission, but Koryn's had to admit – the notion of spilling more traitorous blood had a certain appeal.

Koryn raised his lightning claws, which crackled and sparked in readiness.

'Now, brothers!' he called over the vox. 'Let us see how many of these vile traitors we can destroy!'

Forgoing all sense of subtlety, Koryn took the lead,

charging out of the mouth of the tunnel and directly into the path of a band of seven cultists coming in the other direction. His talons flashed and three of them fell before they had even realised what was happening, torn asunder so violently that they showered Koryn's armour in a dark, fleshy rain. He heard the chatter of bolter fire from behind him and knew that his brothers were there too, as he cut a swathe along the passageway.

'Victorus aut Mortis!' he bellowed over the vox as he opened up the belly of another cultist, before severing a fifth entirely in half at the midriff.

'In the name of the Emperor!' called Argis, whipping his combat blade around so that it opened a broad gash across the face of cultist, slicing through flesh and bone alike and felling the foul man where he stood.

'For Corax!' echoed Grayvus, loosing off a chatter of bolter shells.

As more and more of the cultists spilled forth from the other end of the tunnel, Koryn smiled. He allowed the lust of battle to consume him, to fill his thoughts until he was barely conscious of his own actions, carried along by the ferocious rise and fall of combat, the dance of the raven. Within minutes the corridor was filled with a tide of corpses, as if they had somehow washed up here, deposited and abandoned like unwanted flotsam – a torrent of death left in the wake of the living shadows.

Koryn, dripping blood from his talons, charged on, allowing his intuition to guide him, crushing the enemy as he led his Raven Guard deeper below ground, down towards the heart of the mortuary complex.

When he finally came to rest a short while later, it was beside the entrance to a large subterranean cavern. Here, an ornate doorway had been erected, a vast, steepled arch, towering above even the Space Marines' heads. It seemed incongruous to Koryn to find such a place at the heart of such a dark, oppressive structure.

Immense statues stood proud and silent on either side of the yawning archway, their heads, hands and feet now vandalised, leaving them deformed and unrecognisable. Their blank faces stared unseeing into eternity.

Koryn stepped to one side, pressing himself up against the wall in order to remain out of sight. He glanced round to see Argis's helm looming out of the gloom beside him.

'I sense movement inside,' said Argis quietly.

Koryn could tell that Argis was spoiling for another fight – he'd had a taste of battle and was now filled with the rush of it, with the desire to smite the enemy. Koryn knew, however, that it would be wrong for them to go any further. This was no longer their fight.

'No,' he replied, shaking his head. 'This is a battle our brothers should face alone. We should allow them that, at least – the opportunity to defeat the beast in its own lair. We have done what we came here to do, to lead them to their goal, to ease their path to victory as they once did ours. Now we must leave them to finish it, to taste the blood of their enemies for themselves.'

'Yes, Captain,' said Argis, and if he was disappointed, he did not allow it to show in his voice. 'The Raven's way.'

'And besides,' said Koryn, grinning. 'We need to clear them a path out of here, yet. There are plenty more of those traitorous wretches waiting for us in the tunnels above.'

Argis raised his bolt pistol. 'I am ready, captain,' he said, and Koryn could tell that he was smiling with anticipation behind his respirator.

Koryn turned and made a hand gesture for the others to follow, and then silently the Raven Guard melted once more into the shadows.

# DAED

It had been a bloodbath.

Whatever had happened here in this confined tunnel, it had been carnage. Someone – and having found the beaked helm in the passageway above, Daed was beginning to form an idea of who might have been responsible – had ripped through a swarm of enemy cultists, shredding them limb from limb and leaving behind a slick mess of body parts and eviscerated corpses. It wasn't so much a bloody trail as evidence of a massacre. There must have been thirty or more of the corrupted humans, their wretched, mutated cadavers already rotting where they had fallen. It was difficult to make out their true number – their remains were no longer whole enough to be able to judge.

'What happened here?' growled Throle, and Daed knew it was a rhetorical question, echoing all of their thoughts.

'Help,' he replied, his voice quiet and low. 'We were

wrong to assume we were being led into a trap, or that another foe was engaged in attempting to beat us to our target. Whoever did this... they are allies. Someone is clearing us a path.'

'Clearing us a path...?' said Targus, his voice incredulous. 'But who?'

'There'll be time for that later,' replied Daed, brandishing his axe before him to underline his point. 'We are close to our goal. I can sense it. We must press on. We must make good on the fortune we have been granted.' He turned and charged off along the passageway, his boots sloshing in the spilled blood of the enemy. The others fell in behind him, and together the four Brazen Minotaurs began their final descent into the heart of the enemy labyrinth.

It was not long before Daed, following in the wake of his benefactors, located the entrance to the central cavern at the nexus of the mortuary complex. The path had been made clear to him by the grisly trail of fallen cultists. They were heaped against the tunnel walls or spread out upon the ground, in some instances two or three deep at a time.

Some of them, he'd realised as he'd thundered down the tunnels, were still alive, scrabbling at his legs as they bled out from terrible wounds or tried to push their spilled organs back into their rent-open cavities. He finished many of them as he ran, crushing their skulls with his boots or spreading their infected brains across the walls with a swift shot from his bolt pistol.

Now, in the shadow of the enormous archway, surrounded by wispy green mist, Daed stood shoulder to shoulder with his brothers, ready to face whatever – or whoever – was waiting for them in the dank cavern beyond.

Without a word he stalked forward into the gloom, his bolt pistol tracking back and forth, his footsteps ringing out in the cavernous space. Inside, the cave had been dressed to resemble an elaborate temple, with a corridor of ornate marble columns leading to a raised dais upon which, Daed saw with a quickening of his hearts, their target rested: the supine form of Theseon, the Chief Librarian of the Brazen Minotaurs.

Theseon, apparently unconscious, was lashed to a marble slab, and as Daed watched a number of human cultists worked strange ministrations over his power armour, splashing unguents across his chest-plate and painting runes upon his pauldrons in livid green paint. They were trying, Daed knew, to weaken Theseon so that their psykers could extract the secrets from his mind. He only hoped that Theseon had been able to remain pure during these assaults. It had been days since he'd been taken, captured alive on the field of battle, and Daed knew that he had only two options: to kill the Librarian before Theseon gave himself up to the creatures of the warp, or to save him and return him to his brothers. He hoped for the latter, but as he entered the grotesque temple he began to prepare himself for the former.

Around them, candles flickered in sconces upon the walls, casting everything in a dull, flickering glow. Between the pillars, the remnants of ancient statues watched forlornly as Daed and Targus strode forward, preparing to slaughter the infidels who held their brother captive.

But Daed knew immediately that something was wrong. The cultists hadn't so much as stirred as the Brazen Minotaurs had entered the chamber, hadn't even looked up from their diabolical work at the sound of the Space

Marine's thundering footsteps. Where were the guards?
Where were the former Death Guard, the traitorous Space
Marines of Empyrion's Blight? Surely they would not leave
such a precious weapon as Theseon unguarded by anything but mere humans?

Daed's questions were answered a moment later as he
neared the flight of stone steps that lead up to the dais.
From the darkness off to his left, he became aware of a
wet, rasping laugh and the sound of footsteps splashing
heavily in the poisonous slurry that pooled on the floor.

Raising his axe, Daed turned to see one of the most horrific creatures he had ever encountered emerging from
between two of the pillars. It had once been a Space
Marine, but now it was a disgusting, lumbering, monster.
The remnants of its terminator armour hung off its twisted,
gangrenous flesh, and half of its ribcage was exposed to
the elements, allowing Daed to see through to one of its
black, beating hearts. It had swollen to almost twice its
original size, and a large, bony horn protruded from the
centre of its forehead, erupting through the remains of
its helm. Acid dribbled freely from the orifice that had
once been its mouth, and its respirator had been almost
entirely eaten away by corrosion. Necrotic flesh hung in
loose strips from between the plates of its ruined armour.

In its left fist it clutched a storm bolter, but its right
arm was now a wriggling mass of tentacles – at least six
of them – each of them dripping with glistening venom.
Strange, repulsive creatures, about the size of rats, scuttled over its body, burrowing in and out of its flesh.

The monster was flanked on either side by two Plague
Marines, each of them clutching bolters trained on Daed
and his brothers.

Daed wasted no time. With a bellowing roar he lowered his head and shoulders, raised his power axe and charged.

The creature's storm bolter barked, spewing shells, but Daed charged on, strafing left and right and swinging his axe in a wide arc over his head. It connected with the monster's chest, shattering ancient ceramite and ribs indiscriminately, burying itself deep inside the rotten husk of the former Space Marine. The creature staggered back under the force of the blow, wrenching the shaft of the axe out of Daed's gauntlets in the process, so that half of the weapon's double-bladed head still protruded from its chest.

Then, almost as if the weapon had barely caused a scratch, it came on again, lashing out with its multiple tentacles, whipping Daed's legs from underneath him so that he fell, hard, to the floor.

Daed scrabbled for purchase, attempting to lever himself up before the massive bulk of the thing fell upon him. He could hear the chatter of bolter fire from behind him, and realised that his brothers had engaged the two Plague Marines, keeping them busy while he tackled the beast.

The creature raised its left leg as if to crush him beneath it, but Daed rolled, springing up onto his feet just as the thing was struck by a blast from Targus's heavy bolter, punching a massive hole in its left side and spilling its rotten innards across the floor. Daed raised his bolt pistol and pressed forward, shooting openly into the creature's face so that it howled in pain and stumbled back against one of the pillars.

Hands shot out from the strange, fleshy membrane that covered the pillar, and Daed realised with disgust that there were humans in it, half-subsumed by the gelatinous goo so that they had become one with the walls, their bodies melding into the organic morass. They clutched the former Space Marine to them in their fleshy embrace, and it battered them off, lumbering forward, its storm bolter raised.

It snapped out a reply to Targus's heavy bolter and Daed saw his brother reel, shredded by the explosive rounds as they chewed pockmarks in his chest and face. He fell without issuing a sound, his weapon clattering noisily to the ground.

'Targus!' Roaring in rage and defiance, Daed rushed forward, his bolt pistol flaring. The creature swung around, its trigger still depressed, and Daed felt a sharp pain in his left shoulder as a stray shot burst through his armour, blowing out the top of his arm and rendering the limb useless. Warning sigils flared in his helm display but he charged on regardless, crying out for vengeance, ignoring the pain.

Daed slammed against the rotten bulk of the creature, striking it hard in the face with his good fist. He felt its tentacles lash out in response, curling around his waist and squeezing him with crushing force. He could smell the thing now, even through his respirator, and its stench was repugnant: the very scent of death itself.

Choking as the creature tried to squeeze the life out of him, Daed grabbed for the shaft of his axe, hauling on it with all of his might in an effort to wrench it free. He felt it give as the creature shifted, and he pressed on with renewed vigour, working the blade back and forth until it finally slid free in a spray of sickly ichor.

Daed was feeling dizzy now from the sheer force being exerted upon his body. His armour was beginning to crack under the pressure and he could feel where the creature's acidic spittle was searing his flesh, burning through the ceramite on his chest-plate. He had only moments to act.

With a huge effort, Daed raised the axe as high above his head as his good arm would allow him, and then brought it down in a sharp chopping motion, throwing all of his strength behind it. His aim was true, and the blade struck the creature hard in the side of the throat where acidic discharge had rotted away its armour.

The creature lurched backwards, loosening its grip and allowing Daed to drop to the floor. It staggered back, its storm bolter swinging aimlessly, and then, to Daed's relief, its head slid from its shoulders, the last vestiges of its decaying flesh failing to hold it in place any longer. The head struck the stone floor only seconds before the lurching, spasming body.

Daed clambered up onto his feet, twisting around to see how his brothers were fairing. Throle was on the ground, his leg shattered at the knee, but with the corpse of a fallen Plague Marine beyond him. Bast was standing over the toppled remains of the other, still spraying its now obliterated face with bolter fire.

Daed staggered over to them.

'Targus is lost,' said Throle, matter-of-factly.

'We shall mourn him later,' replied Daed, putting a hand on Bast's pauldron to stay his brother's hand. Bast released the trigger of his bolter, and the last echoes of the battle died a few moments later.

On the dais, the cultists were working furiously to release the chains that bound Theseon to the marble slab, evidently planning to flee.

'Hand me your bolter, brother,' said Daed, passing his axe to Bast and taking his brother's weapon in return. He raised it, took aim, and felled the screaming cultists one by one as they finally acknowledged his presence and bolted for cover, abandoning the Librarian where he lay. None of them made it as far as the door.

'Bast – see to Throle. I'll see to Theseon.' Daed crossed the cavern, taking the steps two at a time as he leapt up onto the dais. There, on the marble slab, Theseon lay unmoving, still wearing his bright blue power armour, covered now in blasphemous scrawl. He was still alive – that much was clear to Daed almost immediately – but he had retreated into a sus-anic coma, disappearing into his own mind in an effort to protect himself and the secrets of his chapter from the foul ministrations of the Death Guard's psykers. Whether he might ever be roused from it, Daed did not know. He hoped it would be so – Theseon's mind was a powerful weapon, and he was needed if the war against the Chaos forces was to be won.

But now was not the time for such thoughts. Daed would have to carry the Librarian to the surface. He only hoped their mysterious benefactors had thought to consider their escape, too.

It was the work of only moments to wrench Theseon free of the chains that bound him. Daed turned to see Throle, upright, resting on Bast, his shattered leg hanging useless and limp. With a groan of agony at the sharp pain in his left shoulder, Daed hefted the bulk of the supine Librarian over his shoulder, and staggered towards the door.

Their passage to the surface proved relatively uneventful, if painfully slow. There was evidence everywhere of the passing of another party; corpses strewn at every junction, tunnels spattered with the blood of both human cultists and traitorous Death Guard. Once again, it was clear to Daed that someone had seen fit to carve them a path to the surface. With the burden of the injured Throle and the unconscious Theseon, it was a much-needed reprieve.

Above, on the planet's surface, the green mist now swirled thicker than ever, cloying and sickly even through Daed's helm. Trusting his instincts, he staggered into the haze towards the Thunderhawk resting amongst the broken spires of the vast temple complex.

Soon enough, the shadow of the vessel hulked out of the fog to greet them. Daed staggered over to the ship, reaching for the control panel that would release the boarding hatch. But his fingers encountered something unexpected there. He glanced down to see something dangling on the end of a chain that had been draped over the release mechanism. It was a tiny, fragile bird's skull, bleached white and stained with spatters of dark blood.

The skull of a raven. He had seen their like before, hanging from the belts of fellow Space Marines, ebon-armoured warriors of the Raven Guard, whom he had fought beside on Empalion II. He cupped the totem in his fist and then thumbed the release control, causing the hatchway to hiss open like a gull's wing.

'What is it, Captain?' asked Bast, standing behind him as he held the raven's skull up to the light. It twisted as it dangled on the fine chain.

'Hope,' said Daed, cryptically. 'Hope that we may yet win this war, and a debt repaid.'

Daed slipped the totem into a pouch at his belt, and then strode purposefully up the ramp towards the waiting vessel. The Brazen Minotaurs would triumph yet in this conflict. They had Brother Theseon, and they had help from the most unexpected of quarters.

Daed grinned as he dropped Theseon onto a bench and secured him into place with the webbing. He wondered if, even now, the sons of Corax were watching from the shadows. The thought filled him with an unexpected mix of confidence and dread.

Seconds later the hatchway hissed shut once again, and Bast gunned the Thunderhawk's engines.

Now, Daed knew, the real battle would begin.

# THE UNKINDNESS
# OF RAVENS

# DAED

*Light and darkness. Darkness and light.*

Around him, the world was described only in the stuttering flashes of muzzle flares; the brief, blooming light of detonating incendiary shells; the flickering headlamps of Land Raiders as they roared over the churned earth, now sticky and sodden with spilt blood.

The traitors had shut off the immense, arcing lumen strips in the rocky canopy above and as a consequence the entire bastion – all several hundred kilometres of it – was shrouded in a dense, artificial night. Even with his ocular implants he was struggling to define anything in the intense gloom, and Daed suspected there were sinister powers at work, somehow altering the very quality of the light, or else his perception of it. He shuddered at the thought of such diabolical things influencing his mind. Daed was forced to rely on his other senses, and on the scant few glimpses of the battle he could garner by the muted light of scattershot explosions and weapons fire.

Around him, the bark of bolters and the echoing boom of exploding mortar shells indicated, along with the screams of the dying, where the battle was at its most fierce.

From his elevated position behind the hastily erected barricade, Daed could survey the entire battlefield, and from what little he could tell – given the gloom and the swirling, miasmic mist that seemed to permeate everything – things were not going well for the Brazen Minotaurs. Two entire companies of his brother Space Marines were engaged in the siege, and had been for weeks. They had suffered heavy losses to both troops and equipment, and he mourned each of them with a heavy heart. It would take decades for the Chapter to recover from such grave losses, and the battle was far from over. They had yet to even breach the bastion walls. Only the Emperor Himself knew what horrors they might face on the other side.

The traitors, by contrast, were legion, and cared little for their dead. They spilled over the bastion walls in their thousands, former Imperial Guardsmen now corrupted by the taint of the Sickening, the rot of Chaos. An inexorable tide of stinking, pestilent flesh, washing over his brothers as they slowly inched their way towards the towering plascrete skirts of the former Imperial stronghold.

Daed had slain hundreds of them in the preceding days, but he had done so without even a mote of satisfaction. That a stronghold so important to the Imperium could fall so easily to the sly imprecations of Chaos left him feeling ill at ease, as if a chill fist had wrapped itself around his primary heart and refused to let go.

Worst of all, amongst the enemy marched ranks of

daemons: foul, one-eyed beasts with pustulant, bloated bellies and sharp, bony protrusions erupting from weeping foreheads. These creatures bore broken, rusted blades that dripped with deadly toxins, and they shambled unerringly across the battlefield, coteries of buzzing insects trailing in their wake. Obscene, fist-sized creatures festered in their rancid guts, scampering about amongst their putrid organs, breeding disease.

Daed had seen his brothers cut down by these grotesque plague-bearers, felled by a single stroke of their poisoned blades. It was not the wounds themselves that brought death, but the vile poisons imparted by their blades. In this war, even the most innocuous graze could prove deadly, if the enemy spores were allowed to fester.

The creatures were difficult to kill, too, and even harder to spot amongst the green mist and frenetic urgency of the battlefield. They leered out of the eternal night, chanting softly beneath their foetid breath, and despite his zeal and determination to face these abominations in the name of the Emperor, to crush them with all the might of the Brazen Minotaurs, Daed feared them.

He did not fear death, nor did he fear facing the daemons in open combat; it was purely what they represented that struck him with a cold sense of dread. He feared the stain such monsters left upon the universe, the corruption and dissention they bred amongst men, and perhaps most of all, he feared failure. He feared the consequences if he and his brothers did not prevail. Such fear as this, he knew, made him stronger, more resolute. This was fear that he could embrace and channel into rage. He would turn it upon his enemies and he would smite them.

Daed longed to bring the battle to a swift end. The war in

the Sargassion Reach had become protracted, the enemy entrenched. He was resolved that he would do his duty – that he would lead the Brazen Minotaurs to victory, or would die trying. He would do so in the name of the Emperor, and he would do so with righteousness on his side. Nevertheless, he craved resolution. A war of attrition did not suit the ways of the Brazen Minotaurs.

Nevertheless, they would do as they must.

The warband Empyrion's Blight, led by traitorous Space Marines of the former Death Guard Legion, had plunged the Sargassion Reach into conflict, devastating entire worlds and leaving behind nothing but seething pestilence and death. These former Space Marines were now given over wholly to the foul taint of Nurgle, and the very thought of their depravity made Daed's blood boil. Their motives were obscure and arcane. Their corruption appeared to extend not only to the physical – the ooz-ing boils, necrotic flesh and parasitic worms that they encouraged to writhe and fester inside their once glori-ous bodies – but to their logical minds, also. Their tactics could not be anticipated. Their goals could not be fath-omed. They appeared to delight only in destruction and death for their own sake. The spreading of the Sickening had become their sole purpose.

Planet after planet had fallen to the contagion, from the mortuary world of Kasharat to the forge world of Plutonis. And now it had come to Fortane's World. The last outpost on the rim of the Sargassion Reach, a bizarre planet with an eccentric orbit that brought it close to the neighbour-ing Kandoor system, a sector of Imperial space teeming with heavily-populated colony worlds. Fortane's World, if not regained, would form the perfect beachhead for an invasion of Kandoor. Billions of human souls would fall to the Sickening if the Chaos forces were allowed to progress. The Brazen Minotaurs were all that stood between Empyrion's Blight and death on an unimaginable scale.

On top of that, Daed knew, came the risk of corruption. Those who did not die in such a mass invasion might instead succumb to the lure of the impure, the deadly breath of Chaos. That would mean a fate much worse than death and, more harmfully for the Imperium, a swelling of the enemy ranks. It had to be prevented. Failure was not an option.

Fortane's World itself was not an inhabited planet. There were no useful minerals buried deep beneath its crust, and the gravitational stresses imposed by its eccentric orbit rendered it unsuitable for the erection of vast hive cities. Nevertheless, the worldlet was one of the most valuable planetary bodies in the system. Its position at the tail end of the Sargassion Reach was paramount – a prime defensive position against the terrors of the warp and the ever-encroaching xenos threat emanating from the galactic rim.

The planet's unique composition aided significantly in this role: half of the world was encapsulated by a vast, rocky carapace, a tectonic umbrella that from space resembled an enormous, half-closed lid, shrouding the planet against the vagaries of the immaterium, and any weapons that might be trained upon its surface from orbit. Beneath this immense, natural shield, the Imperium had constructed a city-sized bastion, and from here innumerable foes had been rebutted in the intervening millennia, from xenos incursions to all manner of warp-spawned horrors.

The bastion was built to be impregnable. No invasion force had ever succeeded in breaching its walls by direct assault or devastating bombardment. As Daed well knew, however, there were other, more subtle, forms of invasion.

The taint of Chaos had come to Fortane's World, worming its insidious way into the weak minds of the men who were stationed there, insinuating itself amongst the ranks of the Imperial Guard. Unbeknownst to the Administratum or the Ecclesiarchy, sinister death cults had begun to spring up amongst the men, in turn blossoming into full-blown dissent and daemon worship. By the time the problem had been identified it was already too late, and the garrison on Fortane's World was in full revolt. Those few who had remained true to the Emperor were sacrificed according to bizarre rites, their bodies given over to become breeding grounds for plague maggots and the poisonous warp spawn that now stalked across the battlefield, spreading their foul contagion.

So it was that when the vanguard had arrived – the festering hulks of Empyrion's Blight – the traitorous bastards of Fortane's World had thrown open the doors and welcomed the Chaos forces inside.

Now, with only two companies at his disposal, Captain Daed of the Brazen Minotaurs needed to find a means to achieve the impossible: he had to breach the walls of the bastion and root out an entrenched enemy that knew the bastion far better than he did, and who outnumbered the Imperial forces by a factor of ten to one.

Not only that, but he was working to a deadline. Within another ten days Fortane's World would reach the zenith of its orbit, bringing it temporarily within the boundaries of the Kandoor system. Once that happened, it would be too late. The infection would spread.

Daed sighed. He lived for battle. He did not know patience. He longed to find himself on the other side of those plascrete walls so that he might take his axe to the traitorous scum who hid behind them.

He spun around, sliding his bolt pistol from its leather holster and squeezing off a single shot. A man-thing – a former Guardsman now bloated and scabrous from the plague – fell back from where it had been scaling the barricade just a few metres away, emitting a plaintive wail as its entrails slumped through the fist-sized hole in its belly. Daed listened as the creature toppled to the ground, just out of view. After a moment, the wailing stopped. Daed dropped his bolt pistol back into its holster.

He glanced across at Bast, the lamp affixed to his golden power armour picking out the glinting shape of his veteran sergeant, ensconced a few metres away amongst the heaped debris of the makeshift barricade. Bast was studying the battle below, his bolter trained on an enemy target that Daed could not discern in the gloom.

Daed watched as Bast opened fire, his bolter chattering wildly as he played it back and forth, showering his target with a barrage of screaming rounds. He heard something large and fleshy thud to the ground close by, and Bast released the trigger, easing himself back with a grunt of satisfaction.

'I'm sure it's getting darker,' he said, over the vox-link. He was wearing his helmet, but Daed could imagine the expression on his face.

'Yes,' Daed replied, his voice low. 'The enemy employs diabolical powers to maintain the gloom.'

Bast shrugged. 'They die just as well in the darkness,' he said, before turning back to his post and searching out another target.

Daed wondered how the Librarians were progressing. A kilometre behind the front line, in a ruined outpost building, two acolytes were furiously working their ministrations over the prone form of Theseon, the Chapter's Chief Librarian.

Theseon lay deep in a sus-anic coma, having retreated inside his own mind as a means of protecting himself from the attempts of the Chaos psykers to pry open his thoughts. Theseon had been captured during the first wave of attacks on Plutonis, spirited away to the dead world of Kasharat, where the traitors had attempted to break his spirit, to crack him open and reveal his secrets. Despite their efforts, throughout his ordeal Theseon had remained steadfast and true, and Daed – with help from unexpected quarters – had been able to affect a rescue, extracting the unconscious Librarian from a subterranean mortuary complex and returning him to his brothers.

Weeks had passed, however, and Theseon remained locked in his unmoving slumber. Nothing more had been seen of the mysterious benefactors who had aided Daed on Kasharat, either, and he was beginning to think that the entire episode had been intended as a diversion, devised by the enemy as a means of keeping him from Fortane's World, from where he was really needed. Now, he was making up for lost time.

'Prove me wrong, Theseon,' he muttered, glancing out over the top of the barricade at the gloomy battlefield below. He needed the Librarian by his side, countering the effects of whatever accursed psychic weapons were

being deployed by the enemy to conjure up the impenetrable darkness.

There was a sudden, massive roar and the ground
shuddered beneath his boots, causing him to reach out
and grasp hold of a jutting spar of metal, once part of
a Baneblade tank, but now just another fragment of the
barricade. The entire planet seemed to tremble, and then
a second booming explosion sounded from high above,
followed by another, and another. Daed cursed, but managed to retain his footing as he lurched to the right, jolted
by the impacts.

The vox-bead in his ear crackled to life, buzzing for
his attention. 'They've started the bombardments again,
captain.'

'So I'd noticed, Throle,' replied Daed, dryly.

'Shall I send orders for them to cease their attack?'

Daed considered this for a moment. 'No. Leave them
to it. If they wish to continue banging their heads against
the wall, let them. It can only aid us if the enemy are rendered unsteady on their feet.'

'Yes, captain.'

The vox-link hissed for a moment and went dead. Daed
glanced up at the dark underside of the rocky carapace
above. If the Imperial Navy thought they would be able
to blast their way through this upper layer of the planet's
crust, they were clearly deluding themselves. Daed had
already tried. The mushroom-shaped carapace would simply absorb or deflect anything they threw at it.

Soon enough, the sphincters on the crust would iris open
and the enemy would return fire. Then the bombardments
would stop for another few hours while the Navy ships
took evasive action, before coming back in to resume their

attack once the enemy weapons withdrew. The pattern had been the same for days. Meanwhile, scores of other Navy vessels were still locked in ship-to-ship combat with the Chaos vessels, drifting plague citadels squatting like crustaceans atop the shattered hulks of ancient barges.

Daed turned to follow the progress of a howling missile as it whistled overhead, punched from one of the Imperial weapon emplacements in the direction of the enemy troops. He saw an enemy Defiler detonate in a ball of orange fire, scattering scores of militia troops and churning great furrows in the loam. He hefted his axe in salute to his brothers. Another hour, he decided, and they would push forwards again, claiming a little more ground. Soon they would be in range of the walls, and the real battle could begin. He would punch a hole in the wall with his fists if he had to.

'Captain?'

Daed turned to see one of his brothers standing by his elbow, a data-slate clutched in his outstretched gauntlet. 'Throle,' he replied, his voice level.

'I think you should see this, captain.' Throle's voice was edged with trepidation.

'What is it?' he asked, failing to keep the impatience out of his voice. He took the data-slate and peered at the grainy image on the screen.

'The image is being relayed from the ruined outpost where we left the Librarians, sir.'

'On the rim of the canopy?'

'Aye, captain. That's the view of the sky above the forest,' confirmed Throle. 'The image is hazy, but they're clear to see. The data-slate is replaying it on a loop.'

Daed watched as three of the stars appeared to detach

themselves from the ink-black sky, hurtling at speed towards the line of trees below. Each of the three glowing specks disappeared a second later, landing somewhere out in the vast arboreal forest that covered the bulk of the planet's dry surface – or at least those parts of it that didn't fall beneath the shade of the massive carapace.

Daed watched as the sequence reset and cycled again, and then again, over and over on a constant loop, the three lights streaming out of the sky and disappearing into the dark woodland beyond.

'Falling stars,' he said, quietly. 'Drop-pods.' He glanced at Throle, handing him the data-slate. 'Either someone's coming to help, or the enemy are bringing in reinforcements to pin us from behind.' He turned, engaging his vox. 'Drago?'

The response was faint, intercut with hissing static and the sounds of distant battle. 'Captain?'

'Can you confirm you've received no communiqués from the Navy regarding reinforcements?' he asked, already knowing the answer.

'Negative, sir,' came the response. 'No communiqués. But then the damn fog has been making it near impossible to raise a channel.'

Daed cut the link. He turned to Throle. 'As I thought. We must assume the worst. Begin preparations. Within the day we're to be ready to receive incoming enemy on both flanks.'

'Aye, sir.'

Throle turned and marched off, already snapping out directives over the vox in order to muster enough of his brothers to begin erecting a second barricade. Fighting on two fronts would slow them down. It meant entrenching, consolidating, not pushing forwards. It meant time that they didn't have.

Daed drove his gauntleted fist into the barricade, sending a shower of debris tumbling over the side. He grunted in frustration, grinding his teeth.

Could it be the sons of Corax? He had thought, after Kasharat, that they might further come to his aid. Could he even begin to hope? Reinforcements could alter the tide of battle and break the pattern of the siege. Most likely, however, the Death Guard were having exactly the same thoughts.

Something shifted on the other side of the heaped wreckage, and Daed leapt up onto the chassis of a downed enemy Helbrute, hefting his axe in one fist and bringing it curling around from behind his back in one, smooth motion.

The creature's head parted from its shoulders and sailed away into the swarm of oncoming enemy troops, eliciting an answering hail of las-fire. The man-thing's remaining torso shuddered and stumbled forwards onto its knees, before collapsing into the mud, spouting ribbons of blood and pus from the stump of its neck.

Daed grinned. Perhaps there *was* satisfaction to be had in despatching these heretical scum. He would spend some time searching for it while he waited.

Soon enough, he would know the nature of the drop-pods and what they contained. In the meantime, there were traitors to be killed.

# KORYN

From orbit the planet appeared to be festooned with gaudy ribbons of orange and gold. They crisscrossed its pallid grey surface, flickering and rippling like shreds of tattered fabric in the wind.

The sight stirred ancient memories in Shadow Captain Koryn, recollections of a time before his indoctrination into the Raven Guard, of primitive rituals enacted in the wooded glades of Kiavahr. There, entwined around the branches, the ribbons had symbolised life and renewal, the blossoming of the forest. Here, in contrast, they meant only death. For these were not ribbons but funnels of flame, each a hundred miles long; splashes of searing plasma exploding from barrage shells; burning outposts and detonating warheads.

Such things as these now punctuated Koryn's existence. He barely remembered that earlier life on his distant home world, although he clung to what memories of it he still retained. Kiavahr was the womb from whence he was born, and echoes of it still lived on in his unregimented thoughts.

The sons of Corax, however, had descended from the stars and granted him a new life. A life beyond the forest, its rituals and the daily toil for survival. They had instilled in him not only the physiological enhancements that had altered his body and sharpened his mind, but also a deep sense of purpose. Now, Koryn lived that life in devotion to the Emperor, smiting the Imperium's enemies in His name.

A thousand battles had been fought and won in the intervening centuries. Consequently, Koryn's time on Kiavahr seemed like an eternity ago. To a human, of course, it was. Not so to a Space Marine.

Koryn clutched a data-slate in his gauntleted fist, studying the planet's ravaged surface as his drop-pod plummeted towards it, the thin shell trembling around him as it gathered speed and momentum. It was the planet, he knew, that was making him think of his old home.

He braced himself in his harness as the drop-pod struck the upper atmosphere and the howl of entry drowned out all other sound. The noise became a tortured, continuous scream, the whine of plasteel rending the air asunder. It was as if the planet was wailing in anger or pain, protesting as its boundaries were irrevocably breached.

Fortane's World had already been breached, though, Koryn thought. This was a world consumed by death.

The Imperial forces here had dwindled in the face of overwhelming numbers and encroaching plague. Below, on the planet's surface, the Brazen Minotaurs were locked in a deadly siege, a last ditch attempt to stem the spread of the Sickening. Koryn knew they were doomed to failure, just as they had been on Kasharat. Given time, he had no doubt their bull-headed tactics and sheer, brutal determination would prove successful; that no bastion wall, no matter how thick, could prevent Captain Daed and his brothers from attaining their goal. But time was a commodity they didn't have, and the head-on tactics of the Brazen Minotaurs would soon come to nothing. All the enemy had to do was delay, and the foul traitors of Empyrion's Blight were not beyond using their newly recruited human militia as collateral to such ends.

So it was that the Raven Guard had come to Fortane's World: not to displace their golden-armoured brothers, but to aid them in breaking the siege and bringing the reign of the Death Guard in the Sargassion Reach to an end.

Koryn and his brothers would employ a different approach, a subtler means of warfare. He only hoped that Daed would welcome such intervention – the history between their two Chapters was long and complex, and grave debts had been earned and repaid by both parties. Time, he supposed, would tell. Koryn had made efforts to communicate with Daed in the preceding days, to warn him that the Raven Guard were deploying to Fortane's World, but the miasmic fog summoned by the traitors was deadening communications across the surface of the planet. He supposed the Brazen Minotaurs would be expecting him anyway. On Kasharat, Daed had learned of the Raven Guard's presence in the Sargassion Reach. He could not believe that Koryn would stand by now and refuse to assist him in his hour of need.

The drop-pod bucked and rattled around Koryn, gathering speed. He glanced across at the figure opposite him, strapped into a harness identical to his own.

Cordae. The company Chaplain.

Cordae stared back at him from the nest of his webbing, his gaze unflinching behind the strange, beaked mask he wore over his helm. Koryn couldn't help thinking that in his full battle regalia, Cordae resembled an animal more than a Space Marine. His ancient power armour was older than even Koryn's own, dating back to a time long before the great Heresy and bearing the pits and scars to prove it, but was now largely obscured by the skeletal fetishes with which it was embellished and adorned.

These totems were the carefully preserved remnants of one of the giant rocs that inhabited the bleak crags of the Diagothian mountains back on distant Kiavahr, fashioned to resemble a grisly, humanoid exoskeleton. The bird's ribcage formed a brace over the Chaplain's chest-plate, while the finer bones of its wings fanned out across the bridge of his jump pack like two sets of spread fingers. Long, hollow femurs were held by clasps to each of the Chaplain's black-armoured thighs, and smaller bones hung from tattered ribbons and chains, attached to every surface, from vambraces to pauldrons.

Most disturbing of all, the bird's skull had been fashioned into a mask that covered Cordae's entire head, the relic now incorporated into the very fabric of his helm. The ivory beak jutted forwards monstrously, accusingly, while its empty eye sockets seemed to peer directly into Koryn's soul.

It was Cordae's belief – so Koryn understood – that the spirit of the deceased roc still inhabited its long dead bones, and that this spirit, tied to his totemic armour, accompanied Cordae into battle, serving as both a guide and a stark reminder of the Chapter's spiritual doctrines. Whether or not it was true, Koryn knew the impact it had on the morale of his brothers, and whatever the truth, Cordae was a fearsome, iron-hearted warrior with few equals. To hunt and kill a roc in unarmed combat was a task that few could achieve. The birds were rare creatures, eking out a harsh existence in isolation, high in the craggy peaks of Koryn's home world. Cordae would have had to live off the land for weeks at a time, remaining unseen and unheard during his long search for the nest. Then there was the precarious approach along the precipice, not to mention the battle with the creature itself...

Most hopeful initiates of the Chaplaincy who set off with such a goal in mind never returned.

Cordae would be an asset during this mission. He would serve as an adviser to Koryn, and he would smite the enemy with a zeal that none of the others could even hope to attain. Nevertheless, Koryn couldn't help feeling a certain amount of trepidation. Cordae's presence might well prove to be a boon, but Koryn was still unsure if he could entirely trust the Chaplain.

Koryn's head snapped to the left at the sudden, shrill cry of a warning klaxon.

'Incoming!' bellowed Argis, and Koryn braced himself as an enemy projectile slammed into the side of their fall-ing drop-pod with a deafening explosion.

The vehicle went into a crazed, dizzying spin, turning end over end, and Koryn was thrown back and forth in his webbing as he struggled to remain orientated in the cha-otic seconds that followed. He could hear the high-pitched whistle of inrushing air and caught stuttering, orphaned images of shredded plasteel and the dark night sky of the planet beyond. His brain hardly had time to register the sight of Borias – one arm and leg entirely missing, blood spraying generously from his ruptured torso, head lolling unconscious or already dead – before he was pitched forwards again, twisting in his harness and feeling a sharp tug on his left shoulder.

Koryn fought to stay conscious, focusing on making sense of what he was seeing.

Through the gaping wound in the side of the drop-pod he glimpsed trees; immense and gangly, receding into the far distance, clutching at the sky with thin, bony branches. Beyond that, looming over the distant horizon, was the dark, ominous shell of the planet's carapace.

The drop-pod smashed into the ancient woodland, colliding with the boughs of several enormous trees, pulverising them into oblivion as it carved a path through their dense foliage. Millennia-old trunks toppled in its wake, cracking and rending with ear-splitting noise. The drop-pod rebounded, shaking Koryn violently in his harness, and then, with a jarring *crunch*, it impacted against the forest floor.

Koryn lolled forwards, dazed, as the drop-pod careened across the ground, churning great furrows of earth behind it. Mud and leafy mulch spewed through the ragged hole in its side, temporarily entombing what was left of Borias and piling up around the others' knees. The air was filled with the fresh reek of damp soil.

Red warning sigils flared inside Koryn's helm, but he blinked them away, choosing to ignore them. He could feel a sharp pain in his left shoulder, and glancing down he saw a spar of metal embedded in the ebon ceramite of his chest-plate. He had been speared by debris during the explosion. The broken strut had pierced clean through his shoulder, pinning him to the wall.

He allowed the webbing to take his weight and, a few moments later, the drop-pod finally shuddered to a stop. Koryn drew a deep breath, pulling himself upright.

The drop-pod was on its side, half buried in the sticky loam. The klaxon was still sounding insistently, like the shrill cry of an angry bird.

'Shut that thing off!' Koryn croaked over the vox-link, and the sound came to an abrupt stop. Koryn glanced up to see Cordae still strapped rigidly into his webbing, immaculate and unmoving, still fixing him with the same blank-eyed stare. Koryn could not even tell if the Chaplain was dead or alive. 'Are you wounded, Cordae?' he said.

'No, captain,' came the low, even response. 'I remain unharmed and fully functional.'

'Argis?' Koryn called.

'Here, captain, and unscathed. But Borias is dead.' Argis's tone was neutral, clipped.

'Corvaan?' Koryn tried to repress the anger in his voice. The traitors would pay for Borias's death. He would make certain of it.

'Minor injuries only, captain.'

'Grayvus?'

'Scratches, sir.'

The rest of the squad confirmed their situations in turn. They had been lucky, sustaining only minor injuries and damage to their armour and equipment – save for Borias, who had borne the brunt of the surface-to-air missile strike that had sent them veering wildly off course.

Eleven of them had come to Fortane's World. Now they were ten. The omens were not good.

'Corvaan, start digging us out of here,' Koryn ordered, turning over in his mind how the next few moments might transpire. Would the enemy be waiting for them in the forest? There was a part of him that hoped they were. He longed to spill their blood, to rend them limb from limb with his lightning claws. To make them pay for Borias, for stealing from him an honourable death on the field of battle.

'Yes, captain,' replied Corvaan, and Koryn heard him disentangling himself from his webbing, cursing as he fought to free himself from the churned up earth that pinned his legs.

'And Cordae,' continued Koryn, 'help me with this shrapnel.'

The Chaplain cocked his head to one side, as if contemplating his response, and then, as commanded, tore away his own harness and clambered free. He scrambled over the mound of heaped earth between them until the beak of his bizarre skull mask was almost touching Koryn's faceplate. This close, Koryn could see that it was pitted and scarred from innumerable battles, and two long scores had been carved into the beak – presumably knife blows that Cordae had struck while the beast still lived.

Koryn fixed his eyes on the skull's empty sockets and gritted his teeth as Cordae wrapped both of his fists around the metal spar and wrenched it free, using his foot to gain leverage against the wall. Koryn gave a grunt of satisfaction as he saw the jagged end of the metal post erupt from the front of his chest-plate along with a shower of dark, red blood.

Immediately his enhanced physique and his armour's systems kicked into effect, stemming the tide of blood and sealing the puncture wounds.

'Thank you, brother,' said Koryn, as he tore at the remains of the webbing with his talons. He flexed his left arm, feeling the pull of the wound in his shoulder. It would slow him, but only fractionally.

'Corvaan, are we free yet?' he called.

'Almost, captain,' came the response, buzzing over the vox like an insect.

Koryn hauled himself up onto the mound of earth, pushing his way past Cordae as he edged his way around the confined space of the drop-pod, clambering over the damaged supporting struts and dropping down to join Corvaan and the others. He heard Cordae following behind him.

Corvaan had almost cleared a path through to the surface, having dug a small tunnel through the damp, compacted earth with his fists. He was currently worming his way up through the small opening he had created, pushing clay and rubble out of his path as he worked. Koryn watched as he hoisted his legs up through the hole, loosing a small avalanche in his wake. He scrabbled to his feet, his bolter at the ready.

Through the opening, Koryn could see only the misty night sky and the shimmering fingers of the nearby treetops.

'All clear, captain,' came the report a few seconds later.

'For now,' replied Koryn, beckoning Argis forwards and indicating the hole. 'Clearly they know we're here.' He placed his hand on Argis's pauldron. 'Move out, brother. And be on your guard.'

* * *

It took only moments for the ten remaining Raven Guard to extricate themselves from the ruins of their drop-pod. Siryan and Kayaan worked to dig free the corpse of their fallen brother, dragging it up through the hole behind them and laying it carefully on the ground at Koryn's feet.

Koryn stood over it now, fighting the rage that was welling up inside of him. Borias was a mess. The explosion had almost fully disintegrated the right side of his body, blowing his limbs and half of his chest away in a shower of flesh, bone and ceramite. Now damp earth was impacted in the empty organ cavities, as if he had just been disinterred after spending years in the ground, rotting inside the remnants of his ebon armour. His head remained inside the cracked shell of his helm, and Koryn could see that his gorget had been torn open, exposing his pale white flesh, now stained with crimson arterial blood.

'Argis. Reclaim his progenoids, if you can. We must think of the Chapter now, as well as our fallen brother,' said Koryn, quietly.

'It would be my honour, captain,' replied Argis, reaching for the small incision tool in his belt and dropping to his knees in order to crack open what was left of Borias's chest-plate.

'He would have wished to die in battle,' said Kayaan, bitterly.

'Then we honour him by allowing his death to mean something,' replied Koryn. 'Fate is a cruel mistress, Kayaan, and today she chose Borias instead of you, or Corvaan, or I. We honour Borias by ensuring our own deaths mean something also. We carry his corvia into battle, and if we die, he dies again with us. Here.' Koryn stooped and swept up the tiny, fragile bundle of bird skulls tied to Borias's belt, tugging them free so that the slender chains snapped in his fist. He handed the fistful of bleached skulls to Kayaan. 'Carry them with you, and return them to the distant soil of Kiavahr, should fate grant you the opportunity.'

Kayaan accepted the corvia without question, taking a moment to secure the fine chains to his own belt, alongside the growing cluster that hung above his right thigh. So many dead, thought Koryn, as he watched his brother knotting and looping the chains. Had it been so long since they had returned home?

'This place stinks of death,' said Grayvus through gritted teeth, standing on the perimeter of their small circle, his back to them as he watched the forest for any sign of the enemy. Koryn left Argis to his gruesome work and went to join Grayvus.

The clearing – or rather the impact site of their now destroyed drop-pod – was surrounded in all directions by towering trees, which formed a dense canopy of twisted, leafless limbs above, filtering even the dim moonlight until it was nothing but a cold, silvery glow. They were deep in the heart of the arboreal forest that covered almost half of the small globe, and Koryn had no sense yet of how far they were from their intended target.

The trees nearby shimmered and whispered in the breeze, and Koryn felt a deep yearning for Kiavahr, to be surrounded once more by the forests of his home world. Fortane's World might once have resembled Kiavahr, but now its forest was a sick, twisted parody of those he had known in his earlier life.

The trees here were warped and gnarled, and their branches appeared to coruscate in the moonlight, dripping with a glossy, pustulant sap. They twisted and groaned, their angular limbs and fat boughs shifting and leaning as Koryn watched, as if they were outstretched hands clutching for the small coterie of Space Marines in their midst, yearning to hold the ebon-armoured figures in their deadly grasp. Where they had broken and cracked open following the violent impact, Koryn could see that they were largely hollow, and a thick, green mist dribbled out of their ruptured innards, mingling with the strange miasmic layer that already hugged the ground by his boots.

'The very trees have been infected by the rot,' said Koryn, glancing over at Grayvus's chalk-white face and hard black eyes. 'Find your helm in the wreckage, brother, and engage your respirator. Do not breathe this foul air any longer than you must. It bears the taint of Chaos.'

'You're right,' said Grayvus, studying the tree line intently. 'It's as if they have eyes, and they're watching us.' He coughed, hacking on the foul air, and then turned and strode purposefully towards the wreckage, disappearing into the makeshift hatch.

Koryn turned to see Argis standing by his side. 'It is done, captain. The gene-seed is secure.'

'Very well.'

'What's to be done with Borias's remains? Shall we leave him to the birds?'

'No,' said Koryn. 'Not today. Not in this foul place. Put him in the wreckage and then set a charge. I'll leave nothing for the inhabitants of this vile forest to pick over.'

'Very good, captain,' said Argis. 'And after that?'

'We move out,' replied Koryn, decisively. 'We head towards the carapace.' He glanced up at the horizon, taking in the vastness of the rocky canopy that curved away above the tops of the trees: a distant, foreboding ridge in the sky, dark and unyielding. 'And beyond that, the battle.'

'Aysaal?'

The vox hissed with unfiltered static, like the subtle entreaties of a snake. 'Aysaal?' Koryn repeated, his voice level. He glanced up at Argis, his pauldrons heaving in a dismissive shrug.

'I fear the worst,' said Argis, scanning the trees intently as if he expected the enemy to be upon them at any moment. He was clutching his bolter firmly across his chest, his finger on the trigger guard. 'If Aysaal's drop-pod was struck in the same manner as our own...' He trailed off, the implication clear.

Behind the flared grille of his respirator, Koryn grimaced. Aysaal's Tactical squad represented an entire third of the Raven Guard's small guerrilla force, and if they too had been lost like Borias...Well, the implications were grave indeed.

'Will we search for the wreckage and attempt to ascertain what occurred?' queried Argis.

'Negative. The mission must take precedence. It is imperative that we aid our brothers in breaking the siege. The bastion must fall,' replied Koryn.

Argis gave a curt nod. Koryn stood, resting a hand on his brother's shoulder. Argis was a veteran of many hundreds of campaigns and understood his duty. He had fought by Koryn's side for well over a century and would see the mission through without question, or die in the attempt. Nevertheless, Koryn recognised the pain in Argis's voice, the need to understand what had become of his missing brothers. To watch his fellow Raven Guard die in glorious battle was a thing to be cherished; to lose them without word in a Chaos-infested forest provoked quite different emotions.

'What of Syrion?' asked Argis. 'Is there word of the others?'

'Not yet,' said Koryn, solemnly. He glanced over at Kayaan, who was heaping damp loam over the remains of their drop-pod, now wreathed in the swirling, unearthly mist. The earth would go some way to muting the sound of the explosion when the charge went off.

Kayaan looked up, noticing that Koryn was watching. 'Preparations are complete, captain.'

Koryn nodded. 'Then let us take our leave of this foul place. There is much to be done.' He glanced around looking for Cordae and caught sight of the Chaplain on the edges of the clearing, studying their surroundings intently. He strode over to join him.

'There is a strange quality to the darkness here, captain.' Cordae's voice was quiet and tinged with melancholy, as though it carried a deeper warning. The thought unsettled Koryn, sending a cold sensation running down the fold of his back. 'There are forces at work on this planet more powerful than we anticipated. We must tread carefully.'

The Chaplain turned to look at him, and Koryn nodded in acknowledgement. 'Darkness and death are our bedfellows, Cordae. We must embrace them if we are to prove victorious.'

'I stand with you, brother,' came the ambiguous response.

'Grayvus, the char–' Koryn stopped suddenly as the bead in his ear buzzed unexpectedly to life.

'Captain?' hissed a distant voice. 'Captain, are you receiving?'

'Syrion,' said Koryn. 'Report.'

'Our landing target has been achieved, captain,' replied Syrion. Koryn allowed himself a momentary grin of satisfaction. 'We are five kilometres east of the carapace, close to the edge of the battle. What are your orders?'

'Proceed with the mission as planned. The bastion must be breached. Maintain vox silence and remain vigilant. May Corax guide your hand.'

'Understood, captain.' Syrion was silent for a moment. And then: 'I witnessed Aysaal's drop-pod go down under enemy artillery fire, captain. Have you made contact?'

'Negative. Contact has not been established with Sergeant Aysaal. Honour our fallen brothers in combat, Syrion.'

'Yes, captain. Emperor be with you.' The vox went dead.

Grayvus was still looking at Koryn expectantly. 'You know what to do, Grayvus,' said Koryn, and a moment later the remnants of their drop-pod – and their fallen brother – were consumed in a superheated ball of flame.

'Now,' said Koryn, standing over the wreckage so that the guttering flames cast dancing light upon his ancient, ebon armour, 'Let us douse our weapons in the blood of traitors. Let us avenge our dead. For Corax!'

'For Corax!' echoed his brothers, raising their weapons in bold defiance, before melting away into the trees. Within seconds there was no trace of the ten remaining Raven Guard, and no sign of their passing, other than the smouldering wreckage of their downed vessel.

Koryn couldn't see the others, but he knew each and every one of their precise movements as the ten Raven Guard moved swiftly through the cover of the trees. They made hardly a sound as they passed, fleet-footed and determined, skilled in the art of silence.

It was two days on foot to the lip of the canopy, and from there, no more than a kilometre, perhaps two, to the base of the siege itself. Or so Grayvus's auspex had indicated. The green mist appeared to be interfering with the instrument, causing ghost readings and false positives, as if the mist itself – or something lurking in it – was instilled with life.

Then, of course, there was the sinister darkness that seemed to cloak everything, affecting even the Raven Guard's acute vision. Not that it troubled Koryn unduly. He could already sense the raging battle in the distance and the darkness offered them cover to move unimpeded through the forest. Koryn had long ago learned to trust his instincts, and he relied on his other senses as much as he did his keen vision. If anything, the perpetual twilight offered the Raven Guard an advantage, rather than a hindrance.

Koryn paused amongst a nest of coiled tree roots, bringing himself to a sudden, silent stop. He had sensed movement, somewhere ahead of them and to the right. He cocked his head, listening intently.

He did not speak, but he knew that the others had responded in kind, coming to a halt around him, taking cover at the unexpected noise.

There it was again – the sound of a footstep, crunching the soft loam nearby.

Slowly, Koryn, readied his twin lightning claws, assuming a defensive posture. He glanced across at Siryan, who was barely visible, crouching behind another nearby tree, his bolter drawn and presented, ready to open fire when the incoming target presented itself.

Another sound, from behind them this time, and then a third, off to the left.

'Captain!' Argis hissed urgently over the vox. 'They have us surrounded.'

'Impossible...' muttered Koryn beneath his breath, but then the forest around them erupted in a cacophony of sound, of pounding feet and terrible, primal screeching, as whatever it was that had managed to encircle them drew its circle ever tighter.

Koryn readied himself for battle, flexing his damaged shoulder as he prepared to face their attackers. He sensed movement to his right, and then again to his left, and caught sight of something massive pounding through the undergrowth, barrelling towards him at speed. He danced back, keeping another tree behind him to protect his flank, fixing his gaze on the dense foliage for signs of where the ambushers might emerge.

Seconds later, the beasts were upon them.

The things that came out of the trees were like no creatures Koryn had ever seen in his centuries-long existence.

They were birds, of a kind, although in no way did they resemble the graceful flocks of ravens that soared high above the leafy canopies of Kiavahr, nor even the man-sized rocs that inhabited the cave systems high in the Diagothian mountains.

These brutish creatures towered over the Space Marines. They were enormous: two-legged monstrosities, with huge barrel chests and ferocious, glistening beaks, sharp enough and powerful enough, Koryn judged, to tear through the toughened ceramite of the Raven Guard's power armour.

Their bodies were covered in thick, downy feathers of exuberant colours: rich indigos, bright yellows and deep crimsons. The colour, Koryn mused of the last, of spilt blood.

They were clearly flightless, with short, useless wings that stirred and buffeted as the creatures thundered through the dense undergrowth, their pounding steps like the rumble of distant mortar-fire. They shrieked and squawked, their heads flitting from side to side as they sized up their quarry.

Subconsciously, Koryn counted them off, his enhanced senses processing every sound, weighing up the odds in order that he might choose how best to react.

Twelve of them. Ten Raven Guard. He only hoped they were easier to fell than they looked.

'Victorus Aut Mortis!' he bellowed, leaping from behind the cover of the tree and directly into the path of one of the charging birds. His lightning talons crackled and sparked as he readied himself, his twin hearts pounding.

The bird gave a shrill, deafening cry as it launched itself forwards, throwing its full weight behind the manoeuvre as its powerful neck snapped around, its beak opening wide as it moved in for the kill.

Koryn jumped, twisting in the air and arcing his back, his lightning claws flashing.

The bird pivoted on one foot, its vast jaws snapping shut centimetres from Koryn's face. It staggered forwards, unable to halt its own momentum, and Koryn thrust his talons at its head, scoring three great furrows in the creature's beak.

The terror bird howled in rage, drawing itself up to its full height as it turned around for another strike. Koryn was waiting for it, however, and rushed in close, slashing viciously across its belly with the aim of disembowelling it before it could attack again.

He felt the bird's flesh part with ease, but the sight that greeted him caused him to reel back in dismay. The creature's intestines spilled out in a steaming heap, but they were black and wasted, infested with writhing maggots.

The stench hit him like a blow to the face and he staggered away, bringing his talons up in defence. The bird, apparently none the worse for having its guts spread across the forest floor, darted forwards again, trailing its organs across the ground. Its beak struck Koryn's left pauldron and sent him spinning to the ground. He landed on his back, the creature looming over him, its beady eyes intent on its kill. It was dripping dark, thick blood from the ragged wound in its belly, and it spattered on Koryn's helm, obscuring his view.

The bird's foot slammed down on his chest-plate before he had time to roll out of the way, and he felt the crushing weight bear down upon him, the ceramite flexing as it fought to spread the load across his ribs. The bird was not attempting to crush him, he realised, but to pin in him place while it readied itself for the kill.

Koryn focused on remaining calm, on planning his next move. He had seconds before the bird took his head off with a snap of its razor-sharp jaws. Practically an eternity to a Raven Guard.

His options were limited. His right arm was pinned beneath one of its talons. His left arm – still burning with pain from where the metal spar had impaled him earlier – was wedged up against the root of a tree, and he couldn't get enough leverage with his legs to roll.

With a grunt of pain, Koryn forced his wounded shoulder to flex, feeling it pull in protest as he moved it in a way it was never intended to move. He gritted his teeth and pushed harder, twisting it until he could feel the joint almost ready to give.

Almost simultaneously, the bird arched back, widening its jaws, and Koryn's arm popped free with an audible crack.

He took the bird's leg off with a swipe of his lightning claws, moving with almost preternatural speed in order to roll out of the way before the creature's torso came crashing down on top of him. It smashed into the ground with the full force of the blow it had been intending for Koryn, screeching in pain and frustration.

Koryn sprung to his feet, turning quickly to face the thrashing beast. It was clawing at the ground with its remaining talons, its beak churning the earth as it attempted to lever itself up.

Now that he was standing over it, he could see that the creature had succumbed to the same fate as the rest of the life in that infernal forest. Parasites crawled over its entire body, burrowing in and out of its necrotic flesh, nestling beneath its feathers. The reek of death was thick and cloying. The bird had been infected by the traitor's plague.

No wonder the thing had proved difficult to kill: to all intents and purposes, it was already dead. He reached down and separated its head from its torso with a quick, sudden gesture. Its body shuddered, and then its remaining leg finally ceased twitching. Its flesh continued to heave and crawl with the movement of the diabolical parasitic creatures, but Koryn had no time to pay them any heed.

Behind him, the forest was alive with the sounds of battle. All around him his brothers had engaged the birds. Close by, Corvaan ducked and weaved in a dangerous dance, armed with nothing but a combat knife and a burning hatred for the pestilence that had infected these once graceful creatures.

Across the clearing, Avias was shredding two of the beasts with repeated bursts from his bolter, while behind him Grayvus was wrestling another to the ground, hacking at it with his blade and sending shreds of brightly coloured feathers drifting into the air.

At the heart of the clearing stood Cordae, silent and unmoving, a terrifying figure in his full totemic battle regalia. His crozius was balanced lightly in his right hand, which hung loosely by his side. Before him towered one of the immense birds, its beak poised no more than a few centimetres from the tip of his bird skull mask. The two formidable killing machines were regarding each other in silent repose, mirroring each other's stance, their heads both cocked slightly to one side. It was as if there was some sort of affinity between them, as if Cordae's bird spirit and the beast were somehow sharing a moment of understanding.

The stillness was utterly at odds with the crazed, intense combat that was taking place all around them, and Koryn wondered for a moment if Cordae actually planned to destroy the creature, or whether he hoped to achieve some other end. The Chaplain could at times be as difficult to fathom as the enemy themselves.

Koryn noticed Cordae's hand tighten almost imperceptibly on the shaft of his crozius, and grinned. The terror bird was still watching the Chaplain intently, its eyes locked on his. Cordae held its gaze for a second longer, drew his breath, and moved.

The blow came so fast and hard that the bird was caught utterly unaware, and the crozius buried itself in its thick skull, spattering blood and bone fragments across the trunk of a nearby tree. The bird's body rocked from side to side for a moment before crumpling to the ground with barely a sound.

Cordae yanked his crozius free, wiping it on the grass by his feet, and then turned to glance at Koryn, as if he had known all along that the captain had been watching his movements. He stood for a moment, as if waiting for some sort of reaction or response, and then, without a single word or gesture, he turned and darted off into the trees in search of other prey.

The sounds of the battle seemed to crash in on Koryn, and he turned, anxious to aid his brothers. Through the trees he saw flames erupt suddenly as Kayae doused one of the birds with his flamer and the hulking creature burst through the clearing, screeching in panic, its feathers alight with searing flames. To Koryn it looked like a mythical phoenix, burning up as it charged away into the forest leaving a trail of smouldering branches and burning undergrowth in its wake.

Closer to Koryn, Siryan was trapped in a deadlock with two more of the creatures, parrying one before turning to fend off the other, making little headway against either. He had lost his bolter and was defending himself with only his fists and his combat knife, and it was clear to Koryn that the two beasts were hunting in concert, trying to wear the Space Marine down until he made an error and left one of them the opening they needed.

Koryn decided it was time to even up the odds. He charged across the clearing to Siryan's side, catching hold of the bough of a tree with his right hand and swinging himself up and around in a wide arc. Both his feet connected hard with the skull of one of the birds, causing it to squawk and stagger backwards, shaking its head. Koryn completed his orbit of the tree, dropping to the ground before the creature with his talons ready. He was breathing hard, adrenaline coursing through his veins.

'A timely intervention, captain,' said Siryan, dropping to one knee as the other bird lurched forwards and he feinted easily to the left. The beast received a sharp blow to the side of its head for its trouble, and it screeched angrily, kicking out at Siryan and raking his chest-plate with its claws, leaving deep score marks across the aquila that adorned his breast. Siryan plunged his knife into its belly in reply, but the creature simply reared back, pulling away from him with the weapon still buried in its guts.

Unarmed, Siryan circled warily, his fists at the ready, keeping his gaze fixed on his avian opponent.

Koryn had his own beast to worry about, however, and he strafed from side to side in time with the bird, watching its head bob with every movement, trying to predict the direction and timing of its next attack. The creature opened its jaws and hissed at him, its livid pink tongue wriggling in its beak as if of its own volition.

Koryn rushed it, spearing it through the breast with both lightning claws, jamming them deep inside its ribcage. It thrashed and shrieked, shaking itself from side to side in an effort to throw him loose. The stench of roasting meat filled the air as the energy discharge from his talons seared the creature's flesh.

The bird gave a sudden, unexpected jerk, breaking Koryn's momentary hold and flinging him against the tree that only moments before he had used to his advantage. He impacted hard, rebounding and rolling across the forest floor, accompanied by the shattered remnants of the brittle trunk that splintered beneath the blow.

The bird thundered forwards and lurched for him, twisting its powerful neck as it thrust its hooked beak towards his head. Koryn waited until it was nearly upon him, until the jaws were just beginning to part – and then struck, jabbing upwards with his right claw and skewering the beast through the skull, embedding his talons behind its massive beak. He yanked his fist back with an almighty effort, wrenching the bird's beak clean from its head and allowing its bulky, twitching corpse to collapse into a heap across his legs. Blood spewed from the terrible wound where its face had once been.

Koryn kicked himself free and stood, turning just in time to see Siryan stagger back, defenceless, as the other bird finally got the better of him, its terrible jaws snapping shut about his waist. Ceramite cracked and fractured as the beast lifted him triumphantly into the air, shaking its head as Siryan beat frantically against its beak with his fists. Then, before Koryn could react, it bit down viciously, severing Siryan neatly in two.

The two halves of the dead Raven Guard slumped from the bird's dripping jaws, and it raised its head to the sky and screeched in bloody triumph.

Enraged, Koryn rushed forwards, bellowing loudly as he charged at the beast. His twin hearts pounded in his chest.

The bird, cawing loudly, turned about to face him, its tiny, useless wings twitching as it clawed at the ground, as if urging Koryn on, anxious for the battle ahead.

Koryn raised his claws, and then swerved suddenly to the right, ducking behind a tree as Kayae stepped out from behind the creature and coated it in a blanket of raging promethium. It screamed and thrashed about in torment as its feathers ignited, until, a moment later, it had been reduced to nothing but a living tower of flame. It staggered towards Koryn, blinded by the heat, and then keeled over into the mud, dead and unmoving. The flames continued to lick hungrily at its grotesque, rotten flesh.

'It is done, captain,' said Cordae, appearing suddenly at Koryn's side. 'The last of the birds is dead.'

'So is Siryan,' replied Koryn, quietly.

'Indeed. I would be honoured to harvest his gene-seed and reclaim his corvia, if you'll permit it.'

Koryn nodded his assent. He watched as Cordae circled the flaming pyre of the dead beast and dropped to his haunches before the ruins of his slain brother.

Nearby, Kayae stood watching, a stark silhouette against the firelight, the nozzle of his flamer still smoking effusively.

'When he's finished, Kayae, burn Siryan's corpse. I will not allow the heretic's rot to claim his flesh.'

'Yes, captain,' said Kayae.

Koryn flexed the tense muscles in his neck. Now they were nine, and they had yet to truly face the enemy. Fortane's World had not welcomed its ebon-armoured benefactors. Nevertheless, he would soon be spilling the blood of traitors, and that would be retribution enough. That would be the means by which he honoured his dead kin.

Koryn stepped back into the shadows of the trees as Kayae moved forwards, readying his flamer. Siryan would burn, and so would the enemy. Even if Fortane's World was nothing but a husk when they had finished.

# DAED

Daed hoisted the two wriggling humans, one in each fist, and smashed their skulls together, spattering bone fragments and brain matter over his arms. He dropped the twitching corpses into a heap of quivering limbs and hefted his axe from where it was slung in a harness across his broad shoulders.

Behind the grille of his respirator, he bellowed wordlessly, equal parts fury and frustration.

He sensed motion behind him and swung around, his filigreed axe head leading the way. Another cultist slumped to the ground, sliced in half at the waist, spilled viscera heaping onto his muddy boots. The man's blood gave off a foul, noxious steam as it fountained onto the muddy loam; evidence, Daed knew, of the vile infection coursing through his veins. Daed would have spat in disgust, had it not been for the fact he was wearing his helm and relied upon its respirator to filter the tainted air.

The enemy were all around him now, swarming in their multitudes. Daed laughed bitterly as he felled another of these former Guardsmen with a single, swift blow from his fist, collapsing the man's skull. No matter their numbers, no matter how quickly they came at him, Daed would not fall. In his shining golden armour he was like a beacon on the battlefield, a flickering flame in the darkness, drawing the enemy towards him as though they were moths.

One of the daemon creatures came at him then, hissing its strange, unnatural curses, its poisonous tongue lolling from its mouth like a hungry, flapping snake. Its single, jaundiced eye blinked rapidly as if distracted by the sheer volume of flies that buzzed around its foul carcass. The stench was incredible, as if the beast was in fact a walking corpse, half rotted and warm, having been raised up from an ancient battlefield and given life.

For all Daed knew, that might not have been far from the truth. Whatever it was, it was an abomination, the foul spawn of the warp, and it had no place on Fortane's World. It had no right to be alive.

The creature moved with an awkward, shambling gait: too slow to pose any real threat of injury. Still, Daed knew that even the slightest lick of its ensorcelled blade would mean a festering, painful death. Or, more likely, a round from his own bolter to the head.

The daemon lurched at him, swinging its poisoned blade in a wide, upward arc, as if attempting to decapitate him. Daed raised his axe to parry the blow, battering away the creature's weapon. He retaliated with a low kick, aiming his booted foot at the creature's distended belly in an effort to send it sprawling to the ground.

Instead, his foot sank inside the daemon's bloated flesh with a sickening crunch, burying his leg up to the ankle. He almost lost his footing as the daemon staggered back, dragging him with it and threatening to overbalance him. He threw a hand out to catch himself and managed to stay upright. He tugged at his foot, trying to pull it free. The sticky, malleable flesh of the creature quivered and gave, but would not yield.

The creature, still emitting its weary litany of ancient, blasphemous words, seemed hardly to notice the Space Marine's boot in its guts, however, never taking its single, baleful eye from its target. It raised its weapon once more, grasping the pommel with both hands and hefting the blade above its head.

Daed dropped his axe and twisted, using the trapped limb to give him purchase. He pivoted, reaching around and sliding his bolt pistol from its holster. He fired indiscriminately into the creature's face, pulping the eye and flensing the soft, pulpy flesh from the cartilage beneath.

The plaguebearer toppled backwards, carried over by the weight of its blade and wrenching Daed's boot free in the process. It came away with a gloopy *pop*, slopping innards and freeing a swarm of strange, rat-sized creatures that had evidently been dwelling inside the daemon's guts. They scampered away, mewling pitifully.

Daed paused, stooping to retrieve his discarded axe. The daemon was still muttering to itself, as if the words – whatever they were – were somehow sustaining it. He cut off its blinded head with a single blow to the neck, silencing it forever.

The autocannons mounted on the bastion walls began to chatter again, filling the sky with a storm of explosive rounds. The bark of their thunderous fire was deafening, drowning out even the nearby screams of the dying.

Behind Daed, one of the Brazen Minotaurs' Razorbacks detonated with a blinding flash as its fuel tanks ignited, punctured by the onslaught from the bastion's defensive emplacements.

The enemy troops fell upon the resulting breach in the barricade within seconds, and Daed saw two of his golden-armoured brothers torn from their positions by sheer weight of numbers. They fought valiantly, despatching scores of the Chaos troops, before succumbing to the overwhelming odds and disappearing from view.

Daed turned on the nearest squad of enemy militia with renewed ire. His brothers were dying, and he would not allow their sacrifice to be in vain. The odds were against them, but the Emperor was at their side.

The last push had proved to be disastrous. The five Razorbacks had led the charge, pushing the barricade forwards, churning up great furrows of earth and riding roughshod over large numbers of the enemy. Brazen Minotaurs had followed in their wake, slaughtering the survivors and chanting hymnals as they drew closer to the plascrete skirts of the bastion itself.

Daed had not anticipated they would gain so much ground in a single push and had urged the Razorbacks onwards, hopeful that the enemy forces were finally showing signs of weakening beneath the constant vigilance of his warriors.

His hope had turned to disappointment, however, when a few moments later he had realised his folly: the Chaos forces had been luring them closer to bring them within range of the bastion's turret-mounted heavy weapons.

The first casualty had been one of the Razorbacks, the tank blossoming into flames as the autocannons had shredded it with their opening salvo. Daed did not yet know how many of his brothers had been cut down by the ensuing torrent, but he had seen Toros dance backwards with the impact of repeated shots, before dropping heavily to the ground. Before he had been able to run to his brother's side, the barricade all around him had erupted in a series of explosions and he had been forced into cover.

Now, what was left of the barricade was near useless as a defensive measure and the Chaos forces were coming on in even greater numbers. The traitorous Plague Marines of Empyrion's Blight had now joined the fray too, perhaps sensing that the Brazen Minotaurs were faltering, and hoping to tip the tide of battle in their own favour. Or perhaps they simply wanted to gloat, and to spill the blood of the righteous.

Daed, of course, would not give them the satisfaction. The Brazen Minotaurs, despite their fallen, were far from finished yet.

He smiled in grim satisfaction at the sight of three golden-armoured land speeders, sweeping across the battlefield, cutting a swathe through the enemy ranks from above. Further back, the remaining three Razorbacks were spitting deadly bolts of energy from their twin-linked lascannons, searing the oncoming enemy until their front ranks had evaporated into gouts of vapour. They had managed to take out one of the bastion's emplacements, too, buying themselves a respite, although the others continued to bark ceaselessly, spitting rounds indiscriminately into the battle below. The gunners seemed unconcerned with how many of their own troops were caught in the crossfire.

Nearby, Archeos – an ancient Venerable Dreadnought, older than even the Chapter Master himself – was locked in a fierce battle with seven Plague Marines. His ornately decorated armour plating was now scored with deep furrows, and the black cloak of Tauronic lion hide that had been draped across his broad shoulders was now nothing but an ashen stain. Totems and rosaries still clung to his bulky flanks, their tails flickering in the breeze.

The Dreadnought's power fist was damaged, hanging limply by his side. His heavy flamer, however, was spraying super-heated promethium into the faces of two of the traitors, incinerating them where they stood as Daed watched. Their flaming bodies staggered back, their weapons firing blindly as their hands convulsed. They collapsed in twin heaps, succumbing to the cleansing fire of death.

The other traitors were engaged in attempting to pry Archeos's casing open with their hand weapons, or pounding him with repeated rounds from their bolters. Daed knew the odds were not in his brother's favour. He watched as Archeos tried to turn his still-gushing flamer on another of the Plague Marines, but found himself unable to turn as the damaged servos in his legs failed to respond.

Daed hefted his axe and set off at a charge, ready to rush to his brother's side.

Two daemonkin stood between Daed and his brother, and they turned to face his charge, raising their deadly weapons in order to receive his attack. Daed swung his axe as he closed in, cleaving an arm from the shoulder of the first daemon and sending the limb spinning to the ground. The strange, putrid flesh of the creature began to slough off the joint where the limb had been attached, sliding from muscle and bone to form a rancid pile at its feet.

The daemon showed no sign that it had even acknowledged its injury as it took a swipe at him with its remaining arm, and Daed was forced to batter the blade away with his wrist, trusting to his armour that the blade would not reach his flesh.

The other daemon had by this time shambled forwards, spouting its ceaseless diatribe, and came at him with a stabbing motion that he hadn't anticipated. He leapt back, dancing out of the way of the blade. He didn't have time to respond before the one-armed beast took another ponderous swipe, but this time his axe split its skull in two, burying itself all the way down to its gristly chest.

He had no chance to free the weapon before the remaining daemon was stabbing at him again with its dripping sword. He parried with the flats of his hands, knocking the weapon aside. He stepped back, allowing the creature to attack again, and mirrored his earlier defensive move. This time, however, he rushed in close, grimacing as he grabbed the daemon's head in his hands and wrenched it free from its shoulders with an almighty roar.

The daemon staggered for a moment before falling to its knees, and then forwards onto its chest beside its dead brethren.

Daed reached for the haft of his axe, glancing up just in time to see Archeos receive the full brunt of a barrage from one of the bastion's heavy weapons.

The Dreadnought's flamer guttered and died as the arm was blown clean off its shoulder mount, popping and sparking where the electrical components were exposed.

One of the Plague Marines shook and shuddered as it was caught in the crossfire, slumping against Archeos as its pestilent flesh was shredded and the remnants of its ancient, decaying armour were blown clear.

Archeos dropped forwards, his mechanical legs finally failing. The bark of the heavy weapons resounded, and Daed saw cracks appearing in Archeos's housing as round after round hammered into the Dreadnought. There was nothing he could do.

The vox-bead crackled unexpectedly to life in his ear. 'Captain Daed?' The voice seemed hesitant, as if it wasn't sure if it would receive an answer.

'Drago,' said Daed, raising his voice over the din of the battle. 'What is it?'

'There are reports of black-armoured figures on the battlefield, sir, near the bastion walls.'

Daed frowned. Was this a new type of enemy he hadn't yet seen? Or possibly...

'Go on,' he said.

Drago hesitated. 'They came out of nowhere, captain, and disappeared almost as swiftly. They were seen to be despatching the enemy in great numbers.'

Daed felt his spirits lifting. So the sons of Corax had not abandoned them after Kasharat.

'It seems we have company, Drago, and welcome company at that.' He hesitated, taking a moment to assimilate the information and the implications of the Raven Guard's arrival. 'Continue to push forwards, Drago. Get us to those walls. It's useless erecting another barricade now. Throw everything we've got at those walls. We'll see this through yet.'

'Aye, captain. May the Emperor guide your hand.'

'And yours, brother.'

Daed turned, his bolt pistol in his fist, and swiftly

despatched the seven pox-ridden humans who had been trying to sneak up on him while he had been talking to Drago. He didn't even give them the opportunity to loose off a shot.

Daed's heart was singing. So, the Raven Guard *were* here, on Fortane's World. Perhaps the odds had just altered in their favour.

He glanced over to see the four remaining Plague Marines, still picking over the ruins of Archeos. His mood darkened at the sight of the Ancient's shattered carapace.

Daed gripped the slender shaft of his power axe. 'Bast?'

'Yes, captain?' came the response, punctuated by the stuttering sound of bolter-fire.

'With me, Bast. We have retribution to mete out before the hour is done.'

'Aye, captain. We do that.'

Daed slid his bolt pistol into its holster. He would enjoy cutting these bastards down, feeling his axe cleaving their infected flesh. 'For the Emperor!' he cried hoarsely, lowering his head and charging, bull-like, at the enemy.

# KORYN

The building was a bleached, skeletal ruin that seemed to grow out of the forest like an organic thing, the remains of some ancient, long-dead beast, now slowly decaying in the shadow of the great carapace. It had likely once been a small, austere outpost building, or possibly a temple – it was difficult to tell from the splintered pillars, broken statuary and shattered walls. The roof had gone and large sections of the remaining structure had collapsed beneath the pounding of mortar-fire. A tall, arched window frame described a jagged smile, the shattered remnants of stained glass still clinging resolutely to the masonry like ferocious teeth.

Koryn had seen a thousand buildings like it before, on as many different worlds, buildings haunted by the travesties that had taken place within their walls. Death had touched this place, and had left behind nothing but a tribute to its own verisimilitude.

It was clear the building had been abandoned long ago, but all around him, Koryn could see evidence of more recent occupation. Or rather, of a recent battle.

The scattered remains of the dead lay all about the ruined structure. The Guardsmen, Koryn presumed, who had once manned the outpost. One of them lay only a few metres from where he was standing, the corpse already half rotten, decayed flesh around its mouth exposing the grinning teeth and jawbone beneath. Creeping vines had insinuated themselves into the body's orifices and the stalks of an inquisitive sapling had already erupted through one of the empty eye sockets, drawing sustenance from the putrefied brain matter inside the skull. Colourful blooms of noxious fungi had sprung up around the sites of the Guardsman's wounds, and Koryn knew that these were not natural but the result of the foul spores that proliferated in the green miasma slowly choking the life out of the planet. The dark god of the traitors had claimed these dead for his own, allowing plague and pestilence to breed inside their husks.

Koryn took a moment to analyse the pattern of the dead, noting where their corpses had fallen, the nature of their wounds, the dropped weapons and broken equipment. It was clear these Guardsmen had not themselves succumbed to the taint to Chaos. At least, not while they had lived. Here, they had defended the outpost until the very last, until it had become too much and they had been overwhelmed by a tide of the enemy's forces. Judging by the evidence, however, they had taken a number of traitors with them to the grave; the remains of at least one Plague Marine were visible amongst the heaped human cadavers. Its fractured, leering helm jutted out of the earth like some prehistoric skull, only recently unearthed.

Something was wrong, though. There was more to the outpost building than first appeared. Koryn was convinced of it. If pressed, the Raven Guard captain would not have been able to describe the nature of his disquiet, but he had long ago learned to trust his instincts above all else.

Koryn sensed Grayvus moving through the undergrowth nearby, returning to report his findings from a brief reconnaissance of the surrounding area. 'What did you find, brother?' he asked.

Silently, Grayvus slid out from behind the dangling branches of a scorched tree on the edge of the clearing, brushing away the sticky webs of sap that trailed from his armour. He came to stand beside his captain. 'On the other side of the ruins there are signs of a more recent battle, captain,' he said. 'A day or two ago at most. Fallen traitors lay amongst the dead, and there is evidence that the enemy are still active in this area. We must tread with caution.'

Koryn nodded in acknowledgement. 'And the building itself?' he prompted.

'I see no sign of any activity, captain, but the fallen masonry provides many opportunities for cover. There may be traitors lurking in the ruins. It appears as if there are still habitable rooms amongst the wreckage.'

'The entire place has the air of abandonment about it,' said Koryn thoughtfully, more of a statement than a question.

'That could be a trap designed to lure us in,' replied Grayvus. 'They may yet show their hand.'

'Indeed,' said Koryn. 'As may we.'

'It will be good to once again spill the blood of our enemies,' continued Grayvus, and Koryn noted how his grip tightened on his bolter as he spoke.

'The base of the siege is close now, Grayvus. You will have your chance to avenge our dead. But remember why we are here. Brute strength will not win this battle. If it were simply a matter of slaying the enemy, our presence here would not be necessary – the Brazen Minotaurs are adept in the ways of death. There are few walls that could block their path.'

'Yet blocked they are,' said Grayvus, and Koryn was heartened not to hear even a hint of derision in his tone.

'It is for us, then, to break the deadlock. Not on the open field of battle, but in the shadows, striking at the very heart of the enemy. We will destroy them from within.'

'From inside the bastion?' asked Grayvus, quietly.

'From wherever we are needed,' replied Koryn.

He had continued to study the ruins as he talked, and had seen no evidence of movement from within. 'We shall pass through the clearing swiftly,' he said. 'Our time runs short. We have only days to break the siege.'

'Yes, captain.'

'We will use the ruins as cover while we ascertain the proximity of the enemy. Remain alert.' Koryn held out his hand and made two gestures in quick succession, knowing that the rest of his squad would be watching from the shadows. Sure enough, he sensed them moving out around him.

The Raven Guard made no sound as they passed; the clearing remained silent save for the distant cawing of birds and the screeching of other, unseen fauna, somewhere deep in the forest behind them.

Suddenly, the chattering report of bolter-fire erupted from somewhere within the ruins, and Koryn heard Kayaan cry out in surprise as his trailing leg was caught by a stray shot, sending him crashing to the ground. Further shots ricocheted off his armour as he rolled for cover, scrabbling for his weapon.

The Raven Guard's reactions were lightning fast. One moment they were flanking the ruined building, picking their way carefully amongst the fractured pillars on its outer fringes, the next they were inside it, indistinguishable from the shadows and homing in on the source of the enemy fire.

It took Koryn only three steps to reach the inner wall of the complex, and then he was slipping through an opening into the dark interior of the building, the stonework around the hole still blackened and blast-stained from the explosion that had originally formed it. By his sides, his lightning talons crackled in anticipation.

He caught sight of movement to his left: a hulking figure in brilliant, golden armour, brandishing an ornately-worked bolter and carefully surveying the nearby line of trees through a fissure in the brickwork. The figure was not yet aware of Koryn's ghostly presence in the room.

Acting purely on impulse, Koryn pounced. He sprung from the shadows, his talons raised, seconds away from decapitating the enemy who had fired upon them.

+Stop, brother-captain.+

The powerful voice filled his head, accompanied by a strange tickling sensation in the back of his skull, as if tiny spiders were scuttling over his brain.

*Psyker*, he thought, and a cold shiver passed unbidden down his spine. He felt his skin prickle with gooseflesh beneath his armour.

With a split-second decision, Koryn made a minute adjustment to the angle of his attack, twisting through the air so that one of his talons passed within an centimetre of his target's faceplate, the other coming down hard and sweeping the bolter from their grip. The weapon clattered noisily to the floor.

Koryn landed neatly and looked up into the face of his opponent, the talons of his left claw resting gently against their gorget, humming angrily as if hungry for spilt blood. One flick of his wrist and they would be dead, their throat gouged out in a spray of gore.

His opponent had not even had chance to react.

Koryn studied the golden-armoured figure before him. His chest-plate was engraved with unfamiliar runes and sigils, but the white pauldrons and bull's head motif were more easily recognisable. As was the thick, black lion's mane draped across his hulking shoulders. He stood taller than Koryn, a gilded giant, stocky and broad.

Boldly, the Space Marine raised his arm and battered Koryn's lightning claw aside. Koryn stood down, a wry smile on his lips behind his flared respirator.

+We are not your enemy.+

The uninvited voice boomed once again inside his skull.

+We are Brazen Minotaurs. We wish you no ill.+

'Then why did you open fire on us?' Koryn growled, his voice low.

'We wish only to protect our brother,' said the Space Marine, answering the question that had been directed at the voice in Koryn's head. 'Your presence here was not anticipated. You were mistaken for more of the traitors.'

Koryn bristled. The very thought that he and his brothers might have been considered traitors was anathema to him. 'We are here to do the Emperor's work,' he said angrily. 'We are here to aid you in delivering death to the enemies of the Imperium and halting the tide of pestilence that stains this planet, along with its sisters in the Sargassion Reach.'

+Then you are welcome, Raven Guard.+

Koryn glanced around. There were two more of the golden-armoured Space Marines in the room, both of them surrounded by Raven Guard who were slowly, cautiously, lowering their weapons. None of them bore the markings of a Librarian. He did not know which of them had spoken to him inside his head.

'Your concealment was impressive, brothers,' said Grayvus, begrudgingly. 'Your presence in the ruins went unremarked until you opened fire upon us.'

'We do as we must to ensure the survival of our charge,' replied another of the Brazen Minotaurs – a hulking, broad shouldered figure who dwarfed even Grayvus with his towering form.

The Space Marine before Koryn – who Koryn now realised bore the markings of a veteran sergeant upon his armour – reached up and unclasped his helm, mag-locking it to his thigh. He shook out his long, intricately plaited beard. His skin was tanned and his eyes were almond-shaped and alert. His head was shaved, and he wore two brass studs embedded in his forehead. 'I am Aramus,' he said. His accent was thick and clipped, unfamiliar.

'Shadow Captain Koryn,' replied Koryn, 'Of the Raven Guard Fourth.'

'Welcome to Fortane's World, Raven Guard,' said the Brazen Minotaur, with little mirth. 'Welcome to hell.'

The ruins of the outpost were more extensive than Koryn had initially realised. The structure extended below ground into a small network of passageways and rooms, within which the Brazen Minotaurs had, it seemed, established a temporary base of operations.

As he followed Aramus along one of these dank passageways, their steps ringing out upon the ancient flagstones, Koryn wondered as to the purpose of the Brazen Minotaur's occupation of the ruined outpost. As far as Koryn could tell, the outpost could offer them no tactical or defensive advantage, being so far from the bulk of the fighting. Nor would it serve particularly well as a lookout for enemy forces attempting to circle around behind the Space Marines' defensive lines: the trees would provide the Chaos troops with too much opportunity for cover to make it truly effective. Unless, of course, there was a whole string of these outpost buildings forming a perimeter beneath the rim of the great carapace. Even so, given what Koryn knew of the battle raging nearby, it would seem unlikely that Captain Daed would commit so many troops to guarding outposts when they would serve him better deployed on the front lines.

No, Koryn knew his instincts had been correct. There was more to this outpost than had first appeared. Aramus had spoken of a 'charge' they were there to protect, and Koryn already had his suspicions as to its nature.

+You will know soon enough, Raven Guard.+ The eerie voice spoke once more inside his skull, and Koryn found himself unconsciously shaking his head in an effort to banish it.

'In here,' said Aramus, coming to a stop in the passageway before a stone archway. Koryn stepped through, ducking his head beneath the man-sized lintel. The room beyond was an ancient crypt with a low, vaulted ceiling and a series of roughly hewn alcoves chiselled into the bare stone walls. Marble coffins – once glorious tributes to their dead, but now buried beneath the dusty detritus of ages – filled these niches, lending the place a solemn, funereal air.

In the centre of the room a bank of bulky equipment had been erected, the winking diodes and flickering hololithic screens seeming incongruous in such an ancient, reverential setting. A large, faint, blue-tinged projection fizzed and crackled in the air above a low table, showing various aspects of the planet from space.

'The war in the skies does not progress well,' said Aramus with an even tone. 'The enemy barges are little more than drifting hulks, but their firepower is unequalled and their ability to withstand damage is beyond even our capabilities.'

'You sound almost as if you admire them,' said Koryn, his voice level.

Aramus offered him a hard stare. 'The only good traitor is a dead one,' he replied, as if that simple statement was enough. Perhaps it was. The Brazen Minotaurs were known for their single-minded approach to a problem. They would not rest until all of the traitors in the Sargassion Reach had been put down, until they had not only won the war, but the enemy no longer *existed*. It was admirable, yet it was utterly at odds with how Koryn himself would choose to approach the problem.

Koryn skirted around Aramus to stand before the hololithic screen. Flickering orbital images of Fortane's World showed scores of Navy ships as they continued to rain incendiary bombs upon the carapace, to little or no effect.

Another section of the screen showed further Navy

frigates embattled with the bizarre, floating cathedrals of Empyrion's Blight. They circled each other in a silent, stately dance, showering each other with missiles, shells and gouts of searing plasma. For every traitor vessel that crumpled beneath the pounding of the Imperial ships, it seemed, two or three of the Navy frigates were sent boiling away into the void.

'The tide is yet to turn in our favour,' said Aramus, and this time the strain in his voice was clearly evident. Koryn saw his fists clench in barely concealed rage as they both watched a Navy vessel break apart as it collided spectacularly with an enemy hulk, splintering into fragments and frozen jets of escaping gas.

'Why does the Navy not commit its other vessels to destroying the traitors' flotilla? It seems clear that even the constant barrage of the planet's carapace is doing little to aid the assault on the bastion. If they turned their focus to destroying the enemy vessels they would surely reap better results?' said Koryn.

Aramus shook his head. 'They await word from below, from Captain Daed. The carapace is puckered with hidden gun emplacements – when they are opened to enable the surface-to-orbit weapons to fire upon the Navy ships, they provide the only means of striking into the bastion from above. If targeted efficiently, any explosives dropped down those open shafts will blow the bastion apart from the inside out. Of course, when the traitors open them periodically it is to fire upon our frigates, and they are forced to take evasive action. Captain Daed plans to get inside the bastion, to open up the gun emplacements and allow the Navy vessels to strike. The ships must remain in place, as they may have only a few moments in which to act.'

Koryn nodded. So Daed's goal was not, as he had thought, to simply lay siege to the bastion until the walls fell and the enemy forces dwindled. It seemed the Brazen Minotaur's captain was more of a tactician than Koryn had given him credit for. Nevertheless, it was clear to Koryn what he needed to do; how the Raven Guard could aid their golden-armoured brothers here on Fortane's World. The bastion walls did not need to be breached. The Raven Guard simply had to get inside and open up the gun emplacements to allow the Navy ships to do their work.

+Such a task will try even your subtle abilities, Raven Guard,+ said the voice in his head. +Yet it is necessary if the battle is to be won. On Empalion II we aided you and your brothers. We provided you with the distraction necessary for you to achieve your goal, at great cost to our Chapter. I ask you now to employ those same skills on our behalf, and in the Emperor's name.+

'Who are you?' bellowed Koryn, frustrated at the calm, unknowable voice. His question echoed loudly in the confines of the ancient crypt, but went unanswered.

Frowning, Aramus turned to Koryn, cocking his head slightly to one side as if listening intently to something – or *someone* – that Koryn could not hear.

'Are you sure?' he said a moment later, and Koryn realised that the Brazen Minotaur was not talking to him but to the disembodied voice of the psyker who had been invading Koryn's thoughts ever since he had set foot inside the outpost.

Aramus stepped forwards, placing a hand on Koryn's pauldron. 'He wants to see you,' he said, quietly. 'Come, I shall take you to him.'

* * *

Further along the passageway from the makeshift map room was a smaller, but equally ancient, antechamber. Here, the low ceiling followed the same vaulted pattern as the other room, but instead of housing a series of hollowed out niches, the walls had been plastered smooth and decorated with intricate decorations of a type Koryn had never seen. The millennia-old plasterwork was fractured and broken now, with parts of it peeling away from the damp walls, but the illuminations were still largely visible.

The artwork was stylised but incredibly fine and detailed, depicting scenes of battle, in which Space Marines strode like giants across the worlds of men. The figures wore ancient armour, older than Koryn's own suit of artificer-engraved ceramite – older even than the corroded models worn by the traitors.

Koryn saw the blue and white warriors of Ultramar standing shoulder to shoulder with bone-armoured Space Marines of the Death Guard Legion, and realised with surprise that the illustrations must pre-date the great Heresy, during which brother turned against brother and the galaxy erupted into war.

Here, in these paintings, the Death Guard were portrayed as benevolent ambassadors, visiting world after world to bring the Emperor's Light to the teeming masses of humanity, or to defend them against the horrors of xenos invasion. Now, of course, the paintings could not be further from the truth. The splintered, corrupted remnants of the Death Guard had been regurgitated by the warp, spat back out of the Eye of Terror in the form of grotesque warbands such as Empyrion's Blight. Now, they bestowed not the Emperor's Gift upon the worlds they visited but the blight of pestilence and Chaos. The very thought of their fall from grace left Koryn feeling nauseous. He could not even conceive of the weakness that had led to their corruption. He hoped vehemently that he never would.

Koryn wondered what perverse mind was orchestrating the warband's attack on Fortane's World, a planet that – judging by the ancient paintings on the walls – had once been one they had saved.

+His name is Gideous Krall,+ said the voice in his head. +A former captain of the Death Guard Legion, lost to the vagaries of the warp many millennia ago. Little more is known of his origins, save that he is named amongst his kindred 'The Infector of Worlds'. He has emerged from the Eye of Terror to wreak havoc and spread the foul rot of Nurgle throughout the Imperium. He must be stopped.+

Koryn turned, dragging his eyes away from the intricate paintings to properly take in the true purpose of the room. A figure lay supine on a raised dais – or, as Koryn realised a moment later – the bastardised remnants of a former marble tomb, now repurposed to support the massive bulk of a Space Marine. A Brazen Minotaur, clad in striking blue armour that was decorated with innumerable scars and imperfections, each telling the story of a past battle. Large patches of the warrior's chest-plate and vambraces had been recently scoured clean, however, removing the blue paint and exposing the bare ceramite beneath. It was as if someone was attempting to remove stains or corrosion, scratching at the power armour to ensure the marks had been properly removed.

The figure was unmoving, its arms folded, its hands resting peacefully upon its chest. A large hood – the hood of a psyker – curled up from behind its head.

Two other Space Marines, both wearing the shining golden armour of the Brazen Minotaurs, were washing the figure with rags and water, working constantly to clean every armoured plate, from the soles of his boots to the top of his helm. Koryn watched them for a moment as they wiped again and again, ceaselessly, working in perfect concert and starting over as soon as they had finished.

'What are they doing?' asked Koryn, and Aramus moved over to stand beside him.

'Move closer and you will see,' said Aramus.

Koryn took another step forwards, careful not to interfere with the ministrations of the two Space Marines who tended the Librarian. At first he wondered if the washing was some form of strange ritual performed by the Brazen Minotaurs, a cleansing rite, echoing a powerful belief from their home world. But as he watched, it soon became clear that this was in no way a ritual; it was a form of defence.

Small globules of green fungus were forming all over the Librarian's armour, bubbling into life unbidden, growing and spreading, crawling over the joints and seams between the ceramite plates as if searching for a means to worm their way inside. It was one of the most disgusting things that Koryn had ever seen: an invasion on a microbial level, mirroring the system-wide invasion that was taking place all around them.

'Our brother is under attack. The foul god of the traitors recognises him for the threat he poses to its minions and works tirelessly to infect him with its appalling rot. Thankfully, he is not alone, and our brothers are just as vigilant in their efforts to ensure the purity of his body,' said Aramus, not even bothering to hide the discomfort in his voice. Clearly, he was as appalled as Koryn by the

sight of the Librarian and the crawling spawn of Chaos
that assailed him.

'Would it not be easier to strip away his armour?' asked
Koryn, as yet another bloom of lurid green matter formed
amongst the concertinaed joints of the Librarian's left
arm, quickly blossoming into a strange, mossy carpet that
spread almost instantaneously, coating his chest-plate in
a matter of seconds. One of his attendants moved around
the dais and swiftly washed it away before it had time to
take hold. Even as he did so, another patch exploded into
being on the prone Librarian's face, and just as quickly,
his brother-attendant was forced to clear it off, rinsing the
foul detritus away in a runnel on the floor.

'We dare not,' said Aramus. 'The integrity of his armour
protects him from the spores. His respirator is as much
a weapon against these insidious traitors as any bolter.
Remove that and he is exposed.'

Koryn stared into the silent face of the Librarian's helm.
'I know him,' he said, quietly. And then: 'I know who you
are.'

+You were on Kasharat,+ came the voice in his mind.
The tone was calm and even, and showed no sign of per-
turbation or strain at the war being waged across his
armoured exterior.

+You were present when Daed fought the daemon-
creature at the heart of the labyrinth.+ It was a statement,
not a question.

*Yes*, thought Koryn. *I was there. I shed the blood of traitors
amongst the ruins of that dead world. I stood shoulder to
shoulder with your brothers in order to repay a grave debt.*

+Your intent was noble, Raven Guard. It will not be forgotten. Your actions allowed my brothers to save me from

an abominable fate. The traitors would have denied me even an honourable death. +

Koryn stepped closer to the dais, staring down at the unmoving figure. He looked somehow peaceful, as if lost in deep meditation. His chest rose and fell only fractionally with each breath.

'Theseon,' said Koryn, aloud. It was the Librarian he had helped Captain Daed to extract from the mortuary world, still locked inside his own body in a deep sus-anic coma.

+I see you recognise me, Raven Guard.+

*You are the weapon*, thought Koryn. *The weapon that could win the war*.

+I am but a tool of the Emperor,+ replied Theseon. +As are we all.+

*But how?* thought Koryn. *What is it that you know? If you can communicate with me now, why not tell us what we must do to defeat the enemies of the Imperium*.

There was a momentary pause.

+Leave us.+ The command was clipped and firm, leaving no room for argument. The two Brazen Minotaurs who were tending to Theseon placed their rags on the ground and stepped away from the dais, turning and leaving the room. Even Aramus retreated to a respectful distance, waiting in the shadow of the archway as Theseon and Koryn shared their private communion.

'But the infection, the rot?' said Koryn, out loud, watching as fungal blooms burst into life all across the prone form of the Librarian, spreading swiftly until he was shrouded in a blanket of hazy green.

+I would show you, Raven Guard,+ replied Theseon, +how zealously the traitors assail me, so that you might better understand my role in the conflict still to come.+

'Very well,' said Koryn, feeling more than a little uneasy as he watched the strange fungal growths proliferate before his eyes, erupting into colourful blooms that withered and died within seconds, degenerating into sticky mulch.

The Librarian's next words were tinged with sadness, the first time Koryn had heard Theseon express any emotion at all. +It is not what I *know* that could help the war effort, but what I *am*. I cannot tell you, nor Daed, nor the Emperor Himself what to do to defeat these minions of the dark gods. That is not within my power. I wish that were not so. +

Koryn frowned. 'What do you mean, "what you are"?'

+There are no secrets locked inside my skull, brother of the Raven. No hidden codes or schematics, no knowledge of the enemy's weaknesses, no strategies that will bring about an end to the conflict. I am a weapon. I am the sword in Daed's fist, the spear in the huntsman's arsenal.+

'I do not understand,' said Koryn, stepping back as the green spores began to spill over the side of the Librarian's armour, crawling in a putrid tide across the dais. Strange fronds and fungal pods were now forming atop the shell of ceramite plate, as if an entire poisonous ecosystem had sprung to life, feeding off his psychic energy and attempting to smother the life out of him while he lay there immobile. Clearly, whatever sort of weapon Theseon represented, the enemy did not want him to survive long enough for it to be triggered. Good enough reason in itself to ensure that he did.

+The power that surges through me is the raw energy of the warp, + said Theseon, slowly. +I am but a vessel, a repository. I can channel it and shape it. I am the bomb that will destroy Gideous Krall.+

'And you're awake, now. Why do you not move? Why do you not use this power to aid your brothers, to help them crush the enemy that swarms across the surface of Fortane's World like the spores upon your armour?' asked Koryn.

+I am yet weak, brother of the Raven. I do not yet have control of my physical aspect, and my mind is locked in constant battle with the psychic insinuations of the dark god's minions. My sphere of influence extends no further than the ruins of this outpost building.+

'But you *will* wake?' asked Koryn, taking another pace backwards as the spreading spores hit the flagstoned floor and continued to inch slowly towards him.

+In time. But the enemy are clever and unrelenting. They know we are here. The outpost comes under constant attack, and my energy and focus are drawn away to aid my brothers in its defence. Even now, the foul warriors of the Death Guard approach.+

Koryn heard Aramus take two steps into the room, then became aware of the sound of running footsteps in the passageway beyond.

Grayvus appeared in the archway a few moments later, flanked by two Brazen Minotaurs, who immediately set about reclaiming their discarded rags and cleansing their brother of the weird flora that now completely covered him.

'Captain?'

'What is it, Grayvus?' said Koryn, although if Theseon was to be believed, he already knew.

'The enemy approaches, captain. A large party of Plague Marines and traitor militia. They're heading directly for the outpost,' said Grayvus hurriedly.

'What? My brothers have reported no sightings of the enemy,' said Aramus. 'It has only been a matter of hours since their previous attack.'

'I have seen them,' said Grayvus, levelly. 'I have been out amongst those twisted trees, watching the perimeter, and I tell you, brother – they approach from the east.'

+Trust them, brother,+ said Theseon, talking to Aramus, but allowing Koryn to hear his words. +The brother of the Raven speaks the truth. The enemy once again draws near. Prepare yourselves for battle.+ He paused, as if considering his next words. +Leave me. I will do what I can.+

Koryn shook his head. 'No,' he said, decidedly. 'Grayvus, how long do we have?'

'Minutes, captain.'

'Long enough. Brother Theseon, continue your work here. The Raven Guard will defend the outpost. Aramus?'

'Yes?'

'We would be honoured if you and your brothers would join us and fight by our side.'

'I would consider it a privilege, Captain Koryn,' replied the Brazen Minotaur.

'Then let us prepare,' said Koryn, moving towards the doorway. 'It seems as if you'll have your chance to spill traitorous blood this day after all, Grayvus.'

Koryn hung from the tree like a watchful predator, scanning the forest below for any sign of the approaching enemy.

He was at least twenty metres above the forest floor, hanging upside down by the crook of his legs. He was perfectly still, his lightning talons folded across his chest like the wings of a bat.

He craned his neck, studying the trees as they shimmered in the breeze. He could hear the traitors now: their
feet stirring the earth; their ragged, laboured breath; the
thumping of their beating hearts. To Koryn, these sounds
emerged from the background ambience of the forest as
clear as warning sigils on the inside of his helm. He was
a hunter, and the traitors were his prey.

Amongst the ruins of the outpost he could see the glinting power armour of five Brazen Minotaurs, their bolters
at the ready. They would stand their ground until the last,
Koryn knew, defending the outpost with their lives.

The enemy would come from the east. They were bold –
arrogant, even – to assume not even the pretence of stealth
or strategy. Koryn wondered whether they were merely
toying with the Brazen Minotaurs, wearing them down
slowly as sport, knowing that they could overwhelm the
small loyalist contingent with sheer weight of numbers
at any time. This misplaced confidence would be their
undoing. Koryn and his Raven Guard would buy their
bull-headed brothers some time. Most importantly, they
would buy Theseon some time.

The first of the hulking monstrosities lumbered into the
forest glade below. It resembled in every way the grotesque traitors Koryn had encountered on the mortuary
world of Kasharat. Its skin was ruptured and covered in
pustulant boils that wept angrily like so many sorrowful
eyes. Its mouth had been replaced with a metal grille from
which dribbled acidic spittle, slowly eroding the thing's
lower face.

Its ancient armour had cracked and splintered, fusing
with its flesh to become part of its atrocious body, and
although the armour had been painted in the colours of

the traitor's foul master, it had been done so crudely that Koryn could still see the iconography of the former Death Guard Legion on its left pauldron. It carried a pistol and a dripping chainsword.

Behind this thing that Koryn refused to recognise as a Space Marine marched a small army of human militia. These cultists of the rotten god had given themselves over to the Sickening. Their bellies were bloated and bulbous, and buboes covered their exposed flesh. Their mouths, too, had been replaced by mechanical vents that belched noxious gases in place of breath. They bore the insignia of the Imperial Guard, but they had daubed their bodies and wargear with the blasphemous triple-circled seal of their dark god.

They fanned out as they entered the clearing, forming a perimeter around the outpost building. There were six more of the Traitor Marines, forming a squad of seven, and at least three further squads of seven humans. At no point had any of them looked up into the canopy, where Koryn and his Raven Guard hung in silence, waiting.

One of the traitors, whom Koryn took to be the leader of the small force, turned to address his gathered troops. 'Remember, we want the psyker alive,' he said in a burbling voice that sounded thick with mucus. 'You can do what you want with the others.' He laughed darkly and hefted his chainsword, and his foul comrades raised their own weapons in salute.

The traitor took a step further towards the outpost building, and bolter-fire erupted suddenly from behind a spar of broken wall. The rounds thudded into the putrid torso of the lead traitor, showering rancid flesh and body fluid over the troops behind him. The Plague Marine simply laughed, however, continuing to march forwards, ignoring damage that would have felled a Raven Guard. The pact these traitors had made with their dark god rendered them almost impervious to harm, in a similar fashion to the infected birds that Koryn and his brothers had fought earlier. The plague they welcomed into their bodies imbued them with a kind of living death, leaving them trapped in a state of perpetual decay. They were no longer sustained by flesh and blood alone, but by the infernal powers of the warp itself.

Koryn knew from first-hand experience, though, that the traitors were far from impossible to slay. He had fought them on the mortuary world of Kasharat, and he had learned that they could be slain. Taking their heads from their shoulders was the swiftest and cleanest of kills, and despite the vile pestilence that coursed through their veins, it had proved effective against their grotesque kin.

Beneath him, a gaggle of humans were blown apart by the detonation of a frag grenade, tossed from inside the shell of ruined architecture with the utmost precision. It obliterated four of the men, leaving a fifth wounded and writhing amidst the mulch on the forest floor.

That's right, thought Koryn. Take out the humans first. Leave the traitors to us. He would enjoy sending the Plague Marines to their death.

The chatter of bolter-fire filled the air like a thousand raw voices, each of them barking death. The Traitor Marines lumbered for cover while the scattering militia were cut down in great swathes, their torsos ripped apart by piercing bolter-rounds, unprotected heads exploding where they were caught in the barrage. More of them were tossed in the air by the force of further grenades, limbs raining down amidst the flora in a bloody cascade.

All seven of the Traitor Marines were still standing.

Koryn glanced across to where Grayvus and Kayaan were hanging from a tree in similar fashion to himself on the other side of the clearing. All around, his brothers were waiting for his signal, waiting to join the fray.

Just a moment longer, he thought, watching the scene unfold below. Just wait until they're all in position...

The bolter-fire ceased abruptly, and the silence seemed almost unnatural after the furore of a few moments earlier. Most of the humans lay dead or dying, joining their fallen kin on the killing field.

Laughing, the seven traitors emerged from their cover, brandishing their own bolters. It was clear they had used the humans as cannon fodder, there to soak up the bolter-rounds as the Brazen Minotaurs attempted to thin their numbers. Little did they know that silent death awaited them in the trees above.

Koryn slowly unfolded his arms, poising his talons above his head and locking his arms so that they pointed directly down at the ground below. One of the Traitor Marines was shambling beneath him. Koryn measured each ponderous, ungainly step.

*Just a little closer...*

He straightened his legs, releasing his grip on the branch. He fell, dropping like a dart, closing the ten-metre gap in a single heartbeat. He speared the traitor in the back, just behind the neck, plunging his talons deep into its chest and impaling both of its febrile black hearts.

Koryn pivoted, using the traitor for leverage as he brought his legs down and around, landing gracefully on his feet. He rocked back on his heels, using his momentum to lift the enormous Plague Marine wholly into the air, still impaled on his sparking claws.

The traitor cried out in shock, just before Koryn closed his fists and wrenched his claws up and out of its chest, ripping its ribcage open from the inside out and tearing its head off in the process. The corpse fell shuddering to the floor, the still-helmeted head rolling away and clanging against the trunk of a nearby tree.

Koryn, claws dripping with gore, glanced up to see each of his brothers drop from their perches in turn, falling upon the remaining traitors. The Death Guard turned, weapons rising, but they were too slow, their cumbersome, bloated bodies unable to react in time.

The Raven Guard tore them apart in a matter of moments, rending their heads from their shoulders with combat knives and gauntleted hands.

Grayvus, on the far side of the glade, was mopping up the last half dozen of the humans, silencing their whimpering by crushing their skulls with his fists as they attempted to flee into the forest.

Within moments it was over, and the traitors lay dead at their feet.

'To our enemy, we are death incarnate,' said Koryn, standing over the corpse of the traitors' leader, his talons still dripping blood. 'We are living shadows, the ghosts that walk. These traitors shall not have the privilege of knowing our faces, but they *shall* feel our wrath. We honour our dead by smiting their enemies.'

'For Borias!' intoned Kayaan.

'For Siryan!' echoed Korsae.

'For Corax!' bellowed Argis.

Koryn stood for a moment, regarding his brothers. Their black armour was splashed with the polluted blood of the traitors. It would not be the last blood they spilled this day. He was sure of it.

He turned at the sound of movement to his left and saw a human crawling away across the muddy ground, raking the leaves with his fingers, pulling up great clods of mud as he sought purchase. One of his legs had been sheared off at the knee in an explosion, exposing a still smouldering stump of burned bone.

He raised his claws, about to spear the pitiful creature through the skull, when a bolter-round did the job for him, spattering skull fragments and brain matter across the ground. One of the creature's eyeballs landed near Koryn's boots, and he kicked it away in disgust, disturbing a plume of wet leaves.

He looked up to see Aramus approaching, the muzzle of his bolter still smoking. 'Thank you, captain,' said the Brazen Minotaur, and Koryn could hear genuine admiration in his voice.

Koryn nodded. 'Let us hope that it provides Brother Theseon with a few hours of respite.'

'Theseon?' echoed Argis, overhearing Koryn's words. 'He of Kasharat?'

'Yes,' replied Koryn, noticing Cordae standing on the edge of the small group, watching him intently from behind his bird skull mask. 'I have spoken with Theseon, and I know what we must do. There is a control room within the bastion that will open the gun emplacements in the carapace,' he continued. 'We must find our way inside and locate it.'

'Inside the bastion?' asked Avias.

'Indeed,' said Koryn. 'But first we must find Captain Daed. This is his battle, and his war. We must work alongside him so that together we might achieve our aim.'

+Thank you, brother of the Raven, + came Theseon's voice, faint now inside Koryn's mind. +May the Emperor's Light guide your path.+

*And your own*, thought Koryn in reply.

Aramus reached out and clasped hold of Koryn's arm. 'For Tauron,' he said. 'For the Emperor.'

'For the Emperor,' repeated Koryn. He turned to signal to his squad to move out into the forest, but when he looked, they had already gone.

The battlefield was as much wasteland as warzone, Koryn considered, as he picked his way carefully amongst the muddy craters and heaped remnants of barely distinguishable engines of war.

Corpses were strewn everywhere like tattered dolls, their limbs broken and frozen in poises they were never meant to achieve in life. Green mist clung to each of them like a cloying funerary shroud, obscuring their faces from view. It rendered them anonymous and unknowable, reduced them to nameless collateral, alongside those countless other billions of souls consumed by the relentless war machine that was Koryn's universe.

*The nameless dead, fighting to protect the souls of their kin from the ever encroaching darkness.*

The battlefield was marked with occasional glints of golden armour, now half buried in the clinging, churned earth, which told Koryn the battle had been fierce, and that the enemy had proved difficult and unyielding.

In the distance he could see the siege was still raging.

He watched for a moment, reading the battle. The muted lights of muzzle flares and the percussive *crump* of detonating munitions told that the fighting was still just as ferocious, still just as desperate. Nevertheless, the walls of the bastion remained unblemished and unbroken. The Brazen Minotaurs had yet to even penetrate the first line of the Death Guard's defences.

The Raven Guard had to find a way in. They couldn't go around the wall, as it circled for kilometres, curving away in both directions. Nor could they go over it, as it had been built into the carapace itself, towering up into the gloom as high as Koryn could see. Only the heavy weapons turrets punctuated the grey, plascrete surface, and from these spewed not only barking fire but torrents of enemy troops. The sheer number of them meant that even the Raven Guard would find it impossible to batter their way through.

Koryn understood now why the fortress here represented such a strategic stronghold; from the battlefield it appeared unbreachable, built to withstand even the most powerful of bombardments. The insidious taint of Chaos, however, recognised no such barriers.

'We'll have to go through it,' said Argis, quietly. He was picking his way around the ruins of an enemy vehicle ahead of Koryn, but his thoughts were clearly on the problem ahead.

'But how?' said Corvaan. 'They're not about to simply open the doors and welcome us with open arms. The Brazen Minotaurs have not been able to force an entrance, even with this amount of concentrated firepower.' He indicated the blooming flashes in the near distance, where Razorbacks and heavy weapon emplacements were still battering ineffectually against the wall. 'They knock, but the doors do not open.'

'We shall find a way,' said Koryn, firmly. 'We have stealth on our side. We can get closer to the target than our bull-headed brothers, and we can exploit the enemy's weakness.'

'Which is?' asked Cordae, and Koryn thought he detected a hint of sarcasm in the Chaplain's tone.

'Their arrogance,' said Koryn. 'Their unfailing belief in their dark god. Their strategies are not unlike those of our golden-armoured brothers – they believe they can win this battle through weight of numbers, through sheer relentlessness. They send wave after wave of their foul troops from the bastion, and each time the wave breaks upon the Brazen Minotaurs they erode that steadfast shoreline a little more. The situation is a deadlock, and a deadlock buys the enemy time. That is their true purpose. But they are not expecting us to strike back at them from within. They believe the bastion to be impregnable. We must ensure that it is not.'

'We stand with you, captain,' said Argis. 'For Corax and the Emperor. What must we do?'

'Find Captain Daed,' said Koryn. 'Then we parlay and lay out our plans.'

'Where do we even begin to look for him, here in the midst of all this?' said Kayaan.

'In the thick of it,' said Koryn, grinning. 'He won't be far from the epicentre of the battle.'

'I fear you put too much stock in the concerns of our cousins, captain,' said Cordae over a private vox-link a moment later, as they trudged across the muddy wastes towards the fighting. Overhead, the thunderous roar of the orbital bombardment proved a constant companion, and the ground trembled disturbingly with every blow.

'What concerns you, Chaplain?' said Koryn, cautiously. 'The Brazen Minotaurs are fellow servants of the Emperor. Do they not deserve our loyalty and support?'

'I do not know,' said Cordae, and Koryn wasn't sure which of his questions the Chaplain was answering. 'Can they be trusted?'

'Of course they can be trusted!' said Koryn dismissively. 'Their customs may be different from our own, but they are nevertheless Adeptus Astartes. They have more than proved their honour, on Kasharat, and Empalion II before it.' The ground shook momentarily as another thunderous barrage detonated on the carapace above.

'They are blunt and ignorant. They rush headlong into battle with little concern for the consequences. They sacrifice themselves too readily, and their lust for blood and war reminds me of the traitors we fought on Cavonios Prime.'

'You speak hastily and without due consideration, Cordae. I will hear no more of this. The Brazen Minotaurs made a great sacrifice on behalf of our Chapter. We will not speak ill of them or their dead. They are as far from the traitors of which you speak as you or I.' Koryn's tone was harsh and pointed.

'Are you *sure*?' said Cordae, quietly.

Koryn sighed. 'It is true that Captain Daed employs a more direct approach than perhaps you or I would wish to adopt, but their Librarian, Theseon, understands the art of subtlety.'

'Theseon who spent time in the care of traitors? Theseon who allows the spores of the plague god to fester upon his body? Theseon who invades your very mind without warning? Yes, I do believe he understands the art of subtle warfare, captain.'

Koryn rounded on the bird-helmed Chaplain. 'Restrain yourself, Cordae, or I will put you down myself for such treacherous words.'

Cordae cocked his bird-like head to one side, in a gesture that reminded Koryn of the giant, carnivorous avians they had fought in the forest. 'It seems you truly do empathise with the blunt ways of the Brazen Minotaurs, captain.'

Koryn fought down his rising anger. 'Save your vitriol for the enemy, Chaplain. Your counsel is not welcome if all you wish to do is spread sedition. I look to build bridges with our allies, where you look to destroy them.'

'As you wish,' replied Cordae, quietly, and he turned and melted away into the darkness.

Around Koryn, the noise of the battle was growing in intensity. Fresh corpses – or at least, as fresh as the traitors ever got – were heaped where they had fallen, cleaved apart by power axes or peppered with the spray of bolter-rounds. To his right the wreckage of an enemy Rhino burned with a fierce glow, stinking black smoke rising in curling ribbons from the ruins of the control pit. The side of the vehicle had been gouged open, a ragged wound Koryn assumed to have been dealt by an immense power fist – probably belonging to a Dreadnought. Inside he could see the remains of at least three Plague Marines, their rotten husks now roasting and spitting amidst the hungry flames.

Koryn became aware of a low, monotonous sound coming from somewhere nearby. It was a voice, mumbling something he couldn't quite distinguish against the cacophonous noise of the battle. He glanced down and saw the head, neck and shoulders of a plaguebearer, dragging itself along the blood-soaked earth, still reeling off whatever terrible litany formed on its gibbering lips. The rest of its stinking body was absent: ripped away, Koryn guessed, by the attentions of an autocannon. He stepped forwards, jabbing down with his lightning talons to pierce its skull and fry whatever passed for its hateful brain. The remnants of its torso quivered and spasmed for a moment, and then lay still.

As Koryn was extracting his claws a moment later, the vox-bead in his ear crackled to life. 'Captain, the target has been located.'

'Acknowledged, Corvaan. State your position,' he replied.

'Towards the barricade, captain,' said Corvaan, 'Close to the wreckage of a Land Raider.'

'Very good,' said Koryn, searching the vicinity for a sign of the location that Corvaan had described. He caught sight of it a moment later, no more than a few hundred metres away. He broke into a run, folding himself into the shadows as he manoeuvered through the desperate fighting, ducking and weaving his way through the massed ranks of the enemy, through the scattered squads of Brazen Minotaurs, before vaulting up and over the barricade to land, perfectly still, before his Tauronic counterpart. His brothers closed in around him, as if coalescing from the unnatural darkness to form a wall of ravens.

Daed turned to face him, lowering his axe until its head was resting upon the ground. He slid his bolt pistol into his holster. 'Bast – keep watch while I speak with our visitor.'

Koryn knew that he must present a peculiar sight to the Space Marine before him: an ebon-clad warrior in ancient artificer armour that bore the names of all those who had worn it before him and died in its embrace, with corvia dangling in fat bunches from his belt and twin, sparking lightning talons at his side. Only a Raven Guard could understand the significance, the beauty and honour of such a thing.

For his part, Daed was like a golden giant, at least half a metre taller than Koryn, his gleaming armour splashed with crimson gore. The thick, black pelt of a Tauronic lion was draped upon his broad shoulders and ribbons and fragments of tattered parchments clung resolutely to his leg braces, honorific records of past victories and triumphs. His left vambrace was damaged where he had clearly taken a bolter round in his forearm, but the wound did not appear to be troubling him. He was an imposing figure, even for a Space Marine.

'You are welcome, Raven Guard,' he said, his voice deep and steady like the rumble of an engine. 'Most welcome indeed.' He showed no outward sign of surprise at the sudden appearance of Koryn and his squad, but there was a definite note of relief in his voice. Koryn couldn't help but wonder if he had somehow been expecting them.

The Brazen Minotaur stepped forwards and clasped Koryn's pauldron. 'It is good to see you, Captain Koryn. Your intervention here on Fortane's World is timely.'

'Thank you, Captain Daed. We have come to assist you in your hour of need, as you once assisted us.'

'How many are you?'

'Nine,' said Koryn.

'Nine squads. Nearly a full company. Where have they deployed?'

Koryn shook his head. 'No,' he said, slowly. '*Nine.*'

'*Nine...*' repeated Daed, incredulous. 'Nine Raven Guard is all that you have to offer?' His sudden alteration in tone spoke of his dismay. 'Then the battle is lost. We cannot possibly hope to breach the bastion walls in the face of such overwhelming numbers.'

Koryn smiled grimly. 'Nine Raven Guard is all that shall be required,' he replied, coolly. 'This battle shall be won with cunning and not by weight of numbers.'

Koryn could hear the scepticism in Daed's response. 'Two entire companies of Brazen Minotaurs have not been able to breach those bastion walls. What makes you think that nine Raven Guard will make any difference?'

Cordae stepped up beside Koryn, his totemic paraphernalia jangling as he levelled his crozius at Daed's chest. Koryn saw Daed bristle, his stance subtly altering as he prepared to defend himself if the bird-faced Chaplain suddenly decided to strike him with his arcane weapon. '*With respect*, captain, this battle is already lost. Your siege has failed. Your golden battering ram has proved itself to be a blunt instrument in the face of overwhelming odds. Sometimes a blunt instrument is necessary and effective. Sometimes a more subtle approach is needed. It is time to admit that now is one of those times.'

'Stand down, Chaplain,' said Koryn, the warning clear in his voice.

Cordae turned to face him, the beak of his skull mask hovering only a few centimetres from Koryn's own helm. 'Yes, captain,' he said, 'but remember that we are here to do our duty, and not to placate our allies. There is a job to be done.'

'Cordae!' barked Koryn. 'You have said enough.'

Koryn glanced at Daed, but it was impossible to read

his expression beneath his helm. 'You understand, Captain Daed, that our ways are different from your own,' he said, in a conciliatory tone. 'What my brother means to say is that we feel a change of strategy may help to resolve the deadlock with which we are faced. I have spoken to Theseon–'

'Theseon!' thundered Daed. 'Then he lives?'

'In a manner of speaking, captain.'

'You've seen him? Where?'

'The ruined outpost,' replied Koryn. 'He is waking, slowly, from his mental fugue. He does not yet have control of his body, and he is weak. Has Aramus not informed you of this?'

'Our lines of communication were severed. The damn mist...' Daed trailed off, lost in thought. 'You said you'd spoken with him?'

'Yes. And he requested the help of the Raven Guard. He spoke of Empalion II...' Koryn paused to allow his words to sink in, 'And the grave debt that is owed to you.' He heard Cordae scoff behind him.

'A debt you repaid, Raven Guard, on Kasharat,' replied Daed. 'Yet I have not forgotten what happened on that day. The losses were grave indeed. My Chapter has yet to recover.' Daed fixed Koryn with a hard stare. 'And now you ask me to do it again? To stand aside and watch your backs while you sneak amongst the shadows. To ask my brothers to give over their lives so that *nine* of you might have a chance to live. I cannot do it.'

Koryn stepped forwards. 'If there was another way...' he said.

'There *is* another way. Stand by my side on the field of battle. Lend me your arms, your strength. Fight with me in open combat, die standing shoulder-to-shoulder with me in the name of the Emperor.'

Koryn shook his head. 'There is honour in what you say, brother,' he replied. 'And one day I hope to die an honourable death on the field of battle. But today is not that day. The bastion must fall. It *must*. No matter how many of those damnable traitors we slay, it will not be enough unless Fortane's World is regained. You must see that we have no choice. One way or another, we need to get behind those walls. The weapon emplacements must be opened.'

Daed turned and hefted his axe above his head, slamming it down against the barricade in frustration, eliciting a shower of sparks and causing the heaped wreckage to shift and groan in protest.

'This is no longer about repaying a debt of honour, captain. It is about winning a war,' said Koryn, quietly. When Daed didn't respond, Koryn allowed the silence to stretch. After a moment the Brazen Minotaur turned to him, leaving his axe head buried in the ceramite and plasteel structure.

'What is it you are proposing, Raven Guard?' he said, in a low, suspicious growl.

'That we blow a hole in those plascrete skirts, captain,' replied Koryn, allowing an unseen smile to creep upon his face, 'And scare the daemons out.'

'I've told you already – we've tried. We cannot get close enough to the bastion walls to bring our heavy weapons to bear, and even then, it's thick enough to withstand all but the most powerful of munitions,' replied Daed.

'I take it you have explosives?' said Koryn, ignoring Daed's point. It was entirely irrelevant: the Brazen

Minotaurs might not have been able to batter a path through the enemy to the bastion walls, but the Raven Guard did not need a path. Koryn and his brothers would simply disappear; they would walk unseen amongst the enemy until they reached their target.

'Of course,' replied Daed. 'Much good as it will do us from here.'

'The Raven Guard will place the charges against the wall. We can move behind the enemy lines unseen. If you trust us, captain, we will breach the bastion. We will crack it wide open.'

'And then?' asked Daed, sceptically.

'And then, whilst the enemy are occupied defending the hole in their defences from your assault, we will steal inside the bastion itself through a second, smaller breach and locate the control room. We will open the gun emplacements and allow the Navy to blow the entire place apart from inside.'

Daed sighed. 'When – *if* – you succeed in blowing this hole in the walls, you're asking me to commit the entire Brazen Minotaurs contingent to attacking whatever it is that spills out?'

'It's the only way, captain. If the enemy are distracted they won't notice the second explosion, and they won't be looking for us. We have the advantage – they do not know the Raven Guard are here on Fortane's World. They'll expect you to attack through the gap created by the main blast. They'll throw everything they have at stopping you. Meanwhile, we'll come around the other side and open their defences. They'll be a sitting target from orbit.' Koryn glanced at his squad, who were gathered behind him, listening intently to the exchange.

THE UNKINDNESS OF RAVENS · 249

'It's a suicide mission,' said Daed, bitterly.

'For both of us,' replied Koryn, trying to keep the frustration out of his voice. 'Once the gun ports are open and the Navy ships begin their barrage, we'll be trapped inside.' Koryn sighed. 'We must do our duty,' he said, glancing away over the top of the barricade at the stuttering lights of the battle. 'We must sacrifice ourselves for the benefit of a billion souls. Is that not our purpose?'

'You're right, of course,' said Daed, turning to reclaim his axe from where it was still buried in the crumpled metal blockade. 'And so is your Chaplain, much as it pains me to admit it. We *are* losing this battle. And we will do our duty. But know this, Raven Guard: where you sacrifice nine, we sacrifice one hundred, in a war that has already taken a hundred of our brothers. Regardless, we will do as you say. We will hold the line as the enemy spews forth from its hiding place, but we will not do so lightly. Our Chapter will rue this day of loss, and our sacrifice will be recorded in the history of Tauron. Do not fail us. Allow our deaths to be glorious and meaningful. Enable our Chapter's Librarians to tell tales of how the Third and Fifth Companies gave their lives valiantly, in combat, to ensure their victory over the Chaos hordes. Use the time we buy for you well, and make sure those frigates up there blow these stinking traitors halfway across the spiral arm.' Daed's axe, which he had been worrying free as he spoke, finally came loose from the barricade, and he hefted it over his head in a salute that Koryn did not recognise.

'We will,' said Koryn, firmly. 'We will make it count.'

Daed lowered his axe. 'Very well,' he said. 'Bast!'

'Yes, captain,' replied another of the golden-armoured Space Marines, coming forwards to stand at his captain's side. Behind him, the chatter of bolter-fire had become a constant, background hum.

'Show our brothers where they will find our stock of explosives, Bast,' said Daed, and Koryn could tell that he was grinning, despite himself, 'They're going to give us some fireworks.'

'Yes, captain,' said Bast, clipping his bolter to his belt and gesturing for the Raven Guard to follow him. 'This way.'

Koryn signalled to the others, and watched as they followed Bast towards one of the Brazen Minotaurs' auto-cannon emplacements. After they had gone, he went to stand beside Daed at the barricade, surveying the killing field before them.

'It will be an honourable death,' said Daed, quietly, without turning to look at him.

'Yes,' said Koryn, without irony. 'Yes, it will.'


They moved like wraiths, ebony ghosts drifting amongst the dying and the dead. If the enemy saw them pass it was only as a fleeting glimpse of living shadow, the ghost of movement, or else the prickle of hairs on the backs of their necks to warn them that death was hovering nearby.

Koryn killed scores of them as his talons flashed out of the shadows, cutting them down before they had even realised what was happening, lopping off their heads or spilling their steaming viscera upon their boots.

Belching war machines spat gobbets of noxious mucus at the massed ranks of the Brazen Minotaurs, and stomping, twisted things that had once, perhaps, been Dreadnoughts stalked across the heaped corpses of the dead, their weapons blazing as they cut down everything around them, Space Marines and human militia alike.

Koryn and the Raven Guard ignored all of this as they weaved their way towards the bastion walls, dancing elegantly past leagues of the walking dead, past Plague Marines and moaning daemonkin. The mission was everything. It consumed them. They killed only where the opportunity presented itself or the enemy blocked their path. No protracted battles, no retribution.

Each of them carried enough charges that any five of them would be sufficient to blow open the bastion wall. If some of them were lost on the field of battle, the mission would not, therefore, be compromised.

There would be two simultaneous explosions. The first would be the larger of the two and would crack open the wall at its weakest point, blowing an opening just big enough that the Chaos troops would be forced to concentrate around it in order to prevent the Brazen Minotaurs forcing their way inside. The second would be no larger than Koryn himself, and would, he hoped, go relatively unnoticed as the enemy swarmed to defend the main breach. It was through this second hole that the Raven Guard would find their way into the fortress and to the control room where they could override the carapace defences and allow the Navy to do its work.

Cordae led the second team, while Koryn ran alongside Kayae, Grayvus, Avias and Argis. Koryn's squad would place the charges for the main attack, and then rendezvous with the others amidst the ensuing chaos.

Then their mission would truly begin, and so would that of the Brazen Minotaurs.

The immense, sloping wall of the bastion hove into view. Koryn slid to a halt against the towering plascrete barrier, churning sodden mud in a long furrow. The stench of decay this close to the enemy stronghold was nearly overbearing, despite the air scrubbers in his respirator, and Koryn grimaced, trying not to imagine what the festering mulch beneath his boots had once been.

He dropped into a crouch, keeping to the shadows as his brothers came to rest around him. All four of them were accounted for. Their passage across the battlefield had gone unremarked by the enemy – or at least those that were still standing.

Planting the charges proved simplicity itself. The Chaos troops were entirely focused on the battle ahead of them and gave little thought to any possible threat from behind their own ranks: it was inconceivable that the bastion could be about to crumble.

The five Raven Guard scaled the sloping wall like so many crawling insects, their ebon armour seeming to absorb even the muted light of the nearby flames that licked at the ruins of a Rhino, or the muzzle flare from the autocannons overhead, chattering away relentlessly across the nightmare landscape behind them.

'Set them to detonate in sixty seconds,' ordered Koryn, jamming the last of his charges into a pitted crater in the plascrete and sliding back down to join the others.

'Sixty seconds?' said Argis, sceptically. 'It's going to kick out quite a blast.'

'Sixty seconds will be ample time to get clear,' said Koryn, firmly. 'Cordae?' he said over the vox. 'Are you ready?'

'Yes, captain,' replied the Chaplain. 'We're ready.'

'Then activate and get clear,' he said. He saw Argis trigger the remote detonator, casting it away and turning to run. He followed suit, charging for the cover of the downed enemy Rhino, his hearts hammering violently in his chest.

Time seemed to slow. For a moment Koryn thought nothing was going to happen, that somehow the detonator – and their mission – had failed. Then he was pitched forwards with the force of the explosion, scrabbling and sliding behind the flaming tank as the rumble of collapsing masonry filled the air, becoming the only sound for kilometres in every direction.

He listened for the *crump* of a second explosion, but heard nothing beyond the grinding roar of rending plascrete as a section of the wall collapsed. He caught his breath, peering hesitantly over the lip of the Rhino.

The gaping hole was immense – far bigger than Koryn had been expecting – with oily smoke and pale dust billowing out, filling the air and obscuring the view. The plascrete around the blast site was blackened and jagged, and Koryn could see where the rubble had spilled out like a grey waterfall, suddenly frozen mid-flow.

Around him, silence had stolen over the battlefield as combatants from both sides were momentarily distracted by the sudden detonation and resulting collapse of a section of the wall.

As Koryn watched, figures began to emerge from the smoke, pouring out from inside the bastion like white blood cells rushing to the site of a wound. The Chaos troops were hurrying to defend the unexpected breach in their defences, just as he had anticipated. So far, their plan appeared to be working.

Then the world seemed to rush suddenly back in again, and along with the nearby bark of weapons fire, Koryn became aware of the buzzing of the vox-bead in his ear. 'Captain?'

'Speak, Cordae,' replied Koryn, dragging his eyes away

from the blast site to glance in the direction of his brothers, further along the wall. He could see nothing amidst the trailing dust.

'The second breach was successful, captain,' said Cordae, and Koryn grinned, noting the satisfaction in the Chaplain's voice.

He turned to Argis, who was crouching beside him, his faceplate under-lit by the spitting flames of the Rhino. 'We're in,' he said, standing. 'Time to give these foul bastards an explosion that will really get their attention.'

# DAED

The hole in the bastion wall was a ragged, open wound, suppurating with the stinking corpses of the walking dead. Daed watched them emerge in their droves, disgorged as if from a rancid, festering maw.

Traitorous Plague Marines in their ancient, corroded armour lumbered ahead of scores of malformed militia. The men clutched their lasrifles tightly as they were ushered forwards onto the battlefield, terrified of both the golden-armoured Space Marines they would be forced to face in open combat, and the grotesque daemonkin that goaded them from the rear. Blight drones – pulsating sacs of rippling flesh mounted on buzzing rotors – flitted like enormous flies over the heads of the traitors' army, trailing noxious gases and stringy mucus.

The enemy formed a wall far deeper than the plascrete skirts of the bastion, and far more relentless. Daed knew, without doubt, that he was going to die here on Fortane's

World, but not before he had cut a swathe through the ranks of the traitors. He would serve his Chapter and his Emperor. He would hold the line while the Raven Guard struck at the heart of the enemy. Only when they had succeeded would he even begin to contemplate death. Until then, there was only one goal: to stay alive long enough to keep the enemy engaged.

Behind Daed massed the hulking ranks of the Brazen Minotaurs, their golden armour glinting in the perpetual gloaming. This was all that was left of the Third and Fifth Companies of their Chapter. Many had been lost, and their engines of war lay broken and smouldering behind them. Two Land Raiders, a Razorback and less than a hundred Space Marines now stood against the might of the Chaos forces. He had assembled them for their last stand, their last assault on the bastion. Together, they were an awe-inspiring sight, a solid wall of golden power armour and rage. The battle would be glorious.

Nevertheless, Daed hoped that Koryn knew what he was doing. He had no doubt in the veracity of the Raven Guard's intentions, nor his abilities, but Daed had been here before. On Empalion II he had stood firm in the face of overwhelming odds in order that Koryn and his ebon-armoured brothers might prosecute a clandestine mission into the heart of enemy territory. He had provided the distraction necessary to enable them to move unimpeded, and they had proved successful in their endeavours – but the cost had simply been too high. The Brazen Minotaurs had lost an entire company in the ensuing battle, and the Chapter had not yet recovered from the blow. He was not yet sure if they ever would. Not only that, but Daed was acutely aware that, if the Raven

Guard were not successful this time, the costs would be even higher.

He couldn't help but feel wary of such risky strategies. He did not understand the ways of the Raven Guard, their desire to always lurk in the shadows, to strike their enemies from behind. Daed preferred to look his enemies in the eye as he struck them down, to ensure that the last thing they saw was the face of his golden helm as he meted out the justice of the Emperor.

Yet the Raven Guard's bird-faced Chaplain had been right. The Brazen Minotaurs had been losing. And if the battle was lost, so was the war. He had been left with little choice but to go along with their plans. To insist on his existing course of action would have been foolish, and only end in death. Koryn had offered him a way to break the stalemate. Now, their only hope lay in keeping the traitors busy long enough that the Raven Guard could do their work.

Daed watched as three immense figures emerged from the splintered ruins of the fortress wall. They were bound together with iron chains and led by one of the Death Guard, dragged along like animals, shambolic and uncoordinated. Abhumans, Daed realised: former allies of the Guard, now pressed into the service of the traitors' despicable god. Their pugilist faces and spade-like hands showed sign of infection by the rot; just like the humans of this blighted world, both the flesh and minds of these ogryns had been corrupted by the Sickening.

Daed glanced behind him at the serried ranks of his golden-armoured brothers. Captain Lumeous of the Fifth was already dead, torn apart by an enemy Defiler as he had attempted to lead a small team of veterans closer to the bastion walls.

That had been days ago, perhaps longer. Daed had lost track of time. Not helped, he thought grimly, by the ever-present night.

To his left stood Bast and Throle, to his right Forteon and Ebula. He could sense their urgency, their desire to engage the massing enemy. He felt it too.

'Emperor be with us!' he called over an open channel.

'For Tauron!' came the deafening response, as each of his brothers replied in unison, raising their weapons above their heads in a defiant salute. They, too, knew they were most likely marching to their deaths on this killing field, but they would do so with relish. If this was to be their last stand, it would be legendary.

'Here they come!' bellowed Bast, levelling his bolter and fixing his stance. 'Prepare yourselves!'

Daed surveyed the enemy lines as the monstrous army charged across the muddy, corpse-strewn battlefield towards the Brazen Minotaurs. They were flanked by daemonkin, the creatures' long, worm-like tongues snaking hungrily from their bloated, ulcerated lips. It would feel good to send the nauseating beasts screaming back to the hell-pits from whence they were spawned.

He raised his axe high above his head, and then let it fall, indicating that the time had come for his brothers to attack.

The Brazen Minotaurs roared as they charged forwards, thundering across the battlefield towards the oncoming enemy, their bolters barking out a symphony of searing destruction. Heavy weapons belched death, showering the tightly packed ranks of militia with scalding plasma; grenades rained down upon the Death Guard, blowing them into oblivion or igniting their rancid flesh into walking pyres.

They kept on coming, clambering over their own dead, trampling their fallen brethren into the loam as they charged.

Daed felt a stray bolter round smack off his helm and spun around involuntarily, fighting to retain his footing. He steadied himself, grasping the haft of his axe with both fists. He heard screaming, and then suddenly the enemy were all around him, swarming everywhere, and the world became a riot of clashing weapons, buzzing chainswords and wailing death.

He swung his axe, lopping the head from the shoulders of a Traitor Marine who had lumbered too close. The corpse staggered forwards another two steps before keeling over, weeping blood and yellow pus from the fleshy stump of its neck.

Daed unholstered his bolt pistol and discharged it five times in quick succession, turning on the spot, each time dropping a former Guardsman with a neat round in the centre of their forehead.

'The abhumans, captain,' came Forteon's ragged voice over the vox, and Daed glanced frantically from side to side, trying to see past the chaotic morass of combat.

They were over on his extreme left, slamming their way through their own ranks in an effort to get at a squad of Brazen Minotaurs who were still holding the line, cutting down swathes of the enemy with their spitting bolters. Daed saw the first of the ogryns bowl a human through the air as it pushed forwards, dragging the others behind it. The second, intent on squashing another human with its fists, yanked angrily on the chain between them, but received only a spade-like fist in its face in reply.

The third had already reached the Brazen Minotaurs, and

Daed saw it heft one of his brothers into the air, wrenching his arm from its socket with a sharp twist. It dropped
the Space Marine a second later when another of the Brazen Minotaurs ripped out its guts with a chainsword. The
ogryn staggered forwards and then toppled over, crushing another of Daed's brothers as it fell.

With an angry cry, Daed charged forwards, swinging his
axe before him to cleave a path through the battle lines.
Militia fell in their droves as he ran, some of them reduced
to bloody ribbons by the swipe of his power axe, others
simply shouldered brutally out of the way as Daed rushed
to the aid of his brethren.

A plaguebearer lurched suddenly into his path and he
swung at it wildly, putting his fist through the back of its
head and dragging it nearly two metres before he managed to shake its juddering corpse from his arm.

Ahead, his brothers were not faring well against the
two remaining abhumans. The plague had rendered the
creatures near-impervious to harm, and while one of his
brothers set about carving great hunks out of an ogryn's
flank with a chainsword, it simply ignored him, continuing to batter another Brazen Minotaur with its fists.

The other was being goaded by its Plague Marine slaver,
pressed forwards into the midst of the fighting. Daed noted
its apparent confusion and saw his chance. He barrelled
forwards, leaping high into the air and swung his axe up
and over his head, bringing it down in a whistling arc upon
the creature's bald head, cleaving it neatly in two. His axe
buried itself deep in its chest cavity, lodging amongst the
splintered ribs and fibrous muscle. Blood sprayed in a
glossy fountain, spattering Daed's helm and chest.

The enormous corpse of the ogryn rocked back and forth

unsteadily and Daed kicked it deftly, sending it keeling backwards with a wet *thud*. The Plague Marine, too slow to get out of the way in time, found itself bowled over by the falling corpse, pinned beneath its massive bulk and smothered by thick, viscous blood, which continued to burble energetically from both halves of the severed torso. Daed clambered unceremoniously over the heap of quivering flesh, coming to stand over the trapped Death Guard. He reached down and grabbed its head in his fists, his fingers sinking into the slick, pliable flesh of its neck. He sought for a solid grip and wrenched, ignoring the hissing protestations of the former Space Marine, twisting with all his might until the head came away with a wet, sucking *pop*. Daed gave a hoarse roar of satisfaction and hurled it into the seething mass of the enemy, still trailing fragments of spinal column behind it.

He stooped, reaching for the haft of his axe. Just as his fist closed around the slender handle, however, something struck him forcibly between the shoulders, knocking him sprawling across the traitor's decapitated corpse.

Daed fell hard, his shoulder taking the brunt of the fall, and rolled immediately to the left, ignoring the warning sigils that flared up inside his helm. Within seconds his bolt pistol was in his hand and he was emptying it into the hulking figure that loomed over him: the third, and last, of the ogryns. It was spinning a length of heavy iron chain in its fist and laughing maniacally as the bolt-rounds shredded its chest. It spluttered and choked up dark blood, but otherwise the weapon appeared to have little effect. The chain lashed down and Daed moved again, rolling swiftly out of the way so that the heavy links struck the earth where his head had been only moments earlier.

He felt his left arm flare in pain as the ogryn's foot pinned it to the ground. He jabbed at its calf ineffectually with his other fist, wishing he had been able to free his axe before this abhuman had reached him. He could see now that it was missing a whole section of its ribcage and belly where a chainsword had chewed massive, bloody hunks from its side, but it had obviously prevailed against the Brazen Minotaur who had inflicted the wounds.

The creature's other foot came slamming down hard upon Daed's chest, and this time he had nowhere to roll, no way of prising his arm free from beneath its boot. Alarms screamed shrilly in his ears as the ceramite flexed and cracked, threatening to give way and allow him to be crushed by the titanic weight of the abhuman.

He looked up and saw the ogryn raise the chain high above its head. And then something unexpected happened. The sun came up.

The false dawn swept across the battlefield like the very breath of the Emperor Himself. The brilliant, white light flared, banishing the almost tangible gloom, boiling it away into smoke that dispersed upon the wind.

The sudden glare caught the ogryn full in the face, momentarily blinding it and causing it to stagger backwards, covering its face with its hands in sudden confusion.

Freed from its grip, Daed scrambled to his feet, his helm more than compensating for the sudden change in the quality of the light. The Ogryn stumbled, catching its heel on the corpse of its dead kin, and dropping to one knee.

Daed sprung immediately into action, charging at the abhuman and grabbing fistfuls of the thick chain that was still draped across its shoulders. He pulled them taught, crushing the creature's windpipe as the links tightened around its throat. It gargled for breath, clutching at Daed, grabbing him around the waist and squeezing with all its might. Daed felt something break inside his power armour, but continued to ignore the insistent warning sigils that flashed before his eyes. He held firm, drawing the chains as tight as he could, his face level with the creature so that he could see the yellow, jaundiced eyes as they rolled back in their sockets. The ogryn gave a last, wheezing attempt at a breath, and then pitched forwards, limp and dead.

Daed turned, taking in the scene all around him. The light was spearing through the roiling clouds of darkness, spreading across the battlefield as he watched, causing many of the traitors to recoil. Some of them scattered in its wake, running for cover, and Daed realised that this was not simply the pure light of day, but something greater, something far more powerful.

*Theseon.*

The Librarian had woken. His power was returning. Daed felt hope flare along with the brilliant, searing illumination. Despite their faltering numbers, despite the odds, they had the enemy at a disadvantage. If Koryn and his Raven Guard had managed to get inside the bastion, the battle might yet be theirs...

Daed staggered over to where his axe was still jutting rudely from the corpse of the ogryn. He was injured, his armour was compromised and he was drenched in the festering blood of the traitors. Yet his hearts were singing.

He yanked his axe free and weighed it in his hands. It felt good. It felt *right*. 'For Tauron!' he bellowed, his lungs burning, before raising his head and charging headlong into the fight.

# KORYN

Behind the immense plascrete skirts of the bastion was a capacious courtyard filled with the walking dead. These shambling, peeling servants of the dark god stood waiting nervously to be marched to their destruction.

These were the human Guardsmen who had once been garrisoned on Fortane's World, defending the planet in the name of the Emperor. Now they had given themselves over to the foul taint of the warp, and were reduced to this, a shambolic half-life as cannon fodder for the traitors' army. This denigration might have seemed punishment enough to the humans, assuming they had retained enough of their former intelligence to understand their fate, but now, touched by Chaos as they were, the only possible outcome was death. The humans would be cleansed, their corpses razed from existence.

Koryn watched a Death Guard bellow wetly at a group of soldiers, shooting one of them down with a quick blast from his bolter in order to underline his orders. Koryn could sense the palpable tension in the air, the sudden panic that was swelling in the enemy ranks.

The traitorous masters of Empyrion's Blight had not come to Fortane's World with a view to winning the war – they had wished only to delay the breaking of the siege long enough to mount their attack on the neighbouring Kandoor system. Now, as the Brazen Minotaurs formed a spearhead to attack the gaping hole in their defences, the Chaos troops seemed suddenly disorganised and unsure of their own aims. The Raven Guard would use that confusion to their advantage. They would strike while the enemy were at their weakest, distracted and threatened by the might of the golden warriors who waited on the other side of the makeshift gate.

From the shadows Koryn watched the militia being goaded unceremoniously through the main breach in their droves. Death was waiting for them on the other side of that wall. Real death, at the hands of the Brazen Minotaurs, not the foul living death of Nurgle. Daed would rip their heads from their shoulders and scatter their foetid remains to the winds.

The bastion itself appeared to be formed of a series of unconnected structures: long, thin barracks where the Guardsmen had slept formed a circular pattern around a central hub, like the stylised rays of a star. The central hub was squat and grey, constructed from dense plascrete blocks, and the entrance, Koryn guessed, was on the opposite side from where the Raven Guard now lurked, their backs to the inner side of the wall.

The courtyard was teeming with the enemy. Aside from thousands of former Guardsmen, traitorous Space

Marines of the Death Guard marched alongside strange, corroded war machines, awkward looking things that trundled along beside their masters, belching green fumes and leaving stringy trails of mucus in their wake. Plague Marines lumbered towards the breach too, as well as scores of blight drones and the perverse, sickening forms of the daemonkin.

It was a mighty army that the dark gods had amassed here on Fortane's World. It would make victory all the sweeter, thought Koryn, as he silently gestured for his brothers to follow him, tracing the edge of the bastion wall as they skirted around the perimeter of the courtyard, careful to remain hidden from the prying eyes of the traitors.

It was Cordae who saw them first. He caught Koryn's attention with a series of complex hand gestures – the silent language of the Raven Guard – and Koryn glanced over in the direction the Chaplain had indicated.

In the centre of the courtyard stood a huge stone column, supporting a towering statue of a Space Marine, rendered in gleaming white marble that was now discoloured from its exposure to the foul emissions of the Chaos army. The figure stood in silent repose, the pommel of a sword clasped in both hands, the tip of the blade resting by its feet. Its armour was ancient and its expression was one of quiet disdain, as if the long dead hero – an Ultramarine – was looking down upon what had become of Fortane's World with barely concealed disgust. What caught Koryn's attention, however, were the six dangling figures that hung from the plinth upon which the statue stood.

The dead Raven Guard had been strung up on chains by

their throats and hoisted up on makeshift pulleys for the entertainment of the traitors, to provide them with something to jeer at, or – judging by the state of his brothers' shattered armour – to use as target practice. Koryn felt his stomach turn. Anger flared behind his obsidian eyes. The sheer dishonour of it...

'In the name of the Emperor!' growled Argis over the vox, his voice so low it was almost a whisper. 'It's Syrion.'

Koryn felt his spirits sinking. He had hoped that Syrion and his squad were still somewhere out there on the battlefield, that they would take their cue from the explosion and use the opportunity to sneak inside the bastion, just as Koryn had. Clearly, that was not the case. They must have been captured and executed shortly after their arrival, brought here to be displayed like vile trophies.

Koryn glanced at his brothers, who stood to either side of him, clinging to the shadows. He could see that they were spoiling for a fight. When he spoke, his voice was quiet and dangerous. 'Stay your hands, brothers. We engage the enemy only when necessary. We will not win this day with our weapons but with our minds. Stealth and strategy will lead us to victory. Remember your duty. Remember we are Raven Guard.'

'But, captain...' said Avias, his voice a mere breath. 'Their progenoid glands. Their corvia...'

'We have no choice, Avias. The risk is too great. We must honour their spirits in other ways, now, by seeing this mission through to the end. Syrion and our brothers died for a purpose. Let us make that purpose our own, our only thought. Let us avenge them by locating the control room and destroying the enemy's grip on this planet.'

'It is not as if any one of us is likely to return to Kiavahr

to honour our dead,' said Cordae, quietly, 'Or as if we ourselves will be honoured according to our customs. But I
urge you, brothers, to put your faith in the words of your
captain. They are wise and true.'

Koryn glanced over at Cordae, unable to read the Chaplain's intentions from his words. He had sounded sincere,
but given his earlier remarks, Koryn was unsure.

Whatever the case, it would wait. Either that, or it would go
unresolved should they both die here on Fortane's World. It
mattered little, provided it did not interfere with the mission.

Koryn glanced back at the swaying forms of his six brothers, dangling high above them, twisting slowly on the ends
of their ropes. He could not allow it to break their spirits. That was the enemy's purpose, and Koryn would not
allow them even that small victory. Now was the time for
action. They could mourn their dead later, if they survived.

He was just about to give the order to cut the vox-link
and move out when everything changed. There was a sudden, disorientating alteration in the light. One moment the
courtyard was overcast and dreary – a result of the unnatural darkness that the enemy psykers had drawn across the
planet like a black shroud – the next, sunlight was streaking
in from above, showering everything in radiant brilliance.
It lanced through the darkness in great columns, pooling
on the ground and burning away the gloom. Koryn heard
men scream in agony as the light burned their flesh, and
saw some of their faces blister and bubble as they collapsed
to their knees, their eyes boiling in their sockets.

He glanced up but saw only the massive geological
umbrella overhead. The light was clearly as unnatural as
the darkness had been. He realised immediately what had
happened: Theseon.

'Quickly,' said Koryn, urging the others to move. 'This light might disorientate them for a short while, but it will impede us and risk our cover. We must get inside the control hub immediately.' He cut the vox-link and set out, not bothering to wait for affirmation from his brothers.

They traced the inner wall of the bastion for what seemed like an age, circling the courtyard and pausing frequently to avoid any unnecessary attention from the guards. Thankfully, the small patrols of militia seemed more concerned with the sudden, searing light and the bad omen it represented, or avoiding being press-ganged into protecting the main breach, than paying any real attention to what might be lurking in the shadows.

The situation changed, however, when they finally located the entrance to the control complex at the centre of the courtyard. Not only would they have to cross the space in the false daylight, but three Death Guard were standing in the open mouth of the entranceway, and appeared both intelligent and alert.

Unlike the Plague Marines who Koryn had slain earlier, these traitorous Space Marines had not yet succumbed fully to the blight. They showed obvious signs of corruption and mutation – horns, weeping sores and pale, pox-ridden skin – but they did not yet have the massive bulk or distended bellies of their kin. Their mouths had been replaced by corroded vents, a trait, Koryn realised, of the followers of Empyrion's Blight, and poisonous gases leaked from twin funnels on their backs.

Koryn knew that to attack them openly would draw too much attention, possibly even bringing the entire bastion down upon them. They needed a distraction.

Reaching for his belt, Koryn grabbed a fistful of corvia

and tugged them free, snapping the fine chains from which they hung. Cordae reached out and clasped a hand over Koryn's, shaking his head as he realised what the captain was about to do, but Koryn pulled away, knowing it was their best hope. There was nothing else, save for unspent explosives from their attack on the bastion wall, that they could use to draw the attention of the three Death Guard.

Koryn signalled for Avias, Corvaan and Argis to make themselves ready, and then, creeping back along the wall a few metres until he was level with a heap of empty ammunition crates, darted forwards in a dark blur. He skittered to a halt behind the pile of crates, breathing rapidly, half expecting to be showered in a hail of bolter-fire. The moment stretched. Nothing. He hadn't been seen.

Koryn peered around the edge of the crates. The three Death Guard still stood silently, their bolters at the ready. He couldn't risk them loosing off a single shot – even that would likely draw too much attention.

Weighing up the bundle of bird skulls in his fist, Koryn brought his arm back, and then pitched them into the air so that they clattered to the ground just a few metres to the left of where the Death Guard were standing. As one, the three traitors turned to look at what had made the sound, swinging their weapons around nervously.

'Wha–' one of them began, but was cut short by the combat knife that slit his throat all the way back to the spine. He crumpled in the arms of Argis, simultaneously with his two vile kin, and the three Raven Guard dragged the corpses hastily into the shadowy entrance of the control hub.

Seconds later, the others joined them. Koryn brought up the rear with one final glance back at the milling Chaos forces, a smile of grim satisfaction on his lips.

Argis and the others were already secreting the three corpses in an alcove a little further along the passageway.

The passageway itself was plain and functional, forgoing the elaborate decorations of most other Imperial strong-holds that Koryn had encountered in his time. Evidence of the traitors was everywhere: a foul-smelling liquid sluiced across the floor, a sickening amalgam of blood, bile and excrement. The walls, too, were draped in great sheets of flayed human flesh, and daubed with livid red tributes to the dark gods. Shimmering mucus dripped from every surface, festering with ripe toxins and disease.

Koryn tried to ignore the trailing strings of slime that attached themselves to his pauldrons as he brushed against the walls, making his way along the passage to stand beside Grayvus, who had just finished pushing one of the Death Guard corpses into a shadowy recess. 'You have the schematic?' he asked.

Grayvus unclipped the auspex from his belt and flicked it on. A diagram of the bastion's layout appeared on the screen a moment later. 'Yes, captain.'

'Then lead on, Grayvus,' said Koryn. 'Find this damn control room and allow us to get this godforsaken mission over and done with. It's time to put an end to the designs of Empyrion's Blight on Fortane's World.'

'Gladly, captain,' replied Grayvus, motioning for the oth-ers to follow behind him as he set off along the corridor, heading into the darkness.

Any traitors who happened across their path as they crept through the dripping tunnels met with a swift and sound-less end. They were numerous, but mostly alone or in small squads of three, and therefore easily despatched.

The Raven Guard had the element of surprise on their side, and in most instances the enemy did not even know what was happening before they were laying in a heap upon the slick flagstones, their throats torn out to prevent them from screaming for help.

The Raven Guard soon became adept at finding nooks and alcoves in which to hide the bodies before moving on, so as not to give away their presence in the complex by the trail of death they were leaving in their wake. Anyone truly paying attention would find them, of course, but Koryn planned to have reached the control room and opened the gun ports in the carapace long before they were discovered.

The passageways, however, seemed to make little sense, veering off at weird angles or forcing the Space Marines to double back on themselves. The Death Guard had clearly remodelled the bastion to better suit their needs, although Koryn could not fathom what those needs might be. He decided it was better not to even try. To attempt to understand the ways of Chaos was to lose oneself to its corrupting power. The enemy were the enemy. That was all he needed to understand. At least for now.

He realised the passageway ahead was narrowing, and signalled for his brothers to stop. He edged along the wall to where Grayvus was inspecting his auspex again. The screen showed they were standing in a large, open room, but instead they were hemmed in by walls on either side, and the passage was growing narrower with every step. A few metres ahead he sensed movement, and motioned to Grayvus to step back. Grayvus silently clipped his auspex back onto his belt and slid into the shadows, his weapon at the ready.

'Help me...' The voice was thin and reedy, and human. 'I know you're there. Help me.'

Koryn saw Korsae glance at him from across the passageway, and shook his head. It was probably a trap.

'Help me!' the voice pleaded pathetically, increasing in volume. They would have to do something, otherwise whatever it was calling out to them risked giving away their position.

Koryn eased himself away from the wall, feeling the clinging flesh and mucus ripple beneath him as he pulled free of its embrace. He suppressed a shudder. Edging along the tunnel, he passed Grayvus, who peered after him into the darkness, clearly preparing himself to fend off an enemy attack.

It was dark here and Koryn had to allow his eyes a moment to fully adjust to the gloom. When they did, the sight that resolved before him almost turned his stomach. The passageway ended in a dead end, which – for a moment – puzzled Koryn as he attempted to identify its purpose. Then, a few seconds later, it dawned on him. The tunnel was a body farm.

This was where the Death Guard forced their human disciples to sacrifice themselves to their cause, to give themselves utterly to the plague, becoming incubators for disease. Naked human corpses were heaped upon the floor or piled against the walls, rapidly decomposing and festering with writhing maggots. Flies buzzed incessantly, disturbed by Koryn's movements.

Worst of all, some of the bodies had fused into the walls, their flesh binding with the fleshy morass to form huge, gelatinous dioramas. Arms, legs and faces jutted out from every angle, and to his horror Koryn realised that one of the limbs – a forearm – was actually moving.

The arm belonged to a man – or at least, what was left of him – who appeared to have slumped against the wall and simply melted into it. Half of his torso and one leg had been subsumed, but his head was still held at an awkward angle. He was staring directly at Koryn now, one eye swollen shut, the other blinking rapidly, as if in desperation. 'Help me...' the man repeated, solemnly.

'I will,' said Koryn, stepping forwards and sliding his lightning talons through the man's face. The body twitched and shuddered, and then was still.

'Shall I burn it, captain?' said Kayae, coming up behind him, flamer in hand.

'No,' said Koryn. 'We must press on. The Navy will level this entire bastion when we open the gun emplacements. It'll keep.'

'Yes, captain,' replied Kayae. He turned and walked back to join the others.

Koryn was just about to give the order to move on, to try to find a way to circumvent the dead end, when he heard Avias hiss 'Incoming!' over the vox.

He sprang forwards in time to see Avias swamped by a swarm of strange, rat-sized creatures. They were green-skinned and covered in weeping buboes, with long, worm-like tails and twin heads, each crested in a short, bony horn. Each head bore a single, milky eye and a fang-rimmed mouth that dripped acidic saliva.

There were hundreds of the beasts, a writhing carpet of them, and they scuttled up and over Avias's armour, gnawing at the ceramite, their corrosive spittle pitting and scarring it as they chewed.

Avias dragged at them frantically, wrenching them off, but more simply took their place. Cayaan opened fire, chewing up scores of them with his bolter, but making hardly a dent in their number.

'Burn them!' called Koryn, kicking at three of the creatures as they darted around his feet, snapping their jaws.

Kayae stepped forwards, igniting his flamer. He squeezed the trigger, squirting a spray of super-heated promethium into the twittering morass. They howled and squealed as they burst into flames, crackling and hissing as their flesh charred. Kayae played the nozzle of his flamer back and forth, blanketing the creatures. Avias was still struggling to get the things off him, and Koryn stepped forwards, intent on coming to his aid.

He lurched back suddenly, however, when a burning jet shot past his face, missing his head by millimetres. He spun around to see Kayae lurch backwards, one of the creatures attached to his throat. It had eaten its way through his gorget as he had been intent on dousing the main swarm with his flamer. Kayae stumbled and fell against the wall, one hand going involuntarily to his throat. The flamer, still spraying searing flame, twisted in his grip, drenching Avias in its orange embrace.

Avias howled in agony as the promethium took hold, licking hungrily at his damaged armour, finding its way into the joints and the holes inflicted by the daemon creatures. He struggled forwards a few steps, his arms outstretched, and then toppled over, a burning heap upon the floor.

Kayae had now slid to the ground too, slumped against the wall, his throat a mess of chewed-out flesh and vocal cords.

The remaining seven Raven Guard stood for a moment in stunned silence.

After a few seconds had passed, Grayvus cautiously approached Kayae's corpse and carefully removed his dead finger from the trigger of the flamer. The flame sputtered and died, smoke trailing from its red-hot nozzle.

On the ground, Avias's corpse continued to blaze amongst the smouldering remains of the bestial swarm.

Cordae moved to the other end of the corridor, back from where they had come. 'It's still clear,' he said quietly over the vox, 'But not for long. We need to locate the control room before they realise what's happened here.'

'Shall I harvest their gene-seed, captain?' said Corvaan, his tone respectful.

Koryn glanced again at the corpses of his two brothers. Avias was still smouldering, his corvia blackened and charred, flames licking at the joints between the partially melted ceramite plates. Koryn's hearts ached to see such loss. But he knew what he had to do. 'No, Corvaan. If we survive this, we will come back for our fallen kin. But Cordae is correct. We must move, now, before it is too late.'

Corvaan gave a brief nod of acknowledgement, his beaked helm dipping fractionally, and then turned and followed after the Chaplain.

'Grayvus?' said Koryn.

'Yes, captain?'

'Get us to that control room. We're running out of time.'

'I don't understand,' said Grayvus, consulting the readout of his auspex. 'According to the schematics it should be here. We should be right on top of it.'

Koryn glanced at the softly glowing display over his brother's shoulder. Sure enough, the faint green blip that indicated their position was hovering in the outline of the passageway beside the entrance to the main control hub.

Something was clearly wrong. They had traced their way here through innumerable corridors, each of them near identical save for more of the mutated remains of humans who had been subsumed by the walls, creating a crazed jigsaw of body parts and rotting meat; a grotesque, decorative patchwork.

'The Chaos forces have warped the very fabric of the building,' said Cordae in disgust. 'They work to confuse us, to prevent us from reaching our target. These tunnels were a maze even before the Death Guard brought their unholy pestilence to Fortane's World. Now they are near unfathomable.'

'No,' said Koryn, absently. 'Something's not right.' He had an instinctive feeling that there was more to their situation than first appeared. What if the map was right, and it was simply their perception that was wrong?

He looked up, examining their surroundings. Just like all the other dead ends they had encountered, the walls here were covered in thick, elastic sheets of flesh. They dripped ichor and were crusted with old blood. Cautiously, Koryn approached the wall ahead of them – the wall that, according to the schematics, should not have existed.

He peered at it closely, and realised it was partially translucent: he could just make out a bank of winking diodes on the other side. He reached out the tip of his lightning claws and gently sliced into the human tissue. It parted like soft butter, revealing a cavity behind. 'This wall is simply flesh,' he said, turning to his brothers. 'It has been erected here to mimic a wall, but the passageway continues beyond it. If the schematic can be trusted, this leads to the control room.' He turned back intending to tear more of the filthy covering away, when he heard something shift on the other side. Before he could react, a massive fist burst through the hole he had created, slamming into his helm and sending him spinning to the ground.

He heard Cordae bark commands as, dazed, he shook his head and picked himself up off the floor. The sheer force of the blow had been beyond even the capabilities of a Plague Marine, swollen and imbued with the power of its sick deity.

Thundering footsteps echoed in the passageway, and he looked round to see his assailer erupt through the fleshy membrane, pawing it away with massive limbs, one of which terminated in a huge heavy bolter. The figure was immense, almost filling the passageway, and while its flesh and armour was twisted and corrupted beyond all recognition – bulging out like some misshapen sack of body parts and technological gadgetry – it did not bear the hallmarks of the plague like its twisted kin. Its face, partially obscured behind twin eye implants, twitched in what Koryn took to be a smile.

The creature raised its weapon and emitted a thunderous barrage of shots. The Raven Guard dropped to the floor, dancing swiftly out of the line of fire, but Korsae, too late, was caught in the hail of rounds. Koryn saw him punched backwards as multiple bolts punctured his armour, shredding him completely before dropping him, sighing, to the ground.

The beast – which Koryn now realised had once been a Techmarine, before it gave itself up to the vagaries of the warp – gave a stentorian roar and charged forwards, swinging its fist in a wide arc and sending Grayvus sprawling to the ground. As Koryn watched, the heavy bolter began to change and morph, twisting before his very eyes into something entirely different: a chainfist. The power being harnessed by the creature was far beyond Koryn's understanding, and it rendered the traitor a truly fearsome opponent. Still, they had little choice but to kill it. The beast was between them and the control room.

Koryn rushed in to meet the creature's charge head on. His talons sang as he carved away chunk after chunk of the creature's flesh. It slowed, raising its arms up before it in defence. Yet every time Koryn opened up a gash, the flesh seemed to close again around it, sealing itself neatly until there was no evidence of the wound at all. He punched forwards, spearing it through the belly, but almost lost his arm in the pliable flesh, which simply bubbled and exuded him, pushing his arm free and sealing itself.

The creature laughed and battered Koryn aside, knocking him easily against the tunnel wall. It pinned him around the chest with its gargantuan fist, raising the buzzing blade of the chainfist.

He struggled in its grip as the beast brought the blade inexorably towards his head. It was slow-moving and ponderous, but seemingly indestructible.

Bolter fire erupted down its left flank, as Corvaan and Argis concentrated their fire, trying to wound it badly enough that the flesh was unable to knit itself back together. The bolter rounds tore at its flesh and armour, but then dropped out again through its belly before they could detonate, pinging off the metal floor even as its flesh morphed and twisted to compensate.

The muted *crump* of a grenade finally got its attention, as Cordae triggered a melta bomb, and it bellowed in fury as the tumbling explosive seared a hunk out of its shoulder. It twisted, dropping Koryn and turning on the Chaplain, who brandished his crozius before him like a talisman, as if the weapon might somehow ward the creature off.

Its shoulder was still smouldering from the explosion, and while the flesh around the wound was stretching and morphing, it seemed unable to knit itself back together again. 'It's susceptible to explosives!' Koryn bellowed. 'Use whatever you've got!'

'The remaining charges from when we blew the wall!' called Kayaan, unclipping one of the devices from his belt and clutching it in his fist.

Koryn nodded, wishing now that he had retained some of the charges himself. 'See if you can get near enough to plant it, Kayaan,' he called, circling slowly, his eyes still fixed on the beast. It took a swipe at Cordae with its chainfist, missing as he ducked out of the way and striking the wall instead, showering the passageway in hot, grinding sparks.

Cordae battered it across the chest with his crozius, and the creature staggered back a step under the force of the blow. 'For Corax!' bellowed the Chaplain, striking it again on the left knee and causing it to buckle.

Kayaan saw his opening and rushed in, punching out with the explosive charge. His fist burst through its heaving belly, disappearing up to the elbow. The creature bellowed and struck out, the chainfist buzzing as it brought it down hard across Kayaan's right shoulder, severing his head and left arm entirely from his body.

The top half of the Raven Guard slid to the floor in a shower of dark blood, but the creature's flesh had already knitted around the arm, holding the rest of Kayaan upright in an obscene embrace.

'Detonate the charge!' bellowed Koryn, as the corrupted Techmarine lurched along the passageway towards them, dragging the remains of Kayaan along with it.

'We can't!' shouted Argis. 'We don't have the detonator.'

'We'll have to trigger it manually,' said Corvaan. He pulled another charge from his belt. 'Keep it busy,' he said, dropping to a crouch. 'I'm going to get behind it.'

Argis and Grayvus dropped back, showering the creature's face with bolter-fire. It seemed to have little impact on the abomination, though it swatted at the rounds puncturing its soft flesh in annoyance.

Koryn, knowing that he needed to buy Cayaan time, rushed in beside Cordae, swiping at its legs in an effort to slow it down. His talons sparked as he thrust them again and again into the creature, severing ligaments and muscles with every attack. It stumbled slightly as it tried to turn, finding it difficult to manoeuvre its vast bulk in the narrow passage. Cordae struck out with his crozius, knocking it back with another blow to the chest, and while it was occupied, Corvaan slipped beneath its legs, leaping up behind it and jabbing his fist into its back.

'Get clear!' he called, and Cordae and Koryn fell back to join Grayvus and Argis a little further down the passageway.

'Corvaan?' called Koryn, realising that something was wrong. The beast twitched and twisted, trying to shake the Raven Guard free from its back.

'My arm is trapped, captain. I can't get free, but I can trigger the bomb,' he paused for a moment, weighing up his words. 'It's been an honour,' he said quietly. 'For Corax!' He depressed the detonator inside the beast.

The creature exploded in a blinding flash, roiling flame

and flying body parts forcing the remaining Raven Guard to the ground. The passageway trembled with the force of the detonation, buckling and twisting out of shape as it attempted to contain the blow. Koryn felt flesh, plasteel and ceramite shower down upon his back in a continuous hail. He didn't wait for it to stop before he was up on his feet, urging the three others to join him. All around him, the scene was utter devastation. One of the walls had collapsed, exposing pipework and circuits, and the four corpses had been nearly obliterated by the force of the explosion. Flames licked hungrily at scattered body parts like a series of tiny funerary pyres.

'If our encounter with the vermin-things didn't get their attention, this certainly did. We must move, *now*!'

He clambered through the wreckage, pushing his way past a hunk of metal that might once have been part of the corrupted Techmarine. He tried not to think of the loss, the fact that three more of his brothers had died. Three drop-pods had arrived on Fortane's World. Now only four Raven Guard survived.

The passageway spilled out into a large, dimly-lit chamber containing a bank of dead screens and three control desks, each of them peppered with winking lights. Koryn crossed immediately to the desk in the centre of the room, scanning the bank of dials and levers in an effort to ascertain how to open the gun ports high above their heads. He heard his brothers enter the room behind him.

As he reached out a hand for one of the switches, he heard a choking sound from the far corner of the room, which broke into a long, hideous laugh. He glanced up to see a Plague Marine brandishing a bolter in his direction. The bloated figure stepped forwards so that Koryn could see him better, and Koryn almost winced at the sight. The former Death Guard was, like most of his kin, bloated and mutated beyond all sense. His intestines drooped in fleshy hoops around his knees, spilled from a ragged wound in his guts, and his faceplate had been broken, exposing rancid flesh and bone beneath. Worms writhed inside his cheeks and jaw. He fixed Koryn with his single remaining eye. 'So, the Raven Guard are not, after all, impervious to ambush,' drawled the Plague Marine, its voice deep and gravelly.

More figures loomed out of the darkness – seven of them, surrounding the Raven Guard entirely. Fury flared inside Koryn. So close, and now they were badly outnumbered. He glanced at his brothers and saw that, like him, they were calculating the odds, trying to envisage the best plan of attack. They would have only seconds to act.

'The irony is quite delic–' The Plague Marine broke off with a sudden, strangled cry. Confused, Koryn watched as each of the traitors simply dropped in turn, choking and pitching backwards, clutching at their throats.

Cordae stepped forwards. 'No...' he muttered, realisation dawning.

Koryn saw seven ebon-armoured figures emerge from the shadows brandishing combat knives. 'Aysaal! We'd thought you lost,' he said, unable to keep the relief from his voice.

'It is good to see you, captain,' replied Aysaal, coming to stand beside Koryn at the console. Koryn was shocked to see that he was missing his left arm, severed at the shoulder and now a bloody stump. 'Our drop pod was damaged. We landed far out in the forest, and we were unable to raise a signal. I decided the only course of action was to continue with the mission. We thought you were dead.'

'Many of us are,' said Koryn, grimly. He put a hand on Aysaal's pauldron. 'And many of us will be.' He indicated the controls. 'We must open the gun ports and allow the Navy to bombard this bastion. They await us in orbit. Time is of the essence.'

'Then do it,' said Aysaal. 'We may die together like brothers, ridding this world of its foul interlopers.'

Koryn nodded, turning to the controls and engaging the vast engines that would iris open the gun emplacements on the skin of the carapace, providing the frigates above with their sitting targets. Their shells would penetrate the carapace, destroying the bastion from within. 'It is done,' he said, solemnly, standing back from the console.

'Then we should run,' said Argis. 'If we die killing traitors it will be an honourable death. I won't sit here and wait for the bombing to begin.'

'Yes, Argis,' replied Koryn. 'There is honour in what you say. Head for the battlefield, and rendezvous with the Brazen Minotaurs if you make it out alive. I will remain here to ensure none of the traitors are able to close the gun ports before the Navy have done their work.' He was jolted by a sudden rumble from below, indicating that the shelling had already begun. 'I wish you luck, my brothers,' said Koryn, glancing at them each in turn. 'And my thanks, Aysaal, for coming to our aid in our hour of need.'

'I did only as you would, captain,' said Aysaal.

'Captain – I should remain in your place,' said Argis, stepping forwards.

Koryn shook his head. 'No, Argis. This is my fight. I will not leave this place until I know the mission is complete. I must ensure the gun ports remain open until the bastion has been destroyed.' He paused. 'We will be reunited on the fields of distant Kiavahr, when our brothers honour us amongst their dead.'

'As you wish, captain,' said Argis, and Koryn could hear the strain in his voice.

'For Corax!' bellowed the Raven Guard in unison, turning towards the door as another explosion rocked the foundations of the bastion.

Koryn watched for a moment as his brothers melted into the shadows of the wrecked passageway beyond. He stepped forwards in order to barricade the door behind them, but then the console beside him buckled and shifted, and he was thrown to the ground, striking his head hard against a shattered lintel that had fallen from above. He pulled himself up onto his hands and knees, feeling the entire bastion trembling around him. He could hear multiple explosions detonating through the plascrete, thrumming through the fabric of the building. Hunks of rubble dislodged from the ceiling and tumbled to the floor, one of them striking his legs and causing him to wince in pain. He looked up to see the doorway was blocked by fallen masonry.

So, he thought, a sense of peace and finality settling over him. This is it. At least my work here on Fortane's World is done. All debts are repaid. All honour is restored. The bastion falls.

He felt something touch his pauldron, and turned to see a golden gauntlet resting there. Surprised, he twisted, scrabbling to his feet. A Brazen Minotaur stood amongst the wreckage, a shimmering visage amongst the plumes of dust and the flame. 'This way, brother of the Raven,' said the Space Marine, indicating a path through the wreckage. 'Brother Theseon is waiting.'

Dazed, Koryn followed behind the shining figure.

They were not out of danger yet, but Koryn felt hope blossom in his breast. He, and, perhaps his brothers alongside him, might yet live to fight another day.

# DAED

At first, Daed barely noticed that the world was on fire.

All he could see was blood and rage. He had given himself over completely to the battle, surviving on instinct alone as he chopped and slashed and punched and roared indiscriminately at the enemy. They fell in great swathes as he carved his way across the battlefield, leaving a trail of sticky blood and shattered limbs.

It was only when the ground began to tremble so violently that he lost his footing and dropped to one knee, that he finally reclaimed his senses and took stock of what was happening all around him. The enemy army was routing. Militia were scattering in every conceivable direction, leaving the Death Guard and their daemonic bedfellows exposed, doing their utmost to rally their followers but failing in the face of the devastation that surrounded them.

Daed turned, watching the bastion erupt into flame as the orbital strikes hit home, cracking the walls from the inside out and causing momentous landslides as massive hunks of plascrete were jettisoned across the battlefield. They bowled through the fleeing army, crushing hundreds of men in their wake.

Daed saw a lumbering Plague Marine emerge from amongst the wreckage, its head and shoulders entirely engulfed in flame. It stumbled a few paces more, then, like a torch suddenly doused, its head burst with a sickening *pop* and it collapsed to the ground in a blackened heap.

Daed tilted his head back and roared in triumph. The Raven Guard had been true to their word. They had succeeded in their clandestine mission. The siege had finally broken, and now the Navy could do their work.

+The enemy have been vanquished, Daed,+ came the calm, yet confident voice of the Chief Librarian in his head. +The Brazen Minotaurs have served the Emperor well.+

*You live, Theseon*, thought Daed. *I had feared you were lost to us, until you woke and banished the darkness.*

+I live,+ replied Theseon. +In a manner of speaking. I am damaged. My mind is assailed on all fronts, while my body remains under constant threat. While one siege breaks, another continues to rage. I am trapped inside the shell of my body, unable to move, unable to risk lowering my defences for even a moment. Yet I was aided by the Raven Guard. You were wise to accept their assistance, Daed. They may not understand our ways, but they have proved useful allies in this war.+

*I did what was necessary*, thought Daed. *I did what I needed to do to win the battle.*

+Your risk has helped to preserve the integrity of our Chapter, brother.+

*And the Raven Guard?* thought Daed. *Did any of them survive? I took no chances and sent some of our brothers through the breach behind them. I had to be sure they would achieve their aim.*

+Some of them live. Our brothers helped to extract them from the wreckage. We shall return them to the outpost here, and then onwards to our barge in orbit.+

*And from there, to whence they came. Back to the shadows like ghosts.*

Theseon was silent for a moment. +No. We may yet require their assistance again. The battle here is over. The Navy frigates currently bombing the bastion will soon redeploy to join their sister vessels in combating the enemy warships. Kandoor is safe for now. But we, brother, must turn our attentions to Gideous Krall. We must find him and terminate him with all due haste. I do not know how long I have left. Our time runs short.+

*Yes, brother,* thought Daed. *The battle may be over, but until Gideous Krall is destroyed, the war is not.*

+I see you understand me, Daed. It is time to withdraw from Fortane's World. The Navy and Guard will ensure the remnants of the enemy army are destroyed.+

*Soon, brother,* thought Daed. *Soon.* He glanced across the battlefield, still panting from his exertions. Plague Marines lumbered amongst the dead, hacking at the wounded with their poisoned blades, and plaguebearers continued with their diabolical incantations, still locked in vicious battle with Daed's brothers. Theseon was right. Gideous Krall was waiting for them, somewhere amongst the blighted worlds of the Sargassion Reach. It was paramount that they found him and put him to the sword. But here on the battlefield there were still traitors, and Daed's axe was yet hungry for blood. Gideous Krall could wait a little while longer.

Daed hefted his axe and fixed his sights on a nearby daemon. 'For Tauron!' he bellowed, breaking into a charge, leaving muddy plumes in his wake.

'For Corax!' he heard a voice echo from close by, and his face creased into a wide, satisfied grin.

# BY ARTIFICE, ALONE

The disrobing chamber was shrouded in a thick, comfortable silence, broken only by the *skritch-scratch* of a knife tip working insistently back and forth across ceramite, and the distant, tortured sigh of the battle-barge's warp engines.

Captain Aremis Koryn of the Raven Guard sat alone, observed by the dead stone eyes of a hundred primitive statues, each of them peering down at him from one of the shadowy alcoves that lined the edges of the chamber.

All around him lay the carefully placed pauldrons, vambraces, and chest panels of his venerable armour, every inch of its surface etched with the names of the long-dead veterans who had once worn it before him. A little pool of corvia – the bleached skulls of ravens, carried to honour those who had died in combat – lay beside the armour, bound by fine silver chain.

Koryn was wrapped in a loose-fitting cotton robe, the

ghostly-white flesh of his chest, shoulders and arms exposed as he sat on the cool marble floor, hunched over one of the pauldrons, worrying away with his blade. His black eyes flicked towards the open doorway at the sound of movement from the passageway outside.

'Come, Cordae. Your loitering makes me ill at ease.'

The Chaplain stalked slowly into the room, his heavy boot steps ringing out like bolter fire in the empty space. 'I thought you had come here to make preparations for the deployment?' said Cordae, standing over Koryn so that his shadow fell across the captain's work.

Koryn stilled his hand and glanced up at the Chaplain. Cordae was still clad in his full battledress, his ebon armour adorned with the skeletal remains of a giant Kiavahran roc. The creature's ribcage formed a brace across his chest, its wings were spread upon his jump pack as if in stilted flight and its skull leered at Koryn like a grim, jutting death mask. Cordae cocked his head in a gesture that mimicked the creature whose spirit he claimed to share. Koryn could not recall the time when he had last seen Cordae without the macabre totems.

'I did,' replied Koryn simply, and returned to his work.

Cordae did not move. After a moment, he spoke again. 'I fear you place too much trust in Captain Daed and the Librarian, Theseon. They have all but taken us captive upon this barge. We labour under the illusion of freedom, captain, but this place is, in truth, a prison.'

'We must place our faith in our brothers, Cordae,' replied Koryn, his voice low and even. 'They fight in the name of the Emperor. Their methods may seem brittle and unfamiliar – ignorant, even – but nevertheless, their motivations remain sound.'

'Can you be sure?' asked Cordae, and it was clear he was not.

Koryn glanced up at Cordae. 'I am sure,' he said, sharply. 'I will hear no argument. We do what we must. Gideous Krall and his foul cadre of traitors must be destroyed, before the whole of the Sargassion Reach succumbs to their blight, their sickness.'

Cordae made a gesture that might have been a shrug, or a nod of acquiescence. 'I understand that Krall has fashioned a floating cathedral from bone and rotten flesh,' said Cordae. 'It sits amongst a flotilla of smaller warships, formed from the lashed-together remains of bloated plague corpses and the abandoned vessels of daemons that have returned to the warp.'

'They shall all burn,' said Koryn, with conviction. 'The light of the Emperor shall banish them.'

'We are few, captain,' said Cordae, with a note of warning. 'Even counting the Brazen Minotaurs amongst our allies.'

'Then we shall fight harder, and longer, and with greater conviction than our enemies,' replied Koryn.

'You speak with the confidence of one who foresees the future, with the certainty that we will triumph. And yet, here you sit, alone and stripped of your armour, scratching your name into a pauldron with the end of a blunted dagger instead of preparing for war. Your actions do not mirror your words.'

Koryn glowered at the Chaplain. He knew what Cordae was doing. Koryn was being tested. This was Cordae's way of preparing him for the trials to come.

'I am etching my name alongside those of my ancestors. It is an honourable pursuit,' said Koryn. 'This is *how* I am preparing for battle.'

'Aren't the artificers supposed to do that when you're dead?' asked Cordae, bluntly.

'We're about to mount a boarding action against the enemy's orbital fortress and attempt to smuggle a living bomb deep inside their leader's palace of flesh and bone,' replied Koryn. 'None of us are coming back, Cordae. The artificers won't ever lay their hands upon my armour.'

'Yet you speak of victory and the light of the Emperor,' said Cordae.

'I speak the truth. I am nothing if not pragmatic. I do not wish to die without adding my name to those of my forebears. My honour demands it. Their spirits walk with me, Cordae, just as you share your armour with the spirit of the roc whose bones you wear. I cannot lead our brothers to victory unless I know that my ancestors are by my side. Unless I know that when I die, I cannot join them in honour.'

'It is not your ancestors that worry me,' said Cordae, 'but our allies.'

'I will hear no more of this, Cordae,' said Koryn, sternly. 'You shall not shake me from the path I have chosen.'

'Then my work here is done,' replied Cordae. 'We shall die together, brother, side by side in glorious battle, as we smite the enemies of mankind.' He placed a gauntleted hand upon Koryn's naked shoulder. 'I shall leave you to your preparations,' he said, then turned and quit the chamber.

The test was over. Koryn was unsure whether or not he had passed.

He waited until the sound of the Chaplain's footsteps had died away, before making the last few strokes with the tip of his blade.

He placed the pauldron on the floor beside its twin and stood, tucking the knife into his belt.

'Calix. I wish to dress for battle!' he called, and immediately heard the serf scuttling along the passageway vacated only moments before by Cordae.

Soon he would be ready. It was, he knew, going to be a glorious death.

He glanced at the pauldron, at the words AREMIS KORYN roughly hewn into the black ceramite, and smiled.

## ABOUT THE AUTHOR

**George Mann** is an author and editor based
in the East Midlands. For the Black Library,
he is best known for his stories featuring
the Raven Guard, which include the audio
dramas *Helion Rain* and *Labyrinth of Sorrows*,
the novella *The Unkindness of Ravens*, plus a
number of short stories.

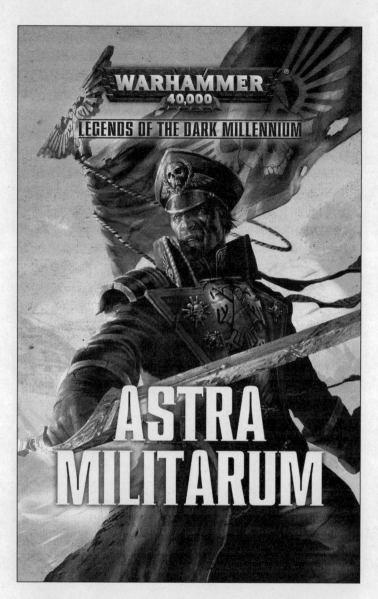